Y0-BCU-231

To Ror...

Enjoy —

Don E. Feingold
June 19, 2015

MURDER IN THE MAKING

BY DON E. FINEGOLD

All rights reserved. No part of this book shall be reproduced or transmitted in any form or by any means, electronic, mechanical, magnetic, photographic including photocopying, recording or by any information storage and retrieval system, without prior written permission of the publisher. No patent liability is assumed with respect to the use of the information contained herein. Although every precaution has been taken in the preparation of this book, the publisher and author assume no responsibility for errors or omissions. Neither is any liability assumed for damages resulting from the use of the information contained herein.

Copyright © 2015 by Don E. Finegold

ISBN 978-1-4958-0544-8
ISBN 978-1-4958-0546-2 eBook

This is a work of fiction. Names, characters, places, and incidents either are the product of the author's imagination or are used fictitiously. Any resemblance to actual events or locales or persons, living or dead, is entirely coincidental.

Published May 2015

INFINITY PUBLISHING
1094 New DeHaven Street, Suite 100
West Conshohocken, PA 19428-2713
Toll-free (877) BUY BOOK
Local Phone (610) 941-9999
Fax (610) 941-9959
Info@buybooksontheweb.com
www.buybooksontheweb.com

Novels by Don E. Finegold

The Samantha Robbins P.I. Novels

Murder in the Making
The Israeli Caper
The Rose Petal Murders
Secrecy and Deception
Revenge
The Investigator

Other Novels

Murder in Leather Town
The Pemberton Murder
The Pact
Interlude

CREDITS

I have a number of people to thank for reviewing my writing and correcting me when I go astray. Chief among these are my sons, Dr. Robert Finegold who edits and offers a critique, and Dr. Jeffrey Finegold who checks for spelling and grammatical errors. Also, my daughter, Ellen Winschel, is happy to check them both, hoping to find something they missed and triumphantly point it out to them. My "Professor" friend, Jerry Rosen, is another important contributor.

My Friday morning breakfast club members offer me encouragement and best wishes, and I need thank them as well: Janice and Harold Cohen, Ruth Lunder, Jerry Rosen, Joan Lisson and Bette-Ann Weisman.

My Monday afternoon coffee-at-the-Mall group, Charlie Lawrence, Pauline Tilas and Bill Tsapatsaris are also big supporters.

And of course, my biggest supporter, my wife Elaine.

Thank you all.

MURDER IN THE MAKING

A SAMANTHA ROBBINS MYSTERY

ONE

Theo Maggio was sipping his morning coffee and reading the sports page of The Boston Globe when his phone rang.

"Theo. It's Giorgio. You still looking for a new car?"

Theo put down his coffee and rested his elbows atop the paper on the kitchen table. "Yeah. You got something good?"

"I've got a two-door late model white Cadillac with low mileage that came into Feldman's pre-owned yard this morning. The owner couldn't keep up with the payments. I got it cheap. I told the boss you'd been looking for a car and he said to let you have it if you're interested. Are you interested?"

"Hell, yeah. My Lincoln's just about had it. How much, Giorgio?"

"Ten grand; but I want your Lincoln as part of the deal. My cousin Leon needs wheels, so I'll fix it up and give it to him."

"Okay. When can I pick it up?"

"You got the money?"

"I can have it for tomorrow."

"Then meet me at Feldman's in Chelsea at seven tomorrow morning. We'll settle the paper work and you can be on your way. Oh, and I want the ten grand in cash."

"Sure. No problem. See you at seven."

"I'll be there."

¥

Theo drove his nine year old Lincoln Town car into Feldman's yard the following morning. He stopped next to a freshly polished white caddy parked in front of the brick office building. The vehicle looked to be in first class condition.

His face beaming, Theo entered the office. The small room smelled of oil, grease, and Lysol. He sat down in front of Giorgio's metal desk and pointed over his shoulder with his thumb. "That's a beauty of a caddy, Giorgio."

"Sure is. We aim to please. You got the cash?"

"Yeah." Theo removed an envelope from the inside of his navy blazer and tossed it on the desk. "Ten grand, in hundreds, like you said. You got the paper work?"

"Right here." Giorgio reached into the briefcase next to his chair.

The smile on Theo's face evaporated when the Glock 19, fitted with a suppressor, came out of the brief case.

Giorgio pointed its business end at Theo's eyes. "What have you been talking to Samantha Robbins about, Theo?"

"Who?" Theo's face blanched. "I don't know what you're talking about."

"Bullshit! And what about the money you've been skimming? That wasn't a good idea either."

Beads of sweat appeared on Theo's brow. "I-I needed a loan. I planned to give it back. Honest, Giorgio, really. I just needed...."

The outside door opened and a muscular man walked in. Tall, dark, and handsome would have normally described him well, but his fuliginous eyes detracted from this first impression, as did the unwholesome leer on his face.

It was evident from Giorgio's facial expression he hadn't expected to see Manny Antonelli.

Theo's mouth gaped wide with recognition and the smell of urine was added to the other odors permeating the office. "I'm-I'm sorry Mr. Antonelli. I've got all your money," Theo stammered. "I-I just needed a short-time loan. Your money's in my basement. I planned to start giving it back over the next three months – all of it, even extra, and…."

"What did you talk to the Robbins woman about, Theo?" Manny said.

"I didn't go to her. She-she came to me asking questions about you, but I didn't tell her nothing. She…she asked me why you killed George Davis and Charlie Curcio and I said I knew nothing about it. She asked if I could find out. I said no."

"Did she offer you money?" Manny asked.

"I…I." Theo hesitated and that was the end of the conversation. Manny took the Glock from Giorgio's hand and fired three quick shots – two to Theo's chest, one to his forehead. Theo's body slipped from his chair and sprawled on the floor, bleeding profusely.

Manny handed the gun to Giorgio. "Clean it thoroughly and then get rid of it. Permanently! Give me your knife." Manny took a red lacquered box from his coat pocket and placed it on the desk. The box had an oriental pagoda in mother-of-pearl on the lid.

Giorgio stood and pulled a switchblade from his pocket. He flipped it open, and handed it hilt first to his boss. He watched, curious, as Manny leaned over the body, sliced through the Theo's belt, and then…

Giorgio sat back down.

Blood dripping from his hand, Manny told Giorgio to open the lid of the box. Giorgio did, and felt his gorge rise as Manny Antonelli, the boss of Boston's drug, gambling, and prostitution "businesses," placed the dangling contents and its two smaller appendages in the box. He had to bend the former to make it fit.

"For such a scumbag, he must have been popular with the ladies," Antonelli said, kneeling to wipe his hands and the switchblade on Theo's shirt. He handed the wiped blade back to Giorgio.

Giorgio's hand trembled as he took it.

Manny pointed at the box. "You show this around to the other collectors, Giorgio." Manny looked down at the body. "Put the rest of him in his car and run it through the auto compactor at the junk yard. Make sure what's left is buried in a deep hole and gets covered over with lots of junk parts. Tell the other collectors what he did, then burn this."

He held up the box. A small mother-of-pearl Chinaman beamed happily at Giorgio from the back panel. "Any questions?"

"N-no, boss. What about the female private eye?"

"In time we'll find a way to kill her. And clean up this office floor. I don't like the sight of blood."

TWO

Steve Grant was a private investigator with an office in Salem, MA. He was forty-five years old, twice divorced and not looking for a third headache.

The divorces were mostly his fault. He'd been away too often the past seven years, with a couple of twelve month tours in Iraq and better than a year in Afghanistan. He was a Master Sergeant during most of that time and more married to his work than to his women. The women wanted kids. He didn't. He figured they had nothing in common other than their love of sex. Hell, you don't need marriage for that. Both breakups were by mutual consent.

Steve got tired of the army.

He didn't like so many kids being killed. He didn't like kids trained to kill by ruthless terrorists who cared nothing for their lives.

He decided to get out at the end of his current tour.

But it didn't happen that way. A roadside bomb shattered both his legs into pick-up sticks.

After a lengthy hospital stay, one leg worked pretty well; the other didn't, even after months of therapy. It worked, but not the way it was supposed to.

He was too crippled to be of use to the army anymore and flushed out of the service.

After a year of daily therapy, you could hardly notice his limp. Then he went to school and became a cop. He didn't win the hundred yard dash competition during training, but he didn't finish last either. And academically he had done well. Ma Grant didn't raise any idiots. Not complete ones, anyway.

He wasn't a loner, but he was picky about who he had for friends. If you were a druggy, drunkard or asshole he didn't want to know you. If you were a regular guy or gal, then okay.

He was a cop in Boston for three years, but the job was too restrictive, so he honed up and went after his PI license. Knowing the right people and his war record helped him.

¥

Work as a private investigator was slow in coming. He initially had taken on a number of sickening abuse cases, and cases for spouses who suspected their significant others were engaged in illicit adventures. Some of those cases were interesting but most didn't ring the bell for him. He was still young and stupid enough to want something more exciting.

¥

His office was on Derby Street, in Salem, MA. He loved Salem, except for the month of October, when busses brought in a zillion tourists, looking for the witches and warlocks and whoever else turned them on. Some locals even dressed like zombies. Can you believe it? The city in October was overwhelmed with traffic, day and night. You couldn't walk without literally being stomped on by some ghoul-seeking revelers.

So okay, the city could use the money, but to Steve it was a pain in the ass.

¥

He got the big paying case he was looking for in November. A smooth looking dude with two associates came to his office on a chilly Wednesday morning. They didn't have an appointment, but that didn't bother them. His secretary, Herb Mellon, looked them over and decided this was money, because the lead guy was dressed in a dark tailored suit, blue shirt, spiffy red tie, and wore shiny black dress shoes like they sell in Nordstrom's. It must have cost the pretty boy a month of Herb's pay. Perhaps three months.

Herb pegged the lead guy as Italian, and had this confirmed when the guy introduced himself as Manny Antonelli.

Herb knew the name, as did probably ninety per cent of the greater Boston community. Manny was mob–big time mob. He was reputedly a killer when in his teens, and had moved up the gangster hierarchy via marriage and ruthlessness. And here he was, standing in front of Herb and, a few seconds later, me, exuding warmth, good manners and Rudolph Valentino looks.

"Thanks for seeing me on such short notice, Mr. Grant," he said, as if he had given me much choice in the matter, "but my friends and I happened to be driving out this way, and I recalled a mutual acquaintance - a Boston cop - had mentioned your name. So I took the liberty to stop by."

"Who's this mutual friend?" I asked.

"Captain Joe Weiss, Mr. Grant; and can we continue this conversation on a first name basis? Mine is Manny."

"That's fine, Manny. I'm Steve. Please sit."

Manny sat and crossed his legs, his smile broadening. His associates stood like statues, eyes alert but bodies unmoving. They looked like they were carved from the same piece of granite from the same Vermont quarry. They were big, homely and intimidating. Steve unconsciously fingered the revolver in the holster attached to the underside of his desk. Then he relaxed. He realized they weren't there to make trouble. They were simply escorts: musclemen to attend the whims of their boss.

"Joe sends his regards, Steve," Manny said.

"Thanks," I said, nodding my recognition of the name Joe Weiss but not showing any emotion. Captain Joe Weiss was a crooked cop working with the mob, and I had that information on reliable authority.

"Anyway, a few years ago I had some dealings with Samantha Robbins, a neighboring private investigator of yours," Manny continued, "and she caused me some problems. I don't need problems, and I don't want her interference in the future. Her husband's a cop in Stanton by the name of Arthur Lite. Do you know him?"

"Yes, I know them both. We're not on the same ball team, or even close associates, but I've met them."

"So I was told, Steve. What I want from you is to track her doings for a while. I want to know all the cases she's working on over the course of the next year or so. That shouldn't be difficult for a man with your skills."

"I'm sorry, Manny. Spying on a fellow investigator isn't ethical, or my cup of tea, and...."

"Fuck ethics," he interrupted, with venom in his voice. Then he lightened up. "You'd actually be doing her a favor, Steve. There are some who don't like her and might harm her. We wouldn't want that to happen. There's fifty grand in it for you, Steve. Cash."

Fifty grand! Shit. I just couldn't help being interested. "Just what are you looking for, Manny?"

"Nothing in particular. You report what she's doing and who for. I'll decide if it's of importance to me. There's no harm in that, is there?"

"I don't know. Your reputation..."

Manny interrupted. "My reputation is no one's business, Steve. I'm a business man, nothing more or less. You shouldn't be caught up in the distortions and lies used to sell newspapers."

His two associates didn't move, but they now wore nasty smirks on their ugly faces.

"I will consider taking the assignment, Manny, under conditions to my liking."

"What conditions?"

"No harm comes to either Samantha Robbins or her husband. I don't like ratting on people in my trade, especially those I know to be good people."

"This isn't the 1920's, Steve. I peacefully work out any differences I have, once I have all the facts. Getting me the facts is your job. That's all there is to it." He smiled warmly to show he meant what he said, but his eyes glinted like ice.

I thought, *If I don't do it, he'll get someone else; maybe someone with fewer scruples. She'd be safer with me.*

"Okay, Manny. With the understanding I stated, I'll take the job. How do I get in touch with you?"

"You don't. You write up a report on your progress once a week." He addressed one of his men without looking at him. "Giorgio, give him a card. You'll mail your report to the address on the card, Steve. If anything real important comes up, you call Joe Weiss. He knows how to reach me. Giorgio will give you his number."

The statue named Giorgio went into motion, and as he approached, pulled out a thick eel skin wallet, removed two cards, and wordlessly dropped them on my desk. He then returned to his prior location. He might as well have been a robot.

I didn't bother to say thank you. I picked up the cards, gave them a cursory glance, and nodded.

Manny stood, reached into an inner jacket pocket, and pulled out a manila envelope. He tossed it on the desk. "There are 10 gees in hundreds in there, Steve. You'll get the rest in quarterly installments. Thanks for seeing me."

He nodded to the two hunks and they followed him out the door. I barely had time to wipe away the sudden perspiration that formed on my brow before Herb barged in.

"Are you okay?"

"Of course," I said, returning my handkerchief to my back pocket.

"What did he want?"

"It's better if you don't know. Forget him. I doubt you'll ever meet him again."

Herb reluctantly let it go, but one of his eyebrows lifted when he noticed the unfamiliar manila envelope on the desk before he left my office.

I opened the envelope and thumbed through the wad of one hundred dollar bills. I didn't bother to count them. I knew it was all there. I was already thinking how I was going to screw Uncle Sam. He wasn't going to give away any of my hard-earned money as perks to a bunch of illegal aliens. I didn't fight in the army for that.

I had a new job–spying on Samantha Robbins. It shouldn't be difficult. All I had to do was find a way to sneak into her office once a week and check and photograph her files. Time consuming, but I didn't sleep well at night anyway. I'd have to do a lot of reading. And I'd have to start with the file she had on Manny Antonelli.

¥

Samantha's offices were in the O'Shea Building in downtown Pemberton. If I remembered correctly, there were small business establishments at street level and two floors of offices above them. I'd visited her two years earlier, but I couldn't remember if she was located on the third or second floor. That wasn't important; I'd go by tomorrow and check. I remembered she had a single secretary sitting out front, an older woman by the name of...of Pauline something. I'm pretty sure it was Pauline. And Pauline would have a set of keys to the office and probably to all the file drawers. So I'd get Pauline's last name, where she lived, case her house and make impressions of all her keys. I'd then have easy access to Samantha's office. That would be easier than having to pick locks every time I visited.

I'd have to check if the office had an alarm system and/or surveillance cameras. Maybe not, because who breaks into a private investigator's office?

I felt the weight of the envelope in my hand and then tossed it upon the desk. Samantha deserved better. She seemed like a nice person, and she could be in danger from this flashy, fancy hood. And that's all he is, just another despicable hoodlum with fancy clothes and capped teeth.

I'll talk to Samantha. I'd be double crossing a mobster, and characters like him repay you in bullets and a cement coffin if they find out you turned on them.

Steve combed his fingers through his hair. *What the fuck, all life is a gamble. I wonder if he's bugged her phones.* He paused. *Or for that matter, mine.*

THREE

O n Saturday morning Steve followed Samantha Robbins and her hubby, Arthur Lite, from their digs to the New Brothers Restaurant & Deli on Maple Street in Danvers. He waited some ten minutes to make sure they and he were not followed. Manny Antonelli had too many assets, including money and manpower, not to be double covering everything he was involved with, and he could have people watching them. It wasn't as if he could make one mistake and get a slap on the wrist. If he made one mistake, he'd likely not be heard from again. At first he feared getting involved, but the fifty grand made him change his mind. Also, if he hadn't accepted Manny's offer, his knowledge of Manny's interest in Samantha Robbins would have been a liability to Manny. Men like him don't allow loose ends. Manny really had no choice. *And all that money won't be any good to me unless I lived to collect it.*

Steve was committed to a risky game but he'd never shied away from danger, and he wasn't about to now. He approached the booth where Samantha was sitting. Her husband was in the long line at the counter, jawing with Ted Kougianos, the Deli's co-owner. Samantha was glancing at the front page of the Boston Globe, but must have felt his presence, because she glanced up. Or maybe it was her sixth sense. He had heard from several sources she was purported to have one. She spoke before he did.

"Hello, Steve; it's been a while. How are you?"

He was surprised she pegged him so quickly. They'd met only a few times, and it was with a crowd of people.

"Fine, "he said. "Would you mind if I joined you and your husband for a few minutes? It's pretty important."

"Of course I don't mind. Grab some breakfast and join us."

"Thanks." I'd already breakfasted at home but I always have room for another coffee and bran muffin.

Moments later Steve carried his tray to where they were sitting, side by side, and plunked down opposite them.

Arthur reached over to shake hands. Arthur was at least 6'4," two-hundred-twenty pounds or so, with a full head of wavy blond hair and great looks. He was a man who undoubtedly could take care of himself, but against Manny Antonelli's organization? Not a chance. Not without his own army.

Arthur apologized for not waiting. "I like to eat while it's still hot." He was shoveling into a huge omelet and home fries while Samantha poked at a single poached egg in a cup with an English muffin on a side dish.

"I'm sorry for the intrusion," Steve said. "I have a problem that concerns the three of us."

"You make it sound ominous," Samantha said, still toying with her food. "What's the problem?"

Steve had their attention. "Manny Antonelli."

He told them in detail about Manny's visit to his office. Samantha and Arthur listened attentively.

"I want you both to know I accepted the job because if I didn't he would have found someone else, and I doubt if he would have liked the idea that I was privy to his doings. Then we would all have been in danger."

Samantha nodded, and then cast a glance at Arthur. "He's right. There's no way around it. We'll have to deal with Manny again."

Arthur muttered an expletive and Samantha frowned at him. "Sorry," he said and nodded.

"I'm having my office and home swept for cameras and bugs, and suggest you folks do the same," Steve continued. "He'll have people watching us. Your secretary will have to let me break into her house so

I can make copies of your office keys, as if I was keeping tabs on you. You decide what info you want me to feed Manny, and we'll string him along. Hopefully, he'll soon lose interest and let us off the hook. That's my suggestion."

Arthur said, "I want to get this guy out of our lives permanently." Samantha placed her hand on his arm. Their eyes met and, after a moment, he lowered the knife he'd been clenching in his hand and buttered his toast.

"Do you have any idea what he's looking for, Samantha?" Steve asked.

She didn't answer right away. He noted the quick glance she gave her husband. Arthur spoke first. "We've both had encounters with Manny and his organization over the past few years. Samantha more so than I. He's bad medicine. Beneath all his charm lies a ruthless killer. He was a hit man for Gino Pintano, but now he's the one pulling the strings and has his minions do the dirty work. He's in strong with the New York bunch, and just about manages every bit of vice in the Boston area. He's no small potato, Steve. Samantha reads him pretty well, which is bad for his business. He doesn't like that."

"I think you're over-stating it, Arthur," Samantha said. "I had dealings with Gino Pintano and with his wife Theresa. I also dealt with their daughter, Manny's former wife, Terri, and her brother Anthony." She paused and ran her finger around the edge of her coffee cup. "They're all dead," she said. "Manny feels I may have been involved in their undoing. That's not the case, however. Manny was the cause, but he has trouble facing reality. Killer that he is, he fears I know things I shouldn't, and he is trying to find out how. He's afraid to kill me because I have certain records of his activities placed with people he doesn't know that could cause him trouble if I should suddenly disappear and they are released. I let him know that is true. In the meantime, I hope to put him and his kind in jail for a very long time, and he also knows that. So it's a battle of wits, and we both want to win."

"Okay," Steve said. "We have our work cut out for us. Are we all in this together?"

"It looks that way, and I really appreciate your clueing us in on it, Steve," Samantha said. "I'll need to tell my secretary Pauline. She's like family to me. Other than her, it'll be the three of us against Antonelli and the mob." She chuckled. "It sounds like a book title. I think we can make it work."

"We'd better damn sure make it work," Arthur said. "We're dealing with pros."

"We're all pros, Arthur," Samantha said. "I'll pick up some throw-a-way phones today and we'll get set up. I'll have a set of office and file keys made for you, Steve, so you won't have to break into Pauline's home. I doubt if Manny will have a twenty four hour tail on you, so there's no way he'll know how you got them. We don't have cameras or an alarm system in my office – we do at home – so that won't be a problem. I'll prepare you a file on Manny and some of his old family – to give some credence to your weekly reports, and I'll make up some notes on mock plans I have concerning Manny and his friends. That should keep him occupied over the next few months – or longer – until we can nail his ass for something that will get him off the streets. This should be interesting. I can hardly wait to get started."

"Don't underestimate him, Samantha," Arthur warned. "He's not highly educated, but he is smart – street smart – and ruthless."

She smiled, but the look in her eyes made me shiver. "So are we."

Steve expected he was in for an interesting few months.

FOUR

That same day Steve called an acquaintance, former Pemberton Police Chief Charlie Lawrence, and invited him to lunch. Charlie joined him noontime at the Wardhurst Grille.

Charlie was a fan of Wardhurst, and would give up just about anything in order to hang there. It was one of those restaurants where everybody knew everybody. Samantha and Arthur were frequent diners there, and were close friends with the ex-chief.

That was the purpose for this meeting. Steve needed to know more about Samantha and Arthur – especially Samantha – as his life might depend on it. He had heard things about her, about her having ESP and having solved murder cases because of it, and he needed to separate fact from fiction.

"Thanks for joining me, Charlie," Steve said as they shook hands. "I hope I'm not inconveniencing you by dragging you away from something important."

"Not a problem. You said you wanted to talk about Samantha and Arthur, and I love them. They are two of the most interesting people I ever met. Especially Samantha, Steve." He shifted his position on the hard bench in the booth he sat in the rear of the main dining room. "She is someone special."

"Why, Charlie?"

"Let's order first. It's a long story, but one I think you'll find interesting."

Charlie beckoned to a waitress. "We're ready whenever you got a minute, Janice."

"I'll be right there, chief."

Charlie was pleased they had chicken croquettes on the menu, and ordered the luncheon special. Steve opted for a BLT and well-done fries. They both settled for a bottle of Miller, and kept the conversation to a minimum while they downed the meal. It was over black coffee that they got to the heart of the conversation.

"I first met Samantha in – I think it was in 2004," Charlie began. "She came to my Pemberton office to introduce herself. She told me she had graduated from the Police Academy in 2003, but after being a cop for less than a year resigned and got her private investigator's license. She didn't give me her reason for becoming a PI at that time. Anyway, she opened her office, hired a friendly ex-schoolteacher as a secretary – a woman who must be in her eighties today, and they locked in on Samantha's business.

"She and Arthur graduated from the police academy together. They started dating a short time later and after a year became a serious twosome. But let me stay with Samantha. I didn't learn her story for a long time, and it's intriguing. Her biological mother was a woman named Kate Winslow. She and her boyfriend, Doug Bidell, were attacked by bandits while on a hiking trip in Guatemala. Doug was murdered. Kate was beaten, raped and left for dead. She was found by nearby village people and brought to a mission house where a padre and nuns took care of her. Her body was healing, but her mind was unable to function properly, especially after she learned she was pregnant. I guess her problem was who impregnated her; her boyfriend or a rapist. Anyway, Samantha was born but Kate died during the birthing. An American couple came through the area months later, fell in love with Samantha, and adopted her, with the blessings of the padre and the nuns. Abigail and Michael Robbins brought Samantha to the States. Sadly, Abigail Robbins was struck by a stolen car when Samantha was four, and died.

"At age five, Samantha first exhibited her gift; a knack for knowing things that she shouldn't know anything about, like a bank robbery and a murder that took place the following day. Her father was concerned, and took her to two close friends, a Dr. Kemper and a Dr. Katcher, a psychiatrist and a psychologist – I don't remember which was which – and after months of testing, they believed that Samantha was gifted with a rare form of ESP: clairvoyance. Her sixth sense was extraordinary, and her father feared it would draw too much unwanted attention. Thus, he and the doctors decided it was in Samantha's best interest not to reveal her abilities to anyone.

"Samantha was intelligent enough, even at that early age, to understand what the doctors and her father explained to her. They called it 'her gift,' but she didn't fully understand what they meant. But she did as her father and the doctors told her to. She spoke to no one about it.

"This gift came to her infrequently in her early years, but intensified after puberty. She wanted to use it to help others and decided she should become a police detective, and went to the academy, graduating at the top of her class. But she found herself too restricted as a female police officer, resigned, and got her PI license...."

"You believe in this ESP stuff, Charlie?" Steve interrupted.

The chief leaned back and eyed him. He took some time before he answered. "Let me explain something to you. I'm telling you all this because I called Samantha this morning and she told me you would be working together and it was okay to fill you in about her. Now to answer your question, I didn't for a long time, but I do now. I've seen the good that Samantha has done, and although I don't understand it all – how it works–I'm a believer. And we don't discuss her gift for her own protection. She's been a target of Gino Pintano, Manny Antonelli's deceased father-in-law, and now of Manny and his New York associates. Arthur and I have suggested that she close shop, change her name and move away, but 'no' is the only answer she gives. She's her own person and makes her own decisions. Her gift, or whatever you want to call it, has helped solve many murder cases."

"Thanks, Charlie. I will keep this conversation as privileged. It sounds like Manny would do her harm because he's afraid of her."

"I agree. Like I said, Steve, I called Samantha this morning and told her you wanted to meet with me to discuss her, and she told me she would be working with you and I could tell you whatever would be helpful, so I've told you everything. Now you make sure you protect her. She's a special person."

'I'll do that. Thanks for joining me for lunch. One last question – hmm – series of questions," he added. "How long have Samantha and Arthur been married?"

"Just a few years."

"Do they have any kids?"

"No."

"Do they work as a team?"

"Only on rare occasions that I know about. He's with the Stanton police, and she's on her own."

"And finally, why is Manny afraid of her?"

"He has good reason to be. Because she can sometimes read him, or he feels she can."

"That will do it, Charlie. Thanks."

FIVE

⌐━━━━┑

S amantha is psychic! Steve had read up on people claiming they had
ESP, and hadn't been convinced, but the ex-chief was no fool and
he was a solid believer. Her gift could be valuable in their dealings with
Manny Antonelli. If she could foretell some of Manny's future moves it
would be a big plus.

Returning to his office, Steve felt somewhat relieved. They could feed
Manny what they wanted and mislead that hood. He was okay with that.
But Samantha and Arthur wanted to nail Antonelli on something that
would put him away for good. That could be difficult…and dangerous.
He had signed on and would have to see how it played out.

He jotted himself a memo to visit the Peabody Institute Library on
Monday to go through everything he could find in the newspaper files on
Gino Pintano and Manny Antonelli, and on ESP.

He met briefly with Samantha the following day and she gave him a
paper bag containing three cell phone throwaways. They were in business.

¥

Steve learned a great deal at the library on Monday, and even more from
Samantha when he next spoke with her. Gino Pintano, like Manny
Antonelli, had been a hit man in his youth. As he moved up in the syndi-
cate, he ordered killings instead of pulling the trigger himself.

¥

He owned a gym establishment in Cambridge and frequented it often. The gym was one of his legitimate businesses, of which he had several, but his big money came from gambling, prostitution, and drugs. He managed big pieces of every illegal doing in Greater Boston, with the backing of the big boys in New York.

¥

His father-in-law, Papa Gardello, had been one of the "big" boys himself.

Gino had picked Manny for his daughter Terri because in Manny he saw a lot of himself.

But there was something strange about the way Gino died in November, 2007.

When Steve called Lawrence and questioned him about it, he was told that Gino's daughter Terri, his wife Theresa, and Manny were all complicit in Gino's assassination. Quite a family!

Six

That same evening, Arthur and Samantha had a quiet dinner at home. She fussed with a five ounce piece of crumb-covered Tilapia and he with a fourteen ounce similarly coated broiled haddock. They split a large sweet potato and shared a garden salad. A bottle of Casillero Del Diablo Merlot had already been disposed of.

"Charlie Lawrence called me today, Arthur."

"Oh? How is he?"

"Curious. He had lunch with Steve Grant, and I was the main topic of conversation. Steve had heard I was psychic and wanted to know about it."

"Damn it! What did Charlie tell him?"

"He told him that I had some ability in that direction."

"I wish he hadn't said anything. Too many people are asking questions about you, Samantha. I don't like it."

"I'm not concerned. I think I'll know when I'm in trouble."

"You think? That's not good enough, Sam."

"S-A-M-A-N-T-H-A, darling."

"Sorry. What do we really know about Steve Grant?"

"He's a war hero, an ex-cop; and single now, with two exes. He's clean; no illicit ties. Besides, I know he's okay." She tapped her forehead.

"Yeah. Well, if you say so."

"I say so, honey. And I welcome this opportunity to do something about Manny Antonelli. The fact that Manny's concerned about me shows there's a weakness in his armor. Let's play on that weakness."

"He's a killer."

"And we're giant-killers, Arthur. He's got to be taken down!"

"Let the FBI do it. Ken Katte will dog the Boston thugs until he gets enough to put them away," Arthur said.

"Katte and his crew have been saying that for a couple of years, Arthur, and have done zilch. Last time I talked to Katte – maybe a month ago – he said they are keeping a close watch on Manny and will move when the time is right. Its bull crap. They're watching him, and he's watching them."

"They have the resources, Samantha."

"And Manny has a person inside who lets him know every move the feds make," Samantha said.

"We know he's got Joe Weiss on his payroll," Arthur agreed.

"Weiss is a Boston cop, Arthur; not FBI. But Manny has a mole in the Bureau as well. I just know it." She tapped her forehead again. "As for Weiss, he's a slick article, playing every side he can as long as there's a buck in it for him."

"So we'll bring him down too."

She nodded. "We'll take him down too."

SEVEN

Manny sat in his office in the rear of Tully's Café in Boston's North End, contemplating. Samantha was a person who concerned him.

He felt she was like Gino had been, somehow able to perceive situations ahead of time. Even more so than Gino. She was dangerous to him, but he simply couldn't erase her. She said she had written and photographic evidence of some of his dealings but wasn't going to use them until she had enough to put him away forever. She had personally told him that.

If Steve Grant became a problem he could easily be erased: But not Samantha Robbins. Unless…!

Antonelli had no intention of spending even a weekend in jail. He needed to get something on Samantha or her husband to use as leverage.

Maybe a murder!

The thought intrigued him. *Who could one of them murder that would give him that edge?*

Slowly, he smiled. *Why not Steve Grant? He had just learned from Weiss that Grant had met up with Samantha Robbins in a deli in Danvers. Was it a chance meeting? Maybe the bastard planned to betray him?*

EIGHT

"You want another coffee?" Pauline asked, after quietly opening the door to Samantha's office.

"No thanks, honey, I'm fine."

"Did you have breakfast?"

"Yes, I had coffee and a prune Danish."

"That's not healthy, Samantha. You need cereal, with berries and a banana and whole milk and…"

"If you don't stop mothering me, Pauline, I am absolutely going to find some ninety year old widower to torment you day and night."

"I'd be more interested in two forty-five year olds," she said, an impish smile on her face. "At least don't forget to have a healthy lunch."

"I will. I'm meeting Arthur for lunch at the North Shore Mall. Now, be a dear and pull out the file on Manny Antonelli."

"Is that goon acting up again?"

"He'll never change, Pauline."

"I thought he was behaving himself."

"He's just been keeping out of the limelight."

"Okay. I'm on my way," Pauline said. "Be right back."

The file Pauline brought in was full of photos of pretty-boy Manny, his ex-wife Terri, their son little Gino, the Pintano parents – big Gino and Theresa and their son Anthony, and some of Gino's and Manny's henchmen, taken in various locations at a variety of events. Newspaper articles covering Manny's doings from the time his name first appeared in print as a teenager, along with Samantha's memos, were filed by date. Escapades Manny was alleged to have been involved with were coupled with Samantha's notes, indicating his complicities in those events. She had enough to cause him a headache, but not enough to see him rot.

She thumbed through the file and made notes she would pass on to Steve Grant a little at a time for him to feed back to Manny. She included a thing or two she made up about how she was attempting to keep up with Manny's doings, including a few possible moves he could be contemplating in the future. There was nothing magical in her line of thinking; she added common-sense moves based on his and the mob's doings. It would be interesting to see how Manny reacted. She intended to suck Manny into the eddy that would become a rip tide, and eventually a tsunami that would wash him out of Boston and into a federal prison.

Setting the file aside, she opened a manila envelope. Inside were listed the names of individuals thought to have been murdered by Manny, or on his orders. There were more than a few names. Finally returning everything into the envelope and resealing it, she held it in her hand a moment.

How could so much evil be packed into such a pretty package?

She left her desk, entered her private lavatory, washed, attended to her hair and lips and was out her office door ten minutes later to meet Arthur. She hoped she could manage to eat after having freshly reviewed the Manny Antonelli file.

¥

Arthur was sitting at a table in the center of the food court, browsing the sports page of The Boston Globe.

"Have you been waiting long?" she asked, tapping him on the shoulder.

"No, hon. Got here about ten minutes ago."

He studied her face. "You look upset. What's wrong?"

She pulled the chair opposite him away from the table, its metal legs screeching against the tile floor, and sat down. "I just reviewed my file on

Manny, and it's quite disturbing. Let's not discuss it yet. What are you having for lunch?"

"I don't know. I was thinking Chinese. That appeal to you?"

"No. I want a salad, and you should think of something healthy too."

"Sounds like Pauline talking."

That elicited a smile. "That was Pauline talking. She gave me that lecture fifteen minutes ago. But she's right."

"Okay. Do you want any special type of salad?"

"Make it a garden salad with light Italian dressing, and have them add a small scoop of tuna, along with a black coffee."

"That sounds good."

"Is that what you're having?"

"No, but I'll find something healthy."

He returned ten minutes later from the Au Bon Pain with her order as well as a sliced chicken, onion and tomato on toasted wheat bread, with a large diet lemonade for himself.

She nodded approvingly. "Good boy, Arthur."

She didn't notice his gaze was on the rather obese woman passing by toting an open cardboard container loaded with Umi chicken, lo Mein, an egg roll and fried rice.

Samantha enjoyed her lunch. Arthur ate quietly, his gaze often on the woman guzzling her Chinese fare at a nearby table.

"So, what bothered you so much today about Antonelli's file?" Arthur asked.

"It bothers me every time I open it. He's a ruthless killer and he's walking around free. He killed his wife, and many others, and he's living like a king."

"You don't know that he killed his wife, Samantha. Rumor was that Lou Adolpho ordered the hit on Terri, and another on Manny, but Manny got to Adolpho first. Ken Katte told me that."

She shook her head. "Antonelli is still free. He shouldn't be."

"I agree. How do you want to start?"

28

"We'll do it through Steve Grant," Samantha said. "We'll feed Manny innocuous proceedings from a few of my more interesting cases – along with things I'm supposedly looking into concerning him. He'll know I'm keeping tabs on him, and I'll be hinting that I believe he killed – or had ordered the killing of – Terri, Gino, and Lou Adolpho. He's not going to be happy with that. It could provoke him to do something foolish."

"Foolish? Like doing something to you? There is no way I'm going to let you set yourself up as bait, so forget it."

"Arthur, he won't come after me. I know he's convinced I have enough information spread among friends that could send him away for five or ten years, and that I won't use it until I have more that will put him away permanently."

"It's risky. I don't like it."

"It's not risky. It's opportunistic, and our best chance to save lives. He won't change his ways."

"No, but even if we get him, someone else will take his place." He placed his hand upon hers. "It's the way of the world, Samantha."

"That's true, but the next boss may not be as vicious. We take one step at a time. That's also the way of the world, Arthur."

He grimaced. He knew he could not dissuade her once her mind was made up.

"So how do we use Steve Grant?"

"I've made up a file titled 'Manny Antonelli – Current,' and filled it with information on where Manny has been seen and who he's talked to. I will add my thoughts as to what he may be up to. This should whet Manny's appetite. I'll add enough side notes that are inaccurate and harmless that Manny will believe I have nothing bothersome about him. He'll eventually call his surveillance of me off. I'll mention some FBI meetings I had that will let him know what he already knows – that the feds are watching him closely, looking to bring him down. Once he believes I'm not on to anything dirty that he's involved with, he might get careless, and we'll jump all over him."

"He thinks you can read his mind, doesn't he?"

"Something like that, Arthur, but he doesn't know to what degree: For that matter, either do I. I just get flashes sometimes. But he doesn't know that."

"Is he still living alone?"

"He's got a couple of girlfriends stashed away in apartments he rents or owns."

"What about his son, little Gino?"

"He's living with Manny's sister Angela and her kids. Manny doesn't see him often, and is probably waiting until the kid gets into his teens before he takes charge. Meanwhile, he pays his sister plenty to see the kid wants for nothing."

"Okay. So that's the plan?"

"That's the plan, Arthur."

NINE

For two months Manny received weekly reports and phone calls from Steve Grant. Steve reported he had gained access to Samantha's office and files but she had a safe that he hadn't as yet cracked. He sent a list of every client's name listed in Samantha's files, as well as current data on Manny that didn't amount to much; mostly places where Manny had been seen, and who he was with. Manny scoffed at some of Samantha's notes about what moves he was going to make and on who she planned to keep tabs.

He believed what he read, and was happy she was so far off base.

Manny also heard from Joe Weiss weekly. Joe had finally landed a reliable source within the Boston FBI who kept him aware of the feds checks on Manny. Between his two sources, Manny felt he was in excellent shape. But he knew he had to be careful, because the man he next planned to have disappear was an established Boston personality. It would be a clean hit, with no witnesses.

A disappearance was treated by the authorities differently from a murder. It clouded the investigation, giving the authorities little to work with. It was part of Manny's new thinking process – leave plenty of doubt as to whether a crime has happened. Let them chase shadows and rumors. Manny smiled these days a great deal more than he used to.

The only time he didn't smile was when he thought of Samantha Robbins. He had to find a way to control the witch that had him in her cross hairs. He had no intention of spending time in court defending himself on what he considered minor transgressions in his younger days. There had to be a safe way to get rid of her, and he intended to find it!

TEN

Giorgio reported to Manny at Tully's on a cold November morning, handing over the manila envelope stuffed with the cash retrieved from Sammy Pickens hiding place. Manny emptied the money on his desk, counted out two thousand, and handed it to Giorgio. "You and Leon share it. You can decide his share, but make it at least five hundred."

Giorgio nodded. "Leon made it happen," he said, posing his right hand as a weapon, then aiming and pulling his trigger finger. "He deserves half. I would have thought after the example we set when Theo cheated it wouldn't have happened again, but some people never learn. I doubt if it will happen again, Manny. But I'll be looking for it."

"You do that. What did you do with Pickens' body?"

"Dismembered it a bit, and then put it through a shredder, or so I told the other collectors. Actually it's in a large trash bag and he's covered with three bags of hydrated lime and buried deep. There will be nothing left of it in a couple of months."

Manny nodded. "Good. Leon is working out?"

"Better than I expected. He's my first cousin, and doing as he's told, Manny."

"Good to hear. I'm flying to New York this afternoon. I want you with me. Pack for an overnight, and pick me up here at the office at 4:00. We'll leave the car at Logan. I've got our usual suites booked at the Waldorf."

"What about hardware?" Giorgio said. "I can't take it with me on the plane. I don't like to go to New York without it. They got bad people there," he said, with a trace of a grin. "Why don't we drive?"

"You won't need hardware, but if it will make you feel better I'll ask Mario to have one of his people leave you a weapon under your pillow in your suite."

"I'd feel better, boss. You never know what can happen in that crazy city."

"I'll take care of it. Pay Leon off, get some rest, clean up and be back by four."

¥

Giorgio did as he was told, stopping only for a quickie with Anna, his twenty year old girlfriend, who worked in the coffee shop across the street from Tully's. She had an apartment on the second floor, above the coffee shop where she worked. Her boss was her mother, only eighteen years older than Anna, and also an occasional recipient of Giorgio's favors. *Why the hell not! Giorgio always left fifty bucks, and they may as well keep the money in the family.*

ELEVEN

M anny had reached a number of the goals he had set his mind to, and hoped in the future his son would take over for him while he traveled the world and saw the sights he read about and was enthralled with in his National Geographic Magazines.

He had no aspiration to move higher in the mob hierarchy – he felt that was impossible – and had expressed his feelings on more than one occasion to his close friend Mario Serino, who reigned with three other New York honchos as heads of the organization. "I'm not competition for anyone to worry about, Mario. Please make sure your friends know that."

Mario almost believed him. He just wished life was that simple.

¥

A stretch limo awaited Manny and Giorgio at the front entrance to Delta Airlines at La Guardia Airport. A sign on one of its side windows, in large block letters, was seeking a "Manny Kennedy." Manny chuckled over Mario's sense of humor, remembering how he had expressed his wishes to Mario Serino, one of the four syndicate heads of New York City, of living as well as the Kennedys' when he retired. Mario had laughed at the time, and told Manny that he'd have to change his name to something Irish, and cut at least three inches off his penis.

Heavy traffic delayed them but the amply-supplied bar in the limo provided them both a couple of Booker's neat bourbons to help pass the time.

The concierge spotted Manny when they entered the hotel, and the man quickly left his desk, greeted Manny warmly, and smiled at Giorgio's refusal to give up their two travel bags. They bypassed check-in and were personally escorted to the two upper floor suites set aside for them.

"I took the liberty of registering you both, Mr. Antonelli."

Manny's thank you was accompanied by a one-hundred dollar bill, which the concierge deftly tucked into a side pocket. "If there is anything else you might need please call my desk, Mr. Antonelli. I'll take care of it personally. I'm on duty until midnight."

"I think we're all set, Frederick. Thank you. Goodnight."

Frederick practically danced out of the suite, beckoning Giorgio to follow him to the suite next door.

After both men refreshed themselves, they met at 8:30 for a late dinner in the Bull & Bear Restaurant. The maître d' rushed to greet Manny.

"Will there be just two this evening, Mr. Antonelli?"

"Yes, Emil," Manny said, smiling as he slipped the folded new fifty dollar bill into a waiting hand. "I'd like a table against the wall, where it's quiet"

"Of course, sir; please follow me."

They ordered bourbons, neat, as Giorgio wasn't into fine wines or champagne, and Manny could have cared less. Tomorrow, with Mario, they would have some good Italian wine. Manny opted for a medium-rare sirloin and Giorgio for the lamb chops, medium well. The meats were from the DeBragga butchery, and were Prime Dry-Aged beef. Their waiter recommended the creamed spinach, and an Idaho baked potato with sour cream complimented their entrees. They made little small-talk, as was Manny's way, and he cautioned Giorgio to hide his weapon better. It bulged under his somewhat tight-fitting sport jacket. Mario had supplied too big a weapon.

When Giorgio got back to his suite at ten thirty, he called the concierge for a hooker, while Manny took off his shoes and stretched out on the bed in his own suite, alone, and began making phone calls. Tomorrow was an important day for Manny: If Mario and his partners gave him their blessing. If they didn't...well, there would have to be some soul searching, and maybe a murder or two in the making.

TWELVE

⌐━━━━┑

M ario Serino arrived for breakfast a few minutes after ten Saturday morning. He was 5'7", slim, and white haired; a well-dressed gentleman with a kind grandfatherly face that dimpled when he smiled. He held out both hands to grasp Manny's shoulders.

He had three of his associates with him. They did not smile, but they were also well-dressed, young, big, of Italian ancestry, and no-doubt legally armed. As it turned out, they were all related to Mario, a smart move noted by Manny, as who could be better trusted, normally, than your own family. His family was the exception.

The three bodyguards sat at a nearby table, in positions to scan every entrance to the restaurant. Manny sent Giorgio over to join them, after whispering to him to behave himself.

Both Mario and Manny ordered large juices, eggs Benedict without Hollandaise sauce, no potato and coffee.

"You got stomach problems, Manny? I see you're careful how you eat."

"No, Mario. I'm just trying to maintain my weight. I don't want my girlfriends complaining I'm too heavy when I crawl on top of them."

He got the muted laugh he expected, as well as a comeback. "Do what I do, let them get on top," Mario said, his face displaying an appreciative smile. "You ain't gonna get married again, Manny? A good looking guy like you can pretty much call his shots and nail whoever he wants."

"I have no plans to, Mario. I kind of like it this way."

"I suppose: To each his own. Me, I got a wife and three kids. I'm married thirty-seven years. My wife still looks like she's twenty years old. To tell the truth, my eyes ain't so good no more." He laughed loudly at his own joke, and then his smile faded and he gazed at Manny intently. "What's so important you want to talk to me about, Manny?"

"Several things, Mario. May I suggest we eat while it's hot and then talk?"

Mario nodded.

The two men dined slowly, savoring the food and freshly brewed coffee. Mario told two jokes and Manny politely laughed.

Mario was a slow eater, primarily because he liked to talk. Eventually he tossed his napkin on the table and took a final sip of water. He set his glass down. "Okay. I'm listening, Manny. What's on your mind?"

"The future Mario. I came from nothing, as you know, and fought my way to where I am today. But I don't want to step on any New Yorkers' toes. I know my place. I'll have enough money when I retire to lead the life I want. What I want to talk to you about today is my son, little Gino. I never really did anything for him because he was far more attached to his mother, and I didn't trust her. She was a bad influence, caring only about herself. And I guess I didn't care because I was too busy. To be honest, I only had the kid to cement my relations with her father, Gino Pintano, and her grandfather, your former partner Papa Gardello. I didn't want kids. Truth be told I don't like kids, but this kid I thought was necessary for the family to have someone to dote upon. Anyway, he's the only one I'll ever have and I feel guilty toward him. He's young now and being brought up by my sister. She has a bunch of her own kids and tells me little Gino is happy living with her. I send her dough every month, so the kid lacks for nothing, but I want to ensure his future. I figure I'll take him in with me when he's thirteen or fourteen. Teach him the business. If he shows the right stuff by the time he's eighteen or twenty, I'd retire and let him take over the Boston operations, with your approval, of course. I know that's years down the road but it's been on my mind and I wanted to throw it by you. I'd need your support to make it work with the others. What do you think?"

Mario didn't want to tell him he thought he was crazy. *I can't plan what's gonna be a year from now, and he wants to go down the road thirteen or fifteen years?*

"Manny, it's a long way off. Don't worry about it. I can promise you this. You keep producing the way you have been and we'll take care of you. I like you and my partners like you. Keep it that way."

"Maybe you could take him under your wing a little bit when he gets older, Mario? If I think he's got the stuff, I'll want you to know him. If he doesn't, I won't send him. I want somebody we can both trust and rely on."

"Yeah, that sounds like a good move. We'll keep it as a possibility. So let it rest for now, Manny. Now I got a request. My wife's got a cousin – she's a good looker, thirty-two years old, got a great body – who saw you at my party a couple of months ago. She's been breaking my wife's ass about meeting you. Are you interested?"

"No. But if you insist, I will."

"I don't insist, but I have to tell my wife something. Personally, I don't think it's such a good idea. I'd like to bang her myself, and I know that's not a good idea either," he added with a chuckle. "I'll tell her you're involved right now and let it go at that. Okay?"

"Thank you, Mario; for everything."

"Yeah. Let it play out. You'll be okay. Don't forget, you're having dinner at my place tonight. We're having a few friends over. Your guy can hang with my people. They'll be playing poker in my game room, and they'll call in for their own food and drink. He'll be okay with them as long as he's got plenty of money to lose."

"He doesn't usually lose, Mario. He's good."

"Good. Then maybe he'll teach them a lesson."

"Your wife's cousin going to be there tonight?"

"No. I wouldn't do that to you."

"Thanks. What time tonight?"

"Eight o'clock. I'll send a car for you at 7:30."

¥

Promptly at 7:35, Manny and Giorgio entered the gleaming limo that arrived at the front entrance of the Waldorf. One of the young men who had attended Mario earlier in the day exited the front passenger side and with a hand gesture invited Mario and Giorgio into the limo. "Good evening, Mr. Antonelli. I'm sorry we're a few minutes late, but it's difficult to gauge New York evening traffic."

"Not a problem," Manny said.

"My name's Tony. I hope your friend has a wallet as big as the weapon he's packing," Tony said.

That remark brought the hint of a smile to Giorgio's normally somber face. "The wallet will be fatter by far when I leave for home," Giorgio said, looking the man in the eye before he took his seat beside Manny.

It took twenty minutes before they arrived at Mario's downtown penthouse. The limo barely came to a stop before two men approached, looked around the area, then opened the limo door to allow Giorgio and Manny to exit. The two men, Manny later learned, were nephews to Mario.

Looks as if he has his whole family on the payroll, Manny thought.

The penthouse was lavish; large and definitely showed a woman's touch. Crystal chandeliers and oil paintings, full-size statues of nude men and women, fabulous huge tapestries depicting Greek gods, custom furniture imported from Europe, Persian rugs – all of which Manny wouldn't have recognized or appreciated if Mario's wife, Sophia, hadn't latched on to him when he entered and insisted on personally showing him around her apartment and explaining everything. Mario gave her twenty minutes with him before he pulled him away.

"Sorry about that, Manny," he said, "but this is her showplace, and if I objected to her showing it off to every new visitor she'd shut me off, and I don't want that," he said lightheartedly.

"She's a charming and very attractive woman."

Mario nodded, but didn't comment on Manny's compliment. "C'mon, we'll have a drink. The other guests should be arriving any minute."

The other guests, three couples, arrived together five minutes later. They were dressed to the nines, the women in long gowns, the men in tuxedoes, and Manny would have felt awkward if Mario had dressed similarly. But Mario was in a dark suit with a white shirt and maroon tie, as was Manny. Manny later learned Mario's guests had just come from a testimonial to a retiring vice-president of a New York private investment company.

The couples were all in their fifties, the women short of stature, the men not much taller. All three men were bankers, and it didn't take long for Manny to figure they were all in the business of laundering mob money. A cozy group–all in Mario's pocket one way or another. The men were attentive to Mario, as if he were handing out bags of candy and they were young boys. *Maybe there's a better reason than that. Mario's probably arranged some indiscretions on their part and they're afraid to do anything but kiss ass. Or maybe he's done what I would have;-threatened to make them disappear.*

The couples were pleasant enough, and Manny decided his inclusion with this group was merely coincidental. *Sophia probably planned this dinner party prior to my contacting Mario for our meeting and Mario simply asked me along.*

It was obvious to Sophia that the other wives were smitten with Manny. They couldn't keep their eyes off him and continually addressed him to find out more about him. Manny played his part easily. He was a Boston business man who dabbled in real estate ventures, and gymnastic companies as a sideline.

Sophia knew better. She knew he was a former hit man who now worked for her husband. She knew a lot of things she wasn't supposed to know because she was beyond inquisitive. She was a schemer like her husband, but far more patient. She had married Mario because she wanted the lifestyle he could provide, and she didn't care how he earned his money. She was faithful to Mario because the money and position were far more important to her than love or sex. And she figured somewhere down the road she would find the man she wanted, and then Mario would have to go. Manny, although young, appeared to be a fit candidate.

¥

Giorgio was having a successful evening. He knew how to play poker; when to bluff, when to bet and when to fold, and in a few hours he was ahead by more than three-hundred dollars in the low stakes game. He was by far the quietest of the five card players, by far the oldest, and by far the smartest. The others all liked to bluff when they didn't have good hands, playing and betting when they shouldn't have, and Giorgio made them pay almost every time. Apparently the money they were losing didn't mean anything, but the idea they were losing to him didn't sit well. By eleven-thirty they had long ago given up on the food they had ordered in, but a couple of them were still downing plenty of beer. The youngest nephew, twenty-four, nicknamed Tito, was the biggest drinker, the biggest bluffer, and the biggest loser. After a particularly bad bluff and big pot loss he snarled at Giorgio. "What the fuck; are you dealing from the bottom?" Giorgio stopped gathering in the pot, and stared at Tito. He said in a controlled but frigid voice, "Do you want to die where you're sitting?"

Tito's cousin Tony was quick to intervene. "Tito, keep your fucking mouth shut. He ain't cheating. Nobody's cheating. You're just a stupid fucking card player and always have been. Now apologize or get out of here."

Apparently Tony's words carried weight. After an ever so brief period, Tito insincerely worded his apology, threw his cards on the table, and stormed out of the room.

"I'm sorry Giorgio," Tony said. "Tito's a lousy card player, and he's had too much to drink. I'd appreciate if you didn't say anything. If Mario got wind of it, Tito would be in real trouble."

"I don't need the fucking money," Giorgio said. "You want it back? Split it up!"

"Absolutely not! You won it fair and square. You know your cards."

Giorgio nodded. "Yeah, I do know...."

The door to the room opened and Tito appeared. "The guests are getting ready to leave. Mario wants you all out front."

¥

It was the same limo driver, Lou, along with his companion, Tony, that returned Manny and Giorgio to the Waldorf. There was little conversation on the drive back, everyone seemingly lost in his own thoughts. When they arrived, Tony was quickly out of the front seat and opened the side door for Manny and Giorgio. He offered his hand to both men and wished them both a pleasant "goodnight."

In the Waldorf lobby, Manny asked Giorgio. "You want a nightcap?"

"Yeah, I think so."

"You don't sound happy."

"One of them prick nephews accused me of cheating."

"Were you?"

"Of course I wasn't. Those dumb bastards don't know how to play. They play every hand whether they have good cards or not. They bluff all the time. It was like taking candy away from babies."

"How much did you take?"

"It was a small stakes game. I took them for about five hundred."

"Good for you. Maybe they won't be so high and mighty in the future."

"The other guys were all right. Just that Tito bastard was obnoxious."

"Any of them say anything of interest?"

"No. Not really. I asked who the other guests were and Tony said they're bankers; nobody of importance. Mario runs them."

"I've got their names. We'll check them out when we get home. Is there anything else I should know?"

"Hmm; no. What kind of a guy is Mario?"

"If he likes you, you live. If he doesn't, you don't."

"They still do things the old way?"

"No. If they want to send a message, the body is found. If not, the guy simply disappears."

"Makes sense," Giorgio nodded.

"It does, and it's the same way we'll continue to do things in every instance," Manny said. "All our enemies will merely disappear."

¥

The plane trip back was uneventful, with Giorgio reading a girlie magazine and Manny thinking about what to do about Samantha Robbins. So far his private eye, Steve Grant, had come up with nothing of interest about Samantha. The cases and people she was working on were not related to him—with the exception of one: Joe Weiss. His name appeared several times, with the reference she knew he was "dirty." But it didn't hint at what she was going to do about it. *Maybe she and Joe Weiss should disappear at the same time. And maybe her husband Arthur Lite would make it a threesome.* Manny smiled at the thought before he dozed off.

¥

They arrived at Logan on schedule. Giorgio went for the car while Manny made two phone calls. The first went to a message machine and he hung up. The second call was answered on the third ring.

"Hello."

"I assume you're free tonight."

"I was hoping you'd call. I'm always free for you."

"Cab over to Abe and Louie's, Maria. I'll meet you there at eight o'clock. Plan to stay with me overnight. You can do?"

"I absolutely can do. I'm looking forward to it. See you at eight."

Giorgio drove up several minutes later. Manny got in the car while Giorgio pushed the windshield washer button for the third time, finally removing most of the droppings some bird had left them. "God-damned birds," Giorgio hissed.

Manny smiled. "Better than elephants," Manny said, being in better humor since making his arrangement with Maria.

"That joke's as old as I am," Giorgio said. "Where do you want to go?"

"Drive to my office. I want to shower and clean up before going to Abe & Louie's. I'm meeting Maria. You grab a bite at the bar and keep your eye on things. Later, you'll drop us off at the Ritz. She'll be spending the night. I'll make the usual arrangements for you."

¥

When Maria entered the restaurant, the maître d' was quick to notice her. He didn't remember her name, but he remembered her body, and whom she had been with.

"Good evening. Are you with Mr. Antonelli this evening?"

"Yes. Has he arrived?"

"Not as yet, ma'am, but he called. Please, come this way."

She followed him, enjoying the eyebrows she raised as she passed through the nearly full downstairs restaurant area. Her low-cut, short, red dress showed about as much as she wanted it to, and there were many looks and smiles as she walked erectly toward the chosen table. The looks and smiles were from the male guests; the females weren't so kind.

"Is that some high-class hooker?" one middle-aged woman queried her husband as Maria passed by.

"Shush," her husband admonished her. "There are all kinds of people who dine here, even criminals, and you don't know who she's meeting."

Maria hadn't heard the comment, and it was a good thing, or the woman would have found her face pushed into the soup she had been enjoying. Maria came from New York originally, and could stand her ground with anyone.

Manny showed up, dressed in gray slacks, a white Brooks Brothers shirt open at the neck, a navy Louis' Boston blazer, and Johnson & Murphy black Cap Toe Oxfords. He had heads turning in his direction as he made his way to the table to join his date.

"You look beautiful, Maria," he said as he gently brushed his lips against her cheek, picking up the scent of the Prada 'Candy 'Eau de Parfum he had recently sent her as a gift.

"Thank you, and you look handsome as ever. I think the ladies here were thankful they were sitting when you passed by. You make half of us weak in the knees." She smiled coyly at him.

"And the other half?"

"Want to spread them."

He laughed. "You have a way with words, Maria. Which group are you in?"

"I'll show you later."

He sat down beside her. "Would you like a cocktail before dinner, or should we go directly to the champagne?"

"Champagne's my favorite, just like you are, Manny."

He smiled and ordered a bottle of Dom Pérignon, one he knew she favored, from the hovering sommelier.

"How have you been, Maria?"

"I'm better than good. I'm happy with my new job. My bosses are good guys, and don't hit on me. There are lawyers in nearby offices who are fresh, but I told them you are my boyfriend, and they just about ran away. I hope you don't mind my using your name, but some were becoming bothersome."

"Are you telling me I'm the one and only, Maria?"

She leaned close to him, smiled, and said, "I don't lie to you. I prefer you. The other two are just rich guys looking for a good time and with the money to pay for it. Frankly, I can't make it with them. If you want me to stop seeing them, I will."

"Hell no, make them happy. We've got to make this world a better place. Spread the love, but be careful." Manny smiled as he said this. This girl was one in a million. She was brutally honest, uninhibited, and fun to be with. She had never once overstepped her position and got into things that were not her business. Manny enjoyed her company.

What Manny didn't know was that Maria had an uncle in New York by the name of Mario Serino.

THIRTEEN

"**S**amantha? Hi. It's Steve Grant. I hope I'm not calling too late."

"Ten is not too late; eleven would be. Are you on one of our safe cell phones?"

"Absolutely."

"Good. Why the call?"

"I'm getting no feedback from you-know-who, or any of his people. It's been a while. I have no feeling as to how we're progressing. Are we accomplishing what we had hoped to?"

"I think so. I suggest we continue what we're doing. I might jazz my info about him for you in the next week or so to lead him further away from the truth but make him want you to check it out."

"Do you think Manny's buying what we've been feeding him?"

"I believe he is – but you never know."

"I thought you would know, based on your…reputation."

"It doesn't work that way, Steve. Sometimes I get a clear picture, other times I don't."

"I can't help being a little nervous, Samantha, dealing with the likes of him."

"Just remain cautious. Things will work out. Wait until this Thursday evening to break into my office. I'll have something of interest for you to find, and you can feed it to him on Friday. Maybe we'll shake him up a little bit."

"Okay. Will do. Sorry to have bothered you."

"It wasn't a bother, Steve. I'll talk to you soon."

¥

"What did he want, Samantha?" Arthur asked as he entered their bedroom as Samantha closed her cell.

"I believe a little reassurance, honey. I think he worries about working for Manny Antonelli."

"And well he might. Manny plays rough."

"I know. I think I'll give Manny something new to think about. I'll leave a memo to myself, something to the effect about checking on women Manny is seeing–who they are, what they do, and can they be used against him. That will give Manny pause–my getting to any of his women. I don't believe he'd have been stupid enough to allow any of them to have any incriminating knowledge of his illicit dealings, but it may shake him up a bit."

FOURTEEN

Friday morning Steve wrote up his report, quoting the memo he found on Samantha's desk. He thought this might be important enough info to pass on to Captain Joe Weiss. He called the cell phone number Manny had given him for Weiss.

"It's Joe. Spill it," a gruff voice said.

"It's Grant. I'm sending you a copy of a memo for our mutual friend, but he may want to be aware of the information right away."

"What's it about?"

"The party in question is looking for information on all our friend's girlfriends, and plans to visit them."

"That would be a waste of time, but I'll pass it on. Anything else you want to add?"

"No."

"Goodbye."

Joe Weiss left his office minutes later and headed across the street. He walked one block south, turned the corner after looking back, was satisfied he was alone, and placed a call to Manny Antonelli.

"Yeah, Joe."

"I just got a call from Grant. He's sending you a memo in his next report, but thought it important enough to call me to pass it on to you right away."

"I'm listening."

"The memo was from the PI. She's going to look into all of the females you've been seeing, and question them."

"It's not a problem. I don't discuss business with any of them. Don't worry about it. Anything else?"

"No."

"Goodbye."

FIFTEEN

M anny put the cell phone into his pants pocket. He had been sitting at his desk at home, and got up to stretch. His body was moving slowly, but his mind was working at warp speed. He paced back and forth a full minute before concluding that none of his women knew anything, and his main woman, Maria, was so crazy about him, she would never say a word against him anyway.

Returning to his desk, he took a second cellphone from the lower desk drawer and called Grant.

"I got a call a short time ago about a memo you're sending. You got that memo handy?"

Steve recognized Manny's voice. "Yes."

"Read it, every word, just the way it's written."

Steve opened the envelope he'd just sealed, pulled his report and slowly read it. There was a momentary pause when he finished.

"Okay. No problem. Send it along. Thanks." Manny hung up.

¥

Steve sat back in his chair and smiled. *"No problem,"* he thought, *but enough of a problem for me to receive a call from the man himself.* He took a few minutes to think about the conversation before calling Samantha.

"Hello Steve."

"Good morning, Samantha. I think we might have stirred something up. I decided to call Joe Weiss about your memo, and he must have felt it important enough to inform Mr. Antonelli right away because I got a call a few minutes ago from the man himself. He wanted me to read him the memo word for word. After that, it took him a bit before he said 'no problem' and hung up. I thought you should know."

"Thanks, Steve. Anything else?"

"No."

"Bye."

Samantha disconnected with a smile on her face. *It's your move, Mr. Antonelli. I wonder which one in your stable of female friends you will consider a problem.*

¥

And that's what Manny was thinking. There were three women he was seeing. Two were strictly for sex, and he could rule them out. He only met them in popular restaurants and taken them afterwards to offbeat hotel rooms, never to any of his regular haunts or living places. Only Maria had visited and stayed over in his residences.

He considered at that moment that it wouldn't hurt to have Steve Grant check Maria's background. He began to reconsider his relationship with Maria. Maybe she was too perfect. She had found him, now that he thought about it. He hadn't found her.

SIXTEEN

F riday evening Samantha and Arthur, along with Billie and Anne Tsapatsaris, sat in a back booth at the Wardhurst Restaurant.

Billie and Anne were old friends and of a different generation. They were into their eighties, some fifty years senior to Samantha and Arthur, but the disparity in age did not seem to matter. Billie had been a well-respected member of the Peabody Police Department, a detective lieutenant now retired, but with extensive experience in all phases of police work. Samantha and Arthur often consulted him. Tonight, however, was hopefully to be more social than business, but Samantha didn't mind mixing business with pleasure, and she knew Billie loved the mixture.

Billie was holding court with two long-time waitresses, Vicky and Anna, who stopped by to greet the group. After a few minutes, they broke away to get back to their tables, and Janice approached to take their drink orders.

"It's like old home week," Billie said, displaying his ever-present smile. "Every time I come here for dinner or lunch I see a lot of people I know."

"And he hates the attention," Anne quipped, with the hint of a smile.

"Of course I do. I'm just a quiet, unassuming, lovable soul by nature," Billie said, and then broke out in laughter. "But that's enough talk about me. What have you two been up to?"

"Work, work and more work. You know what it's like being a cop," Arthur said. "Fortunately at present there are no serious problems."

"That go for you too, Samantha?" Billie asked.

"Pretty much, except for one headache that's out there."

"Who or what might that be?" Billie said.

Samantha held off before answering, allowing Janice to serve the women their glasses of Merlot and the men their bottles of Sam Adams. They placed their food orders, and Samantha continued after Janice departed.

"My problem is a very difficult character by the name of Manny Antonelli, Billie. This topic has to be kept amongst us folk, as I can't have it get out. He's put a watch on me for one reason or another. He's spying on me. I need to return the favor. I let word get to him that I was going to check on the women he's seeing just to see if I could shake him up, and now I think it was a good idea because it did shake him up. I may be able to get something out of one of them. I need to know who they are, their backgrounds, and everything about them. I was wondering, Billie, if you still have connections in Boston who can discretely get me some information without stirring up a maelstrom. I can't afford to get into a battle with Antonelli; he has far more resources than I do, so it has to be done carefully and discretely. My question to you is can it be done?"

"That could be a tall order, Samantha, but not impossible. Let me think about it overnight. I've got many sources, but not that many I fully trust. I'm not positive that a leak wouldn't somehow reach Antonelli. He throws a lot of weight and a lot of money around, and it's impossible to know who he's got in his pocket."

"Take all the time you need, Billie," Arthur said, feeling the need to enter into the conversation. "Anybody involved in dealings with Antonelli has got to watch his backside, including you. If you think it's too dangerous we don't want you involved. We'll find another way."

"Exactly what I was about to say," Samantha said. "We've got to have totally reliable people or not chance it. Please understand that."

"Like I said, let me think about it. I'll call you tomorrow, Samantha, and give you an answer."

Samantha reached into her pocketbook and pulled out a small notepad and pen. She jotted down a phone number, tore off the page, and handed it across the table to Billie. "You can reach me at this number."

He took the paper and stuffed it in his jacket pocket. "You think he's monitoring your office phones, Samantha?"

Billie's still sharp as they come, Samantha thought. "I wouldn't put it past him, Billie. In fact I'm pretty sure he is. I'm having my office phones swept every week, but there are ways around that. I'm now using a series of throw-away phones to conduct the parts of my business concerning him."

"Smart move. I'll ask around and I'll check in with you as soon as I have anything."

"Thanks Billie. The number I gave you is safe to call, and I only answer that phone outside my home or my office."

Billie nodded. "The games we have to play, Samantha. With all the new technology available, we have to forever be on guard. I'll call you soon." He raised his beer and toasted. "To the two most beautiful women in the world: Stay as you are. I assume the business portion of the evening is now concluded?"

"It is," Samantha said with a smile.

"Then let's enjoy. Skoal."

¥

On their way home, Samantha and Arthur were pensive, having talked themselves out over dinner. "Arthur, I'm not sure I did the right thing in asking Billie to get involved. Manny has too many sources, and if he finds out a retired cop from Peabody is asking questions about him, he'll want to know why."

"A retired cop in his mid-eighties won't pose a threat to him, Samantha; but yes, he'll want to know why, and possibly find a connection to you, but so what. He already knows you're keeping tabs on him. I wish you hadn't clued anyone in that you were going to check on his women."

"On hindsight, I wish I hadn't either, but actually I think it was a good idea. I may find something important. Manny's afraid to do me any harm, Arthur. But he may want to send me a message by way of Billie."

"Unlikely. I don't think he wants to stir anything up with a retired cop, or you."

"He's afraid of me, Arthur? Is that what this is all about?"

"I don't think he's afraid of you. I think he's wary of you. That's why he hired Grant. Let's see if he contacts Grant to check on Billie. Grant will tell us. If he doesn't, you won't have to worry."

Samantha reluctantly agreed. Billie was capable of getting her the information she wanted. But she made herself a mental note to put something about Billie into the info that would reach Manny, and follow up with a memo a week later with the result he had come up with nothing.

SEVENTEEN

Billie had two people in mind as he pondered how to help Samantha. He knew the two agencies most likely to have a fix on Manny were the Boston police and the Boston FBI, and he had friends currently or formerly within both organizations. But it was no secret to him that both groups had people who likely supplemented their incomes by doing small favors for cash for people outside the law. Billie decided to take the weekend to think about it.

¥

He had his low acid orange juice, poached eggs, toast and coffee while still in his Celtics pajamas and white terrycloth robe. While he glanced at the Globe's sport pages, Anne talked about what a nice evening they had spent with Samantha and Arthur.

Billie was still very much with it, although advancing age had made him slightly forgetful at times, and his body required the use of a cane. But when he dressed his six foot plus thin frame in his extended wardrobe and flashed his captivating smile, he appeared and acted years younger than most octogenarians. His eyes didn't miss much, as Anne had often noted when they walked the North Shore Mall and a pretty girl walked by. He remained a fun guy. But his line of work had always been demanding. He had been a good cop, an honest cop, a hard working cop, and served his community well. And now he had been asked for help against a mob big shot, and he was inwardly pleased to become involved.

Damn right I'll help.

Monday morning he called the FBI office in Boston and asked for Ken Katte. As expected, Katte wasn't available, but the name Tsapatsaris was left, along with a brief message and a phone number. He knew Katte would get back to him.

His second call went to an ex-Boston cop, Justin Ryan, another retiree whom Billie had known since Boy Scout camp. Justin had been with the Boston Police Department since his twenty-sixth birthday, served as a beat cop in the North End in his early days and had risen to the rank of lieutenant. He retired somewhat early only because he was injured in the line of duty and forced into a desk job he couldn't talk his way out of. He didn't care anymore, though. He liked retirement. He frequented many Red Sox, Celtics, Patriots and Bruins games gratis because he knew the right people, having done favors for many of them. He had done the little favors, like taking care of parking tickets for certain people, seeing that their kids' parties were properly supervised and protected–the little things that respectable people with money were concerned about in a city where divergent gangs were eager to cause trouble. Justin would not take cash payoffs, although many lowlifes had tried to buy him off, but free tickets to events passed his moral standards. He hadn't made many enemies, did have many friends, and knew what was going on in the city - or could find out through his many connections. Billie knew Justin was the right man to contact, and he had his address and phone number because they still hooked up two or three times a year.

Justin answered on the second ring.

"What can I do you out of, Billie?"

"How'd you know it was me?"

"C'mon, Billie. Even an old fart like you knows your name will show up on the TV screen if you have the right service."

"I'm not that much older than you are."

"Maybe not if you figure in years, Billie, but I'm prone to figure the difference in hours and minutes."

"You always were a wise ass. How're you doing?"

"Doing great, feeling great, and lying a lot."

"That's about par for you. I got some serious business to discuss. Can we meet?"

"I ain't driving anymore, so you'll have to come and get me."

"Will you take the subway and meet me at Wonderland? I could pick you up there and we'd go to lunch…"

"Can I pick the spot?"

"…and, yes, you can pick the spot."

"And order whatever I want?"

"You're getting to be a hard ass, Justin. The answer is 'yes', and I'll also say yes to eating a lobster roll, fries and a coke while sitting in the car at Revere Beach in front of Kelly's. Does that satisfy you?"

"Absolutely! When do we meet?"

"Tomorrow. I'll pick you up noontime."

"Are you still driving that same piece of junk?"

"It's not junk. It's more like an antique."

"Ha. Okay, I'll see you tomorrow at noon. Pick me up on the beach side. I don't want to climb all the steps…."

"Okay, old man, on the beach side. See you at noon."

¥

It was twelve-ten p.m. when the subway rolled into Wonderland, its last stop north on the Blue Line. Justin had gotten a ride from a neighbor to Government Center and hopped the MBTA from there. Some twenty minutes later he ambled toward the beach and was greeted by Billie, who was wearing a winter parka, its hood up, and leaning on his cane.

"What the hell, do you think its winter, Billie?" Justin snapped in way of a greeting.

"It sure as hell isn't summer; not along the beach, anyway. I've been standing here ten minutes and I'm freezing my ass off. C'mon; my car is across the street, illegally parked and I'm sure a cop will be along soon."

The two men made small talk as they shuffled along to where Billie had parked, and entered the car. The engine turned over first try and Billie smiled gratefully.

"What is this car, Billie, an Edsel? It ain't the Model T you used to have," Justin quipped.

"You know nothing," Billie joshed. "It's a Bentley, and you're lucky I even let a guy like you sit in it."

Billie made the U-turn to put him on the beach road and headed towards Kelly's. Five minutes later he parked in a handicap spot, shut off his car heater and engine and breathed a sigh of relief. "The heat felt good."

"You're a nutcase. There are plenty of people walking the beach today."

"True, but look how they're dressed. They're all wearing long johns."

"Those are tights and jogging pants. You are a panic, Billie. But enough talk, let's eat. I skipped breakfast, looking forward to this."

Billie looked in his side mirror before exiting the car. "You want coffee or a coke?"

"I want coffee: A big one, with no sugar and three creams; and extra cocktail sauce and ketchup. Wave to me when the food's ready and I'll come across and help you carry it."

"That's damn white of you, Justin," Billie uttered as he left to cross the street.

Twenty minutes later they were barely talking as they sat side by side in the front seat, relishing their meals. "Damn, Billie, this is as good as ever," Justin said after he swallowed a mouthful of lobster roll, set the roll down on the console bench separating them, and reached for his coffee. "I haven't had lobster in a while and this is a real treat. I could do this every week."

"I'm sure you could, especially if I'm paying."

"Ain't that sweet, Billie. I don't care what all our mutual friends say about you, I still think you're a nice guy."

"Still the wise ass," Billie said with a smile.

Justin picked up the rest of his lobster roll and Billie watched it disappear in two bites. A few minutes later Justin washed it down with a final slug of coffee. He gathered his and Billie's paper plates and wrappers and stuffed them in the empty bag the food came in, then added the leftover ketchup and cocktail packets and exited the car heading for a trash barrel. When he returned he was all smiles. "Okay, now to business. Who do you want bumped off?"

"Get serious, Justin. What can you get me on Manny Antonelli's stable of women? I want to know which one he's seeing most often and where he seeing her and the others."

"That's all you want?" Justin said sarcastically.

"For starters, yes."

"Can you give me a couple of days?"

"As few as possible, Justin."

"By the end of the week, if not before," Justin said, "I'll give you what I can get. Does that suit you?"

"Yes. We thank you."

"Who's the 'we'?"

"Just me. Leave it at that, okay."

"That's fine. Can I buy you an ice cream?"

"Nope. I'm full. I'm surprised you're not."

"I am, but I just wanted to contribute something to this meeting."

"Another day, Justin. Thanks for coming. I'll take you back. It's almost time for your nap."

EIGHTEEN

I t took Justin two days to get the information on Manny Antonelli's lady friends. Manny had two hookers – beautiful women who were at his beck and call – and one "awesome babe," per a freckle-faced bellhop, who Manny saw more regularly. The doorman concurred. This last woman, "Maria" he'd called her, was the only one who Antonelli took to his several hangouts and personal quarters on a regular basis – she was his number one girl. And yet she was somewhat of a mystery. A cabbie told Justin she worked at an insurance agency on Beacon Street, and Justin had the man drive him past the place: World Wide Insurance. After checking for a full day Justin could find no one who knew her background, which he found strange. He decided her fingerprints were a necessity, and set out to get them.

On Monday morning at eleven forty-five, he entered World Wide Insurance. Two partners' names, Luigi and Carmen Romano, were stenciled on the glass-paneled door. He waited in the hallway some thirty feet away from the front entrance and was rewarded with the sight of two young women leaving three minutes past the noon hour. One woman was short and dumpy; the other was easily describable as a knockout. Tall, thin, busty, and great legs. *It has to be Maria,* Justin thought, and smiled. As soon as the women were out of sight, he entered the office.

¥

There were three desks aligned in a row and five filing cabinets. Several Boston Celtics sports pictures adorned the walls. A large Red Sox wall clock and four black leather chairs surrounded a low-slung wooden table in the waiting area. Behind the desks, two closed doors led to what he thought would be a pair of private offices.

"Can I help you, sir?" asked a petite, parrot-nosed woman sitting at the rear desk. She wore a name tag that read "Linda."

"Are either of the Romano's in?" Justin asked.

"They won't be back until two p.m. sir."

"My name is Robinson. Carmen was to leave an envelope for me."

"He didn't say anything to me. Maybe he told Maria or Rita. Let me check."

She rose, and with a noticeable limp made her way to the nearest desk and looked around. "It's not here on Maria's desk." She moved to the third desk, shuffled through some correspondence and finally shook her head negatively. "There's nothing here, Mr. Robinson."

"Would you mind checking on Carmen's desk, please? It would save me the trouble of coming back," Justin said, exuding a warm smile.

She returned the smile. "Of course," she said and hobbled off to one of the private offices and disappeared inside.

Justin deftly picked up Maria's coffee cup with his handkerchief, emptied the left-over coffee into her wastebasket, and stuffed the cup into the plastic bag he had in his pocket. He moved back to his prior position and waited for the woman to return.

"I'm sorry, Mr. Robinson. I can't find anything with your name on it," Linda said when she returned a half minute later.

"Well, thank you for your help. I'll call Carmen later this afternoon and have him overnight me the information. Thanks again."

Justin took a cab to the FBI office building at Government Center. He passed the cup with her fingerprints to Katte. When its prints were entered into the federal data base, Katte would have an answer for him, and hopefully some useful information to pass on to Billie Tsapatsaris.

NINETEEN

Ken Katte called Justin Thursday morning at eleven. His voice carried an air of excitement. "I pushed the prints from the cup through the data file, and I'm quite surprised by the results. You mind telling me what this is about?"

"They're from a person of interest I'm investigating for a friend, Ken. Can we leave it at that for now?"

Katte paused. "I would like to know more."

"Why?"

"Why? Because the prints belong to a woman named Maria Ashley, who I just learned is a niece of Mario Serino, one of New York's mob bosses. 'Big Time' Mario is someone we are certainly interested in."

As soon as Justin heard the name Mario Serino his innards constricted. Billie was asking about the niece of Mario Serino? And she was a lady friend of Manny Antonelli, going by the name of Maria Ashley? *Does Manny know who she is, or is she a plant of Mario Serino keeping tabs on Manny?*

"Ken, I'll get back to you as soon as I can. I think the party I'm working with will want to meet with you. I'm going to buzz off. Thanks."

Justin called Billie Tsapatsaris.

"Hello?" said Billie.

"It's me. With news."

¥

Billie recognized the voice. "I'll call you back within five minutes."

Billie selected a cell phone, and called him back.

"Hi, Justin. We're playing the game. You've got something?"

"I sure do," Justin said. "Manny's favorite girlfriend, Maria, last name Ashley – and that's her real name - is mob boss Mario Serino's niece. That immediately pegs the question does Manny know?"

"My first thought would be he doesn't," a surprised Billie Tsapatsaris voiced. "Mario is keeping a close eye on Manny. Why?"

"My thought as well," Justin said. "So what are you going to do? Katte wants in on it. I'm sure he suspects I'm getting the information for Samantha, although I didn't tell him."

"Let me think on it, Justin. I appreciate your help."

"Okay, pal. Bye."

Billie was on the phone a minute later to Samantha's office. Pauline transferred the call.

"Hi Billie, what's up?"

"Samantha, call me back."

She did, on one of the throw away cell phones. Billie couldn't get the words out fast enough. "Antonelli's main girlfriend, Marie Ashley, is Mario Serino's niece."

It took Samantha several seconds to react. "Wow!"

"Wow is right. Who's using whom?"

"Good question."

"I'll find out."

"I have a favor to ask of you. I got her fingerprints and Ken Katte got me the information. I would bring him into it, Samantha. You've got the smarts, but he's got the manpower. I think you'll need him."

"I'll think on it. Thanks again, Billie."

"You're welcome. And Samantha, I'm available to you any time. Just don't tell Anne."

"You are priceless, Billie. I'll be in touch. Bye."

TWENTY

That evening Samantha and Arthur sat at the kitchen table having coffee and fruit. The discussion centered on Maria Ashley and Manny Antonelli, and who was playing whom.

"I've got the answer, Arthur. It came to me this afternoon in my office, and in the usual way."

The "usual way" was Samantha going into a trance and viewing a bright light through a ship's porthole into perhaps a different world, or at least a different dimension, and "seeing" things that others couldn't see. Or maybe it was just a sixth sense that fed her information she was otherwise not privy to. Doctors had tried to explain it, but nobody had all the answers. It was a gift of sorts that was often disturbing and unwanted, but in her case unavoidable, and she had learned long ago she would have to live with it. Now she accepted she could do well with it when properly applied.

"So what's the answer, Samantha?"

"Manny doesn't know she's Mario's niece; and if and when he finds out, there's not a lot he can do about it other than drop her. He certainly can't harm her in any way, and she and Mario both know this. Most likely he'd play dumb and find an excuse for breaking the relationship. In the meantime, I'm sure he's not leaving any of his dealings out in the open for her or anyone else to latch on to. He learned the hard way by dealing with Gino Pintano, and he's not the type to forget those lessons."

"So where does that leave us?"

"Not where I hoped it would. I could always leak the information about Maria so Manny would find out, but for now I don't think it pays. I'll just follow up in my notes for Steve that I found nothing of interest in Manny's women, and will follow a different trail. I'll string out a lot of nothings for a few weeks, and see if Steve gets the word from Manny to drop the surveillance."

"Steve said Manny hired him for a year, Samantha. He's not going to drop...."

"Why not? Manny's not wasteful. He could call it quits anytime."

"That's unlikely. The money means nothing to Manny. Okay, so what's next on this night's agenda?"

She reached her toe to rub the side of his leg. "How about a little lovemaking?"

"There's no such thing as a 'little' lovemaking, Samantha."

She laughed. "Well, be romantic and sweep me out of this chair and carry me into the bedroom. For some reason I'm in the mood."

"It should happen more often," Arthur said as he rose from his chair, approached her, and lifted her bodily into his arms and made for their bedroom.

"Piggy, piggy," she uttered, as she hugged him and then kissed him with urgency.

TWENTY ONE

"Uncle Mario? It's Maria. Can we talk?"

"Maria, darling. Of course we can talk," Mario said, as he sat at his desk in his Manhattan penthouse apartment Tuesday evening. "Is everything all right?"

"I don't know. Something strange I can't explain happened recently, and I thought I'd better throw it by you."

Mario leaned forward in his desk chair. "Okay, pitch it."

"It has to do with my coffee cup. I had come back from lunch and I couldn't find my cup. I asked the other ladies in the office and they said they hadn't seen it. I know I had left it on my desk. I looked all over and it was gone. I checked my waste basket the next day and I saw what appeared to be dried-up coffee stains on some of the waste paper. I figured someone had been to my desk and accidently knocked over my cup, but there was no broken glass in my basket, or in any of the other baskets in the office. Luigi and Carmen had taken the day off, so it couldn't have been either of them. But there was a man who came in during lunch hour, asking for Carmen. My friend Linda was the only one there, and went into Carmen's office looking for a package or a letter for the stranger. There wasn't any, and the guy took off. I asked Carmen about it the next morning and he didn't know what I was talking about. I've let it ride for a bit but it continues to strike me as strange, and...."

"As well it should," Mario said. "Thanks for the call; and don't worry about it. I'll look into it."

Mario remained at his desk, tapping the four fingers of his right hand rhythmically on his desktop. *Someone may have wanted Maria's fingerprints. It wouldn't be Manny; he could get them any time. Maybe the feds were poking around? They could have gotten a lead somewhere. I better do some checking."*

TWENTY TWO

B y Wednesday Samantha had made up her mind. She couldn't
burden Billie Tsapatsaris with a battle against the mob. She called
Katte by cell phone at eleven o'clock.

"Katte here," came his response.

"Ken. Samantha Robbins. Have you got time for me?"

"Always. I was hoping you'd call. I think we have things to discuss."

"We do. Can we meet, tonight or tomorrow night?"

"Tomorrow night would be better for me. Where?"

She paused to think. "Away from Boston. How about Wardhurst at
seven p.m.? Would that fit your schedule?"

"You still go there?"

"All the time. I'd like to have my husband and Billie Tsapatsaris join us."

"Fine with me. I'll see you at seven."

Her next call was to Tsapatsaris, and he answered. "Billie here. How
are you, dear?"

She smiled at his jocular greeting. "Billie. Arthur and I are having
dinner tomorrow at 7:00 p.m. at Wardhurst. We're meeting up with Ken
Katte, and I thought you might like to join us."

"Works out great, Samantha. Anne's having her gang of witches over
at seven for a couple of hours of bridge. I'd be pleased to get out of
the house."

"Do you want us to pick you up? It's not a problem...."

"It's not necessary, Samantha. I drive short distances at night to places I'm familiar with. See you tomorrow at seven. Thanks for the invite."

"See you tomorrow."

¥

Samantha and Arthur arrived at six-fifty and found Billie sitting at the bar with the former owner, Peter Routsis, and the ever-present Bill Brennan, a local historian. Apparently something Tsapatsaris said had them in stitches. Their loud laughter filled the surrounding area. The bartender, Jimmy, had a big smile on his face as he brought a bottle of Bud Lite and placed it in front of Billie, who nodded his thanks.

"Oops, here come my people," Billie said. "I'll take the bottle over to our table with me."

"I'll bring it over for you," Paula offered as she served a nearby customer."

It took nearly ten minutes for Samantha, Arthur and Billie to break away from the bar. They were seated in a back booth less than five minutes before Ken Katte wandered in.

¥

Katte was wearing a ten-gallon cowboy hat, a la Dan Blocker, the original Hoss Cartwright character from the *The Ponderosa*, and caused a lot of eyes and smiles to turn his way while he searched out their table. He spotted the group, whipped off his chapeau, and saluted them with the brim. "No disparaging comments, please; I'm traveling incognito."

He had a big smile on his youthful face, and it brought the expected guffaws.

"You look like a young Robert Redford," Samantha said.

"I was thinking of Matt Damon," Arthur said.

"I'd say more like Boris Karloff," Billie chirped, and could not contain his laughter.

Ken slipped into the booth beside Billie, placing his hat carefully on the bench beside him. "I understand that you small-town people are not used to the way big city folk dress, so I'll ignore your comments. Anyway, it's nice seeing you all."

"You want beer or wine, Ken?" Samantha said. "We're a little ahead of you in the drink department."

"A cold beer would hit the spot nicely. You're all looking great, especially you, Billie," Ken said, knowing the old timer would like hearing the comment.

"And you do too, Ken, no matter what the others among us think," he added, with that sly smile so becoming to him.

Ken's drink was ordered, and with the amenities finalized, the earnest talk began.

Samantha took the lead. "I have it on good authority that Manny's closest girlfriend, Maria, is mob boss Mario Serino's niece. I'm quite certain Manny doesn't know. It's Mario's way of keeping tabs on his New England interests, because Mario, like Manny, doesn't trust anybody. I'm debating how *we* can use that information to our advantage. Ken, Manny is having a local PI, Steve Grant, spy on me. But Steve is a friend and working with me. I think this gives me an edge. I must admit I want to put Antonelli away for a very long time. My question is how can we bait Manny into a situation where we can nail him good?"

Drinks were sipped as the four of them mulled the question. It seemed forever before Samantha broke the silence. "Obviously there is no easy answer. If Manny finds out about Maria, there's not much he can do about it without offending Mario. Manny could break off with Maria, but he knows Mario will use someone else that he may not be able to finger, so it would be better for him to play dumb and to keep Maria, and just be careful what she can learn and pass on. It also doesn't make sense to clue Maria. Mario would pull her away and use someone else, so *we'd* lose out. I think, Ken, if you can get permission to wiretap Maria's home phones maybe we could get some information on her and Mario Serino's doings. Again, it may give us nothing because they may only converse on secure lines, but you never know."

"I don't think it makes much sense to put a team on Maria Ashley, Samantha," Katte said. "At the moment, she's not important enough. I know my boss wouldn't go for it. I don't know exactly who's covering Mario from the New York office, but I can check. Maybe somebody has info on this Maria Ashley that could be helpful to us, but that's probably a long shot."

"At the moment our concern is not nailing Maria Ashley or Mario Serino," Arthur said. "We're after our local headache, Antonelli. Manny has a watch on Samantha and that bothers me. Until he calls off his surveillance, I think we should focus only on Manny, and also keep an eye on Steve Grant. Steve is playing a dangerous game."

"Just what do you know about this Steve Grant?" Katte asked.

"Not enough to completely trust him," Arthur said before Samantha could answer. "I know he told us about Manny's interest in Samantha, and Samantha feels we can trust him – and she's usually right – but I'm not convinced like she is. He could be playing both sides."

Samantha shook her head. "I think he's okay."

Billie had been listening intently. "Samantha, you're probably right, but I side with Arthur on this. You can never know, and Grant's a newcomer."

Samantha didn't agree. She knew. Her sixth sense told her Grant was okay, but she knew she could never convince them.

It was Katte who settled the issue. "Let's keep Grant in the 'not sure' category for the time being and move on. Our number one concern is Manny Antonelli, and how to get to him. Samantha, why don't we come up with a mysterious stranger who calls you and feeds you some information on past killings he thinks Manny was involved with? You told me you're feeding Grant information to pass on to Manny, so let's feed him stuff to upset Manny. We'll go back in the records to who we think Manny took care of personally in the old days, and pass on some weird truths or half-truths that may shake him up. Maybe we will get him to make a mistake."

"I like that," Billie chimed in. "Let's suck him in and maybe he'll do something foolish."

"Worth a try," Arthur agreed.

"It would have to be pretty convincing information," Samantha said. "He's not easily taken in."

"There were several murders in the past that we tried to tie to Manny," Katte continued. "When I get back to my office I'll pull out his file and pick out some likely cases to feed Grant for Manny's eyes. We'll have to converse outside our offices and homes, Samantha, so get me a secure cell phone number for you, and I'll give you mine," he said. He pulled out pen and paper and began to scribble. "Pick out a convenient time of day when you'll be outside and I can talk to you. I'll call you tomorrow with some information and you can word it anyway you want to pass on to Grant. Let's see what we can stir up."

"I'll call you tomorrow at six p.m.," Samantha said. "I'll elaborate in my file what I want Grant to pass on, and we'll see what happens. And Ken, I think I already have two likely victims of Manny's. I'll let you know."

That seemed to satisfy everyone.

"Let's order dinner; I'm hungry, Samantha said."

TWENTY THREE

K atte was halfway through the F.B.I. file on Antonelli the next morning when he came across a picture of Terri Antonelli, Manny's deceased wife. He shook his head, the memories flooding back. It was only three years earlier that he had met a lovely girl in a Boston bar. He thought he had picked her up, but it was actually she who had eyes for him, or so he thought. Imagine the shock when he found out several days after their first date that she was married to, though separated from, the mobster Manny Antonelli. He knew he had to report this to his superiors, but had delayed telling them, trying to figure a way to make it seem unimportant. But it was important, and his superiors wanted him to continue the relationship to find out what he could about Manny. He finally had to break it off a month later because the relationship was becoming complicated. He felt she wanted him to kill Manny! He wondered now who had been using whom? In the end it was Terri who was killed.

A stab of pain in his jaw made Katte wince. He unclenched his teeth and rubbed his left ear. Samantha didn't have to beg for his help. She wanted "to nail" Manny Antonelli. He wanted to wield the hammer that drove the nail in.

¥

Samantha wrote in her fake file notes for Steve that she had received a mysterious letter claiming that Manny Antonelli had murdered both a man named George Davis, an intimate friend of Manny's wife Terri, and Charlie Curcio, a lawyer acquaintance of Terri's. The letter also claimed that Manny was involved in the assassination of Terri's father, Gino Pintano. The writer wanted fifty thousand dollars in old twenty dollar bills and, in return, he would provide proof of the information. She thought material like that, passed on by Steve Grant to Manny in his verbal and written reports, would certainly provoke Manny into some form of overt action. She ran her idea by Arthur when he came home that evening. He was usually negative when it came to duplicity, but he was a good sounding board and she valued his opinion.

"Well, what do you think?" she asked when she finished explaining what she wanted to do. "That should get a rise out of him."

Arthur was tired. "Jesus, Samantha, I just walked in the door after an unusually tough day and you hit me with something like this? Give me a chance to unwind. Give me a chance to think. Let's have dinner and a drink and then we'll discuss this…this idea of yours."

"Okay, darling; I'm sorry. Go wash up and I'll make you a martini. Dinner won't be ready for another half hour or so. We'll talk afterwards."

Arthur said nothing as he hung up his coat and headed for the washroom. He knew it was going to be a difficult evening.

The more Samantha thought about her idea the more she liked it. A few years earlier a killer had taken the lives of George Davis, Terri's then boyfriend, and Charlie Curcio, a lawyer friend of Terri who secretly handled some of her monetary affairs unknown to both Davis and her husband Manny. Terri had learned well from her grandfather, Papa Gardello, even more so than from her father Gino, and had trusted no one.

She recalled vividly the day of the Davis and Curcio murders when her "gift" had enlightened her: Manny had killed both men. His driver Guido had been with him. But Samantha couldn't prove a thing.

¥

"Okay, Samantha, let's hear it," Arthur said after downing his last drop of the martini and then running one finger through the last bit of pork drippings and licking it before pushing back the plate. "I'm sorry I snapped at you. It was just one of those days."

"I get them too," she said. "Anyway, you recall a few years back when I told you I had a vision that Manny himself had gunned down George Davis and Charlie Curcio, and Manny's man, Guido, had been his driver?

I think Manny would believe it if someone was looking for money for fingering him."

"He probably would, Samantha, but you're fingering Guido. Manny might kill him."

"Guido died of prostate cancer more than a year ago."

"I didn't know that. So who would he blame?"

"I don't know, and I don't think I care."

"He might go on a killing spree, Samantha."

"So we clue in Katte, and he puts a team on Manny to watch him. Maybe we catch him in an act of retaliation."

"Hmm. It might work. If you get Katte's approval and cooperation it's worth a shot."

She called Katte on his secure cell phone fifteen minutes later.

¥

Ken Katte placed his beer on the ring-stained end table beside his recliner and pressed the mute button on his T.V. remote.

"Yeah? Who is it?"

"Ken, its Samantha."

"Don't you ever rest?" he said, noting his Timex digital.

"No. I'm a workaholic, just like you are. I have a plan, and I want to throw it by you right now."

Ken leaned back into his recliner and picked up a lined pad of paper and Flair Paper-Mate pen. He shifted into a comfortable position. "Okay, Samantha, I'm all ears. What's on your mind?"

She told him about having Steve Grant pass on the information that she'd been contacted by letter by someone who would pass on proof of Manny's culpability in a couple of murders for fifty thousand dollars."

"Why would he fall for that?" Katte said.

"Because I know he committed the murders," she said.

"You know but you can't prove it; is that it?"

"Yes. But if he *thinks* someone will provide the proof to me, he'll show his true colors."

"And what are they?"

"Several shades of red; blood red."

"Jesus, Samantha. You want to start a blood bath?"

"No! I want to put Manny away forever. I want *you* to prevent a blood bath."

"And how am I supposed to do that?"

"By having your men watch Manny twenty-four-seven for a few weeks. Once he gets the information someone is trying to sell him out, he'll go on a rampage. You're the one with the capable manpower, Ken. It will be a hell of a feather in your cap to nail him."

"You flatter me, Samantha."

"I don't care about flattering you, Ken. I just want to interest you."

There wasn't much of a pause before his answer came back. "You do interest me, Samantha. Give me a day or so to convince my superiors that we have a hell of an opportunity to bag Mannie Antonelli, and I'll get back to you."

"Do a good selling job, Ken."

"I intend to. Ciao."

¥

It took Ken the entire day. He volunteered to be part of the team, emphasizing his belief in the importance of this stakeout.

Twenty-four seven for three weeks was more than he hoped for, but he got it. Manny Antonelli was a big fish, and if the Boston branch of the FBI could nab him on a murder charge, there would be abundant promotions at all levels.

Ken contacted Samantha at her office within an hour of the approval. She had been just about to call it a day and head home.

"Yes, Ken. Good news or bad?"

"It's a go, and for three weeks."

"Good job. I'll get the ball rolling from this end tonight. Our target will have word of it sometime tomorrow morning."

"We'll be in place by then. Hope for the best."

"I will, Ken. Thanks. Keep in touch. Bye."

¥

Samantha left a note for Steve suggesting he call Captain Weiss and get the ball rolling.

She left the letter in the front of Manny's file and, smiling, left her office.

PART TWO

Twenty Four

S teve Grant surreptitiously made his way to Samantha's private office in the O'Shea building that evening. It was nearly midnight, and he saw no one as he used his key to the rear entrance to the building, and wondered if Manny did or did not have someone watching him. He spotted Samantha's note in her middle desk drawer, read it, and understood what she had left him was of such importance that he should call Captain Weiss that evening. He quickly made his way to the filing cabinet holding Manny's file, unlocked it and, with pen light in hand, removed the uppermost paper from the Antonelli file. Retreating to Samantha's desk and chair, he sat and carefully read the unsigned letter. A chill ran through his body. He read it a second time before he made his own handwritten copy and then read it again. He returned the original letter to the file and the file to the file cabinet, made sure the drawer was closed properly, stuffed his copy into a pocket, and returned to the desk to place the chair exactly where it was supposed to be. He shone the penlight across the desk top, making sure all was in order, and then made his way out of the office and building. *Having the right keys makes it a lot easier,* he thought. He walked to his car, which was parked near City Hall, and drove home, his mind on the thrice read letter stuffed in his pocket.

It was one a.m. when he called Weiss. The phone rang for a long stretch before a disgruntled voice answered. "What the hell do you want this time of night, for Christ sakes?"

Steve didn't bother to apologize. "You just listen, and do with it what you want. I found a letter in our girlfriend's possession an hour ago. I made me a copy and I'm going to read it to you. Listen carefully. I'll send it out in my report tomorrow, but our gentleman friend will want to know about this right away." Steve read the contents of the letter to a now alert listener.

"Shit!" Weiss said. "Wait a minute; I want to write it down."

He was back on the phone in less than a minute. "Go ahead and read it again. Talk slowly."

Steve did. Minutes later, Weiss said, "Okay, I got it. I'll pass it on," and hung up without a goodbye.

"And screw you too," Steve said to the empty room.

¥

Weiss waited until eight a.m. before he called Manny.

"Yes, Joe; what do you want? Be quick. I'm heading to the gym."

"Our lady friend got a letter yesterday," he said, and he read Manny the letter.

There was an overly long pause before Manny spoke. "No name? No hint of who sent the letter?"

"No."

Manny was seething, but was not in the mood to share his thoughts. "You need to find out!" and he hung up."

¥

Manny picked up his empty coffee mug and flung it. It shattered against the refrigerator, denting the metal door. The noise brought Maria rushing from the bedroom.

"What happened?" she said, as she took in the sight of broken glass.

Manny, a scornful look on his face, blurted out "someone's trying to fuck with me, and the bastard is gonna die."

"Who? What's happened, Manny?"

"Never mind, it doesn't concern you."

Maria came closer, resting her hands on the table edge beside him, but not daring to touch him. "I just want to help, sweetheart," she said calmly. "Don't be angry with me."

"I'll discuss things with you tonight, Maria," he said.

His voice sounded calm, but cold, very cold, and Maria noted his fists were still clenched where they rested atop the table. He stood.

"I've got to go: We'll talk later. I'd appreciate your cleaning this up." He picked up his keys and jacket and hastened out the door.

¥

Whoever called him really shook him up, Maria mused. She walked to his den office, noted the Weiss cell phone was missing, and nodded to herself.

Returning to the kitchen, she cleaned up the broken glass and then, checking the time on her watch, called her uncle.

"It's Maria, uncle."

"And to what do I owe the pleasure of so early a call from so charming a person?" Serino said. She heard his lips smack and the sound of him sipping a drink.

"Am I disturbing your breakfast? I can call you back."

"That's okay dear. Just sipping my coffee and munching on a donut, but don't tell anyone. I'm not supposed to have donuts." He sounded amused. "What's on your mind?"

"Manny got an early morning call that really upset him. I think it was from his cop friend. He wouldn't talk to me about it he was so angry, but I'm staying with him for the weekend. I'll see if I can find out more about it tonight. Do you have any idea what it could have been that pissed him off?"

Uncle Serino's voice no longer sounded jovial. "No, and I don't like foul language coming out of such a pretty mouth."

"Uncle! At least I don't use the word 'fuck' any more in your presence."

"You are incorrigible, young lady!" he said, but then she heard him sigh. "But I still love you. Let me know when you get more information. Anything else?"

"No, uncle."

"You need any money?"

"No. I'm in good shape."

"Be careful."

"Always. Bye."

¥

Manny skipped the gym and headed directly to Tully's bar. He let himself in the rear door, made sure the door was securely locked, and headed for his private office. The door to his office was solid steel and required two keys to unlock it. There were no windows. The room was temperature controlled and well lit with fluorescent lighting. Signed photos of Red Sox and Celtics players and a framed number 12 Patriots jersey hung on the wall behind the desk.

An oversized glass-topped desk was in the middle of the room, with a comfortable black leather desk chair on wheels behind the desk. Two wooden, padded chairs faced the desk, and a three-section black leather couch spread the length of one wall. To the right of the desk, a door led to his private bath. The bathroom was fully equipped with a shower, toilet, sink, telephone and its own closet for storage of bath and hand towels, facial tissues, toilet paper, bars of soap, extra razors, shaving cream and sundry items. It also held a loaded shotgun.

The closet had a secret panel that was an emergency exit. Manny liked to be prepared. Only Guido had known of it and now that he was gone, Manny kept the information to himself. He had learned long ago you can trust some people with some things, but you can never trust anyone with knowledge about everything – not if you wanted to live a long life.

An hour later he emerged from his office and let his employees in the bar room know he was there. It was often the way he appeared, and caused no surprises. The only difference this morning was that Manny had used his early arrival to make a phone call, to a man none of his employees knew; a man named Steve Grant.

"Are you at a good place to talk?" were his first words to Steve.

"Yes, I'm alone."

"I need to know more about that letter. I need to know who wrote it."

"I understand. I think I should be calling on our lady friend more than once a week, but more visits means a greater chance of being discovered."

"I think you'll have to chance it, at least for the next week or so. I must know who contacted her."

"I understand. I'll do it."

"As soon as you have anything of importance you call me directly. I'll give you a number you are not to write down. You memorize it." He gave Steve the number.

"You have it?"

"Yes."

"You get me a name and there'll be a healthy bonus for you."

"I'll work on it."

"Don't call me unless you're sure of what you got. Do you understand?"

"I understand."

"Goodbye."

TWENTY FIVE

F ifteen minutes later, Steve drove leisurely to *Maria's Place*, a restaurant on the corner of Jefferson and Jackson Streets in Salem. He smiled at the name, *Maria's Place,* because the name Maria was popping up frequently in his investigation.

Pam was his waitress, a sweet and charming woman whose smile erased a decade off her forty years. He ordered his usual Western Omelet and tea with lemon and then scanned the room, looking for people he knew or may know him. He didn't see anyone. He picked up a copy of the Boston Herald someone had left on an adjacent table and scanned some of the middle pages. His tea came, and his breakfast plate appeared in less than five minutes. If taste and speed was the name of the game, *Maria's Place* was hard to beat.

He needed to tell Samantha about the call he had received from Manny, and how anxious and angry Manny had sounded about the letter. He discarded the newspaper and rushed through his breakfast.

He made the call twenty minutes later from inside his car. Samantha answered on the fifth ring.

"Hello, Steve."

"Hi. I think I shook up our friend Manny a great deal when I read him the letter you left for me. I would have liked to have seen his face, but the tone of his voice would have frozen hell."

"I'm not surprised. Manny give you any instructions?"

"He mentioned a bonus if I come up with the name of the letter writer."

"I'm sure he'll come up with his own list of people who might betray him, so we should move into the action phase relatively soon. I think I'll be hearing from the letter writer again soon."

"Do you know who it is, Samantha?"

"I can't answer that yet, Steve. We'll have to wait and see."

¥

Manny sat at his desk, pen in hand, an 8x12 inch pad of lined paper in front of him. In the last ten minutes he had picked up the pen and slapped it down four times. He'd written down only two names of people he thought could be the letter writer selling him out. He thought there should be more, but he didn't know who. The two names were Joe Weiss and Mario Serino.

He had never specifically told anyone who his victims were, but he suspected these two men knew at least some of them. Guido knew; but Guido was gone – dead and buried. Manny wondered now if Guido would have told anybody, or left anything in writing. He had no immediate family, no particular woman friend, no one he trusted besides Manny. *Could there have been someone…?*

Manny didn't handle the unknown well. He'd kill someone with a gun or knife, or order killings, without a twinge of guilt. He'd done it several times and never lost a minute's sleep. When he was in control, there was no second guessing. But Samantha Robbins had a hold on him and he needed to break it, and that meant getting rid of Samantha Robbins…and probably her husband, Arthur Lite. *And perhaps a few more of their acquaintances. No bodies to be found, just disappearances. A little more difficult work, but more confusing for the authorities to fathom.* He would give Steve Grant one week to find the writer of the letter, and if he couldn't…he would handle the situation himself.

¥

It was Thursday afternoon when Samantha constructed the next letter and left it for Steve Grant to find. It was similar in form, asking for the same amount of money, but now giving a deadline for them to agree to terms.

"...you have one week from today to agree and supply the money. One week only!"

Steve visited Samantha's office Thursday evening and called Manny an hour later at the number Manny had given him to memorize.

"Yeah?" Manny answered gruffly.

"I found another letter tonight. No signature. He gave her a week to agree to terms, and said 'one week only'."

"Do you think she will?" Manny snapped.

"Yes. I do."

Manny didn't say so, but agreed.

"Who the hell is this guy, Steve? Have you found out anything?"

"Not yet. I've been on it night and day. The letters were mailed and cancelled in a local post office, and anybody could be dropping them off. They are written on paper found in any pharmacy and the envelope was handled by a number of postal people, so forget about prints. I doubt if the writer left his prints on the letters themselves, but only the Robbins woman would know that, and she's left nothing in her office to clue me in. I'll try to find out when the payment will take place, and maybe we can do something about it. Frankly, it doesn't look good at this point...."

"I don't want to hear that," Manny snapped. "Get me whatever information you can!" He hung up.

Steve heard the anger in Manny's voice and intended to report that to Samantha. He knew Manny was upset, and he got an uneasy feeling about the FBI being able to protect her from the retaliation that was sure to come. Manny was a killer and would go after Samantha. She had to know that, but she hadn't shown concern. Could she possibly know what Manny intended to do? Is her psychic ability for real? She and her close friends say it is, but he was skeptical of such things, especially when your life depended on it.

He voiced his concerns to Arthur the following morning.

The Stanton desk sergeant put his call through when he said it was important.

"Good morning, Steve, What's the problem?"

"Arthur, I relayed the information Samantha wanted me to give to Manny last night. He was seething. I'm concerned he's not going to wait to see this charade play out, but instead go after your wife. Are you sure you trust the FBI to handle this?"

"I appreciate your concern, Steve, and I must admit that I'm always concerned over her doings, but I trust in Samantha's abilities."

"Okay, Arthur. I just felt I had to ask. Bye."

Steve shook his head. *All I can do is sit and wait. It's up to Samantha. I pray her abilities are as good as they say they are.*

TWENTY SIX

"Manny? It's Mario. Is this line still secure?"

Manny squeezed and released the Obie stress toy Terry had gotten him many years before. He'd found it at the back of his desk drawer, behind his Glock. He liked how its blue eyes and red ears thrust out each time he squeezed it. "Yes this line's secure. Is there anything wrong?"

"Not on my end, but there is on yours. I got a call from a friend who tells me your local feds have a twenty-four/seven watch on you. What's going on?"

"I didn't know that. It appears your sources are better than mine. I'll be sure to sharpen things up on my end."

"I would do that. Now tell me what's happening, and how it will affect us."

"It won't. I will take care of the matter within a few days."

"Does this have to do with that Samantha Robbins woman?"

Manny was surprised.

"You know of her? How?"

"From several sources, Manny. One was your father-in-law, Gino; and another a mutual acquaintance, a Greek shipping magnate."

"Ari?"

"Yes. Gino was afraid of no one, with the possible exception of that woman. The same goes for Ari."

Manny felt a cramp in his hand and looked down at it. He was squeezing the Obie so hard, that its eyes and ears thrust an inch out of its head and trembled as if about to pop. "I've done nothing about her up until now, Mario, but feel I have to do something soon. If something damaging is released about my past, I'll need trust it can be handled by my lawyers. I pay them enough. I might make her disappear, Mario."

"Risky. Others must know she's putting pressure on you, particularly her cop husband, and then she disappears? And you have the feds watching you. They're not fools. If they catch you in anyway approaching her, they'll pounce on you. In fact, she may have just arranged it that way. Did you think of that? You had better check it out before you make a move."

Manny set the Obie on his desk. It looked at him accusingly. "You may be right. It could be a trap."

"Yeah, it could. Don't let your Italian get you up. Think first. Call me in a few days and let me know what's going on. I don't want anything upsetting our New England businesses. Right?"

"Yes, Mario, right. I'll get back to you. Goodbye." He sat back in his chair and its wheels squeaked. *It could be a trap,* Manny conceded. *All of a sudden she gets letters from someone wanting to rat me out? Why now? She may have discovered someone is checking her files and is laying a trap.* His eyes narrowed. *Or is Steve Grant double crossing me and they're in cahoots? Or is her damn ESP for real? I've got to know. Weiss should know more about what's going on. I'm paying him enough. And he should have tipped me off about the FBI. He's got people there. I'm going to chew his ass out....*

¥

Weiss placed a steak, still sizzling from the pan, on his wife's plate and then his own and returned the pan to the stove. Sitting, he sprinkled the meat with pepper and picked up his fork and knife.

His cellphone rang.

Sighing, he put down his utensils and took out his phone.

"Weiss here."

"You know who this is," Manny said. The words were clipped, angry. Weiss sat up straighter.

"Yes."

"We've got to meet."

"When?"

"Now."

"It's after eight. I was just sitting down to eat."

"Fuck eating. I want to see you in half an hour, in the usual place."

Weiss knew he had no option. When Manny sounded like this you dropped everything and did as you were told. "I'll be there as soon as I can."

"I said in a half hour!"

"Yes, that's what I meant, in half an hour."

Weiss heard the disconnect signal and hung up. For a big man, he could still move fast when he had to and he knew this was one of those times. "I've got to go out for a while," he snapped at his wife. "I'll be back as soon as I can."

"You've got to go out now?" she said with disbelief. "We haven't eaten."

"Now!" he snapped back. She shook her head as she began to put their meals into the oven to keep them warm.

"No! You eat now. I'll grab something later. I may be awhile."

"Drive safely," she said. She covered his dish with foil and placed it in the refrigerator.

Weiss threw on a heavy jacket after donning his shoulder holster, and left the house. He took his wife's Ford and headed for Tully's Bar Room, in the North End. He didn't know why he was summoned or what to expect. He focused on remaining cool and subservient. There was too much at stake to do otherwise.

¥

"You made good time," Manny said as Weiss entered his office.

Weiss merely nodded as he took off his leather jacket, hung it on the back of the chair, and sat down in front of Manny's desk. His shoulder holster and Glock handle were quite evident. Manny ignored them.

"Do you know I've got FBI teams following me every hour of the day?"

Weiss' brow furrowed. "No. I didn't know. But they've done that before."

"Not in a long time. Why now? And why didn't you know?"

"They have different teams doing different jobs, Manny. One team often doesn't know what the other is doing. I don't have an in with every team."

"Why not?" Manny interrupted. "I've told you to pay out what you had to. I need to know whenever the feds take an interest in me."

"We can't buy Katte to come on board. I tried about everything…"

"Then get someone else."

"It isn't easy. One wrong word and they'll take an interest in me. Then where would you be?"

"You haven't tried hard enough," Manny barked.

Weiss had no answer, and was quiet momentarily. "I'll try harder, Manny."

"You do that. Do you think Samantha Robbins or Steve Grant know they're being tailed by my people? Could they be playing us?"

"The people you're using are good – I've recommended them all – but there's really no way to know."

"Find a way! It's too important to mess up on this. You understand?"

"Yes. I'll try to come up…"

"No! You *will* come up with something. I need to know who I can trust and who I can't. I don't play games unless I'm the winner. Always the winner. Do you understand me, Joe?"

Joe Weiss nodded. He felt sweat collect between his shoulder blades. "Yes, Manny, I'll get the answers for you."

"Good!" Manny smiled. "How about a good steak and a couple of beers? We'll eat them in here. We can't be seen together."

"Fine with me, Manny. I'm starved."

A half hour later two waitresses brought in their food. They were cute girls – early twenties – blonde, built, and obviously smitten with Manny. One of them placed a table cloth over a cleared section of Manny's desk while the other laid out silverware and cloth napkins. They set a pitcher of beer and two frosted mugs on the table, all this happening without a word being said or even a glance from Manny. The two men ate quietly.

Joe Weiss didn't know what Manny was thinking, but he himself was worried. He didn't like dealing with an angry mob boss.

TWENTY SEVEN

M anny returned to his apartment after eleven p.m. Maria was
already undressed and in her nightgown and robe when he
walked in. He merely gave her a nod as he hung up his leather jacket in
the hall closet.

"Can I get you a scotch, honey? Or do you want a cup of coffee?"

"No. Nothing," he said hostilely as he disappeared into the guest
bathroom and closed the door.

He came out four minutes later and sat down in a chair opposite her.

"Everything okay, Manny?"

"I'm fine," he muttered, but she knew he didn't mean it.

"Do you want to talk about anything?"

"No!"

"How about we get into bed and I'll relax you?" she said with a smile.

He almost never said no, but he did tonight. "No. I'm just tired and
I want to get some sleep. Goodnight."

And he was up and heading to the bedroom as she watched in disbelief. She lit a cigarette and sat watching the bedroom door. Ten minutes
later, she snuffed it out and walked into the bedroom. She went into
the bathroom and prepared herself for bed, expecting he would change
his mind, but when she came out fifteen minutes later he was asleep, or
pretending to be and ignoring her; she couldn't tell.

Manny slept fitfully. In his dreams he stood over the bodies of several people, all dead, and his gun warm and smoking in his hand. That wasn't the part that disturbed him. What disturbed him was the face and figure of Samantha Robbins standing in the background, paper and pen in hand, smiling and taking notes.

Manny awoke in a sweat shortly after 6:00 a.m. He turned to see Maria's pretty face next to his, but didn't disturb her. He slipped out of bed, and shaved and showered. Back in the bedroom he dressed in a solid blue dress shirt, sans tie, brown slacks, brown socks, and tan Dexter shoes and quietly made his way to the kitchen. From the fridge he poured a large glass of Tropicana Low Acid Florida Orange Juice and placed it on the kitchen table. He switched on the TV to Channel 4. He sat and sipped his juice and watched the station meteorologist predict a seasonally comfortable day. The news was the usual mix of automobile accidents, stabbings, and robberies – things that once interested him but no longer did. He had more important things on his mind.

I have to make Robbins disappear!

NO! If she goes, the cops will swarm over her files and find the letters. Then they'll come for me. No. I got to make her want to bury the letters and this guy herself.

He raised his glass to his lips, but paused before sipping. *I've got to take someone she loves and make him or her disappear. I've got to show her that she can't screw with me.*

He would have liked to discuss this with someone, but with Guido gone he had no one that close. Mario was smart and could be helpful, but then Mario would have something over him and he didn't want that. Maria was always offering, but the less she knew the less he would have to deal with in the future.

I'll use only Giorgio and Leon. They'll be no big loss if I have to get rid of one or both of them later.

It was in a muddled frame of mind that he left his apartment and drove to his Tully Street office. He again entered through the rear door. He was not in the mood to talk to anyone. He locked the door, something he almost never did, and anyone trying to get in would get the message.

Removing his jacket, he tossed it on a chair and sat at his desk. He unlocked his lower right desk drawer, looked inside and took note of the three different colored cell phones — and the one Glock 17, with its suppressor and ammo clip in place. He felt reassured by their presence and sat back in his chair, closed his eyes, and relaxed. This is what he did when he had a problem. This is what he did before he killed someone.

TWENTY EIGHT

M anny walked into the bar, got his own cup of coffee and moved to the corner table where Giorgio and Leon were having their second cups. They nodded their greeting as he sat down, but said nothing, knowing Manny preferred it that way.

"I've got a job for the two of you," Manny said in a voice barely above a whisper. There was no one else in the room, but Manny chose to deliver his instructions as if a dozen sets of ears were privy to the conversation.

"Giorgio, you remember the lady secretary that works in the Robbins woman's office?"

"Yeah."

"Her name is Pauline something. You check it out. She's a widow, lives alone in Pemberton or Peabody; I don't know which. You find out."

"Okay, boss. What else?"

"Make her disappear. No trace, you understand? Put her somewhere. I don't care where, but I don't want her found until I say so."

"Yes sir," Giorgio said compliantly.

"And Giorgio, be careful; no clues," Manny continued. "Not a trace of anything, understand?"

"Yes. When do you want this to happen?" Giorgio said.

"Tonight or tomorrow night. Use a stolen car or a stolen license plate. It's got to be completely clean. No blood, no mess in her home, no nothing. She just disappears. I don't want to know any of the details."

If Robbins could truly read his mind, he wanted to know as little as possible. He didn't know what the bitch was capable of.

Giorgio stood up, stretching out his huge body. Manny could see he was excited. It had been a while since he'd sent anyone on a hit. Giorgio was no Guido, but he showed promise.

"I'll call you when it's done, boss."

"Discretely, Giorgio. No names, no places, no linking me to any of this when you call. Do it between nine and midnight tonight or tomorrow night. I'll make sure I'm with prominent people during that time who will alibi me. Any questions?"

"No. Consider it done."

"I'll consider it done after it's done," Manny said. Without another word, he got up and returned to his office. The two men watched him leave.

"He ain't in no good mood, Giorgio," Leon said. "I ain't seen him like that before."

"I have. Leon, we got to do things exactly as he says, or we ain't gonna be around long. I'm telling you this because I want you to learn – and think. He didn't get to be where he is by being Mr. Nice Guy. He's cleaned up his act, but in the old days he personally sent a lot of people to the graveyard. You pay attention when he talks, and don't overstep yourself. It ain't no game we're playing."

Leon took Giorgio's talk seriously. He knew Giorgio could kill people with his bare hands and supposedly had, and he wasn't about to confront the man. Giorgio was his access to the big bucks. He had to be patient and learn by following Giorgio's every move. Someday soon he wanted to be Manny's number one guy.

¥

Later that day Giorgio and Leon were in Pemberton, having an early lunch at a McDonalds. From there they made their way into the O'Shea Building, and up the stairs to the second floor. On the opaque glass of an office door, the words SAMANTHA ROBBINS PI, Office Hours: 9:00 a.m. – 5:00 p.m. were stenciled in gold lettering. Leon entered the office.

An older woman, grey-haired and with crow's feet at the corners of her eyes glanced up at him. She had glasses on a chain around her neck but the skeptical glance she gave Leon suggested to Leon that this woman was one who saw things clearly.

"Hi," he said, a warm smile on his face. "Is this the office that called about getting an estimate for a paint job?"

"Not to my knowledge," Pauline said, frowning.

Leon scratched his head and pulled a folded paper from his pocket. "Isn't this The Legal Society office?"

"No. That's in the next building over."

Leon placed the paper back in his pocket. "My apologies, ma'am." He smiled at her again.

"No problem," Pauline said, and smiled back at him.

Leon rejoined Giorgio in the hallway. He knew what his victim looked like and her office hours. They'd return at 4:45 p.m. and follow the woman home and, that evening or the next, pay her a visit. An unfriendly visit!

¥

Shortly after 5:00 p.m., Leon watched Pauline exit the rear door of the office building that opened onto the parking lot.

He followed her at a safe distance, and was on his cell phone to Giorgio. "She's getting in a green Honda CRV. She'll have to come in your direction to Main Street. It's the only exit. I'm on my way to you now," he said. He hastened down the narrow alley between two buildings that led to Main Street and got into Giorgio's car.

The green Honda pulled out and turned west. They followed it at a safe distance some fifteen minutes until it turned into a driveway off Lowell Street in West Peabody. The property had a ranch house that was amply surrounded by tall elm and fir trees and a six-foot stockade cedar fence.

¥

Giorgio smiled. There was lots of privacy, with neighboring homes some distance away. As long as she didn't have a dog in her home, it should be an easy hit. And if she did have a dog, he'd take care of the dog as well.

"Do we do it tonight, Giorgio?" Leon said, quivering slightly with the anticipation.

"No. Tomorrow night. I want to come back here tomorrow when she's at work and check the place out."

TWENTY NINE

Pauline peered through the peep hole of her front door when the door bell sounded slightly after ten p.m. on Friday night.

"Yes, what is it officer?"

"Had a call from your neighbor about a prowler in the area, ma'am," he said. "I'd like to check your house and use your telephone if I may."

Pauline unlocked the door without a second thought and allowed the police officer in.

With one swipe of his gloved right hand, Giorgio knocked her unconscious. He gagged her with several layers of masking tape as she sprawled on the floor inside the doorway, blindfolded her, tied her thin wrists behind her back, shut off the outside light that she had turned on when she'd opened the door, and then carried her out. He lowered her into the back of the stolen Mercury van. Leon had removed the dome light and this was all accomplished in the dark, with the only sound being the closing of the vehicle's doors.

¥

Leon drove, putting on the headlights when they were half a block away. He headed in the direction Giorgio told him to, a place Giorgio had been several times before. Twenty minutes later they stopped at a remote home on the outskirts of Reading, where a retired employee of Manny's lived. He was an old, crippled hoodlum who, for one hundred bucks, would keep Pauline locked up and fed for a night or two until she could be transported to a farm in New Hampshire for long-term keeping.

Manny had decided against killing Pauline because she could be used as a bargaining chip with Samantha. If not, he could always do away with her at a later date.

¥

It was eleven-thirty-two p.m. when Manny, sitting at his desk at home, got the phone call.

"Yes."

"It's done, and no problems," the voice said.

"See me in my office tomorrow, between nine and ten. Come alone."

Manny smiled after he hung up. *Tonight I'll sleep. Tomorrow Samantha Robbins will have something to think about.*

THIRTY

Samantha arrived at her office at nine a.m. She was surprised to find the office door locked. It took a bit to find her office keys in her oversized shoulder bag, but she did, unlocked the door, and expressed a quizzical look as she headed for Pauline's empty desk chair. She scanned the desktop for a note, but apparently Pauline hadn't made it in this morning. She checked the message machines – hers and Pauline's – and they were empty.

Where was Pauline? And then it hit her! The flash of light! The ship's porthole swathed in blinding light. Her head snapped back; her eyes misted, her pulse pounded, her blood pressure skyrocketed.

Through the "porthole" she saw the face of Pauline, her mouth gagged and a purpling bruise on her right cheek. The face grew smaller, fading, as if pulled farther and farther away.

The vision vanished and Samantha stumbled and let herself fall into Pauline's chair. Tears rolled down her cheeks. Pauline had looked dead! Was she?

Samantha didn't know how, why, or when; but she knew. The woman – almost a mother to her – was in trouble. She pulled herself together and ran out of the office, and drove to Pauline's home. From her coat pocket she pulled a handkerchief, and shielding her hand, turned the doorknob. The door was not locked. She entered, calling out "Pauline," knowing there would be no answer. Samantha's eyes took in the room, and although there were no outward signs of a struggle, she instantly envisioned the scene: a man entered the house, struck the unsuspecting woman a heavy blow to the face, bound her, and carried her away. Away to where? Samantha didn't know; but he disposed of her somewhere in a wooded area.

Samantha vowed she would find the perpetrator. She had seen the man who took her in her vision. He was a cop: or dressed as a cop!

THIRTY ONE

The police arrived after receiving Samantha's call, led by the chief himself. The only other call Samantha had made was to her hubby, Arthur. Arthur would have no jurisdiction in this case, since he was with the Stanton Police, but he was well known to the locals and had worked closely with both the Peabody and Pemberton police a number of times.

"Samantha. Are you okay?" the chief said, noticing both the strange look on her face and the unnatural manner in which she moved back and forth in the rocker she was sitting in.

"No, chief," she answered tersely. "I love that woman."

"There's no sign of a break in, or forced entry, Samantha. Perhaps she was called away suddenly and didn't have a chance to notify you."

She looked the chief full in the face. "You know me better than that, chief. If I thought that, I never would have made the call to the police. She was forcibly removed from this house –kidnapped."

"But how do you…?" The chief didn't bother to finish his sentence. Retired Chief Lawrence, his predecessor, had filled him in on Samantha's abilities and he himself had benefited from her unusual "insights" on cases the past three years. How she did it he didn't care, but she had been proven right in each instance. "Okay, Samantha. What can you tell me?"

"I can't tell you anything. Did the station get a call or report of a prowler in this neighborhood last night?"

"Not that I saw on any of the reports this morning."

"Was there a patrol car covering the area for any reason last evening?"

"Not to my knowledge, but I'll check on that as well. Why?"

"Because a cop, or a man in a policeman's uniform, gained entrance. Pauline let him in!"

"How…?"

She didn't let him finish. "Pauline wouldn't have allowed anyone she didn't know to enter her home, daytime or nighttime, other than the police. She was too cautious to have done otherwise."

"Are you sure of that?"

"Dead sure," Samantha answered, her pretty face marred by the intensity of her answer.

"Do you have any idea who did this, or why?"

"I'll answer the second question first, chief. The 'why' is because someone wants to send me a warning. The 'who' is probably Manny Antonelli."

The chief appeared surprised, and merely shook his head.

¥

Arthur arrived and rapidly made his way into the room, stopping their conversation. As soon as Samantha saw him she was out of her chair and into his arms. Her tears flowed silently, and he held her tightly for several moments while she strained to regain her composure. The chief took this time to converse with two of his men, who reported they had found nothing of interest, either inside the home or outside, and that nearby neighbors had neither seen nor heard anything out of the ordinary the prior evening.

Samantha and Arthur moved to the kitchen table to sit down, and the chief joined them.

He and Arthur exchanged a brief handshake.

"My men have found no clues, and the neighbors reported nothing unusual last night," the chief said. "This house is pretty well shielded from neighboring homes, and nobody heard a car arriving or leaving here last evening. We've got a big nothing to start out with."

Samantha stared at him. "We're going to leave now, chief," she announced quietly as she rose. "I will be in touch with you shortly, I promise you."

THIRTY TWO

Samantha, devoid of thoughts other than of Pauline, followed Arthur on the drive home. They parked their cars, and hand in hand entered their dwelling.

"Do you want a drink?" Arthur said after they had shed their outer garments and made their way into their comfortable den.

"Yes, but nothing too strong. Do we have a Zinfandel?"

"We certainly do, and that sounds perfect."

Arthur returned several minutes later with two glasses of wine, and they sat side-by-side on the couch. It was a while before he spoke.

"What do you think happened, Samantha?"

"That bastard Manny is sending me a message."

"But why her?"

"You, Pauline and my father are the closest people to me."

"You think a second message would involve me or your father?"

Arthur had asked without emotion or fear, and she answered him in the same manner. "Yes. But I'll never let that happen. I'm taking him down."

"I don't like the sound of that. Just what do you intend to do?"

"Out think him, outsmart him, and destroy him; and all inside the law."

"Explain yourself, Samantha. How are...."

"Arthur! I can't give you the answers right now, but I will in short order. I've had it with him…."

She stopped talking, and her tears flowed. He moved toward her, but she raised an open palm and he stopped. He picked up his wine glass, and sipped slowly as he sat back, his eyes riveted on her tearful face, allowing the silence to calm the situation.

It was some minutes before she spoke again. "Thank you, Arthur. I'm fine. I'm going to shower and take a nap. I'd like to have dinner at home tonight – just the two of us – and we'll talk. Is that all right with you?"

"Sounds perfect. I've got to get back to my office. Anything I can pick up for you on the way home?"

"A lemon meringue pie would be nice."

"My favorite."

"I know," she said, and smiled.

Arthur left for his office, knowing Samantha needed time to herself, but concerned how she was going to take on Antonelli. Manny was a killer, with a host of underlings ready to do his immoral biddings. A formidable opponent with unlimited access to both respectable and unrespectable people. If he had an Achilles' heel, no one had yet found it. If anyone could, it would be Samantha. But she would need help – all she could get – if she would allow it. And he and Ken Katte were her best chance of remaining safe. And maybe Billie Tsapatsaris could help, along with Tony Bottone, an old friend – a retired Medical Examiner – who had been involved in many of Samantha's past cases. These people, mostly senior citizens – had the smarts and the connections Arthur thought could be useful. When he was inside his Stanton office he began making his calls.

THIRTY THREE

Katte was out. Arthur left a message and phone number for him to call. Billie Tsapatsaris, however, answered on the second ring, and Arthur brought him up to date about Pauline's abduction and Samantha's belief that Antonelli was behind it. Billie was only too eager to help.

Tony Bottone was slow to answer. Arthur waited for his answering machine to kick in. It did, but Tony was on the phone seconds later. They waited for the machine to finish its spiel, and then Tony said, "Sorry about that. I was on the floor doing pushups, and couldn't get to the phone fast enough. Is that you, Arthur?"

"Yes. Can you talk now, or do you want to call me back?"

"No, I'm all done doing that crap. I don't think it helps anyway. These old bones are still creaking, and I ain't moving a hell of a lot better than I used to. Wading in a warm pool at the YMCA feels a lot better."

"I'm sure it does, especially to an old timer like you."

"And screw you too," came the retort. "But nice hearing from you. What's up? How's Samantha?"

"That's why I'm calling, Tony." Arthur told him about the abduction. "Samantha doesn't want help, Tony, but she's going to need it. I thought you, me, Billie T. and Ken Katte could team up to help her."

"Damn right! When and where do you want to meet to discuss it?"

"How about one p.m. tomorrow, at The New Brothers Restaurant in Danvers?"

"Sounds good. I'll see you there."

¥

Billie Tsapatsaris agreed immediately after Arthur called him, and Ken Katte did as well when he returned Arthur's call later that afternoon.

Everyone arrived on time the following afternoon, with the exception of Katte. He had the longest distance to travel and the heavy traffic to deal with, and Arthur expected as much; but he was only ten minutes late. The four men took a corner window booth after being greeted by the affable owners, brothers-in-law Kari and Ted. They left their coats on their seats and then filed in turn along the counter, opting for deli sandwiches and cold drinks, with Arthur signaling the cashier to give him the bill.

It took time to finish their meals because of the catching up talk. When they finished, Arthur signaled the woman tending tables to clear their dishes, leaving only the cold drinks. With small talk done, Arthur directed the conversation to the abduction.

"Okay. Thanks for coming. Samantha's secretary, you all know Pauline, was, we believe, forcefully taken from her home the other night. No witnesses, no clues, no reason we know of, other than she's Samantha's close personal friend and secretary. Samantha's worried she may be murdered. There's no proof of that, but Samantha thinks it's a possibility, and we all know what that means. She feels the kidnapping was ordered by Manny Antonelli, as a warning to her. Samantha has to be near the top of the list of Manny's most hated. And the feeling is mutual. But Manny fucked up. She hasn't been scared by Manny; he's made her pissed and she's going to do something about it. What exactly? I don't know, but *I'm* worried. Worried about her! I need help. I can't watch her every minute; nobody can. But through some of your contacts maybe we can learn what Manny has in mind, and maybe we can stop a war between the two of them. That's why I asked you here."

"Jesus, Arthur. You've got to hold her back," Katte said.

"Ken. You know her. How do I hold her back?"

"You can't," Billie said. "We all realize that. The real question is what can we do to help? They're both strong-willed and uncompromising, but he's a killer with lots of underlings and Samantha's a party of one who's going to need all the help she can get. And that's us. We've got to come up with a plan."

Katte said. "I will help in any way I can, but officially my hands are tied."

"You have any informers in Manny's group?" Arthur asked him.

Katte shook his head. "I had one, but they killed him nearly a year ago. I've had nobody since."

"How did they find out?" Billie asked.

"I think Weiss fingered him."

"Shit. Weiss is another one that's got to go," Billie said. They all nodded their heads in unison.

"Manny's our number one priority," Arthur said. "How do we put him away, or at least keep him from harming Samantha?"

"Someone ought to poison the bastard," Tony offered.

Billie nodded. Katte and Arthur did not. "Everything's got to be done legally," Arthur said. "I took an oath to that. I want you to think about it. Let's meet again Saturday morning, for breakfast. Are all of you good for Saturday, say ten a.m., back here? I'll spring for the breakfast."

They all nodded in the affirmative.

"Then thanks for coming. See you Saturday morning. And I'm keeping our little meeting a secret from everyone – especially Samantha. Mums the word, guys."

THIRTY FOUR

Samantha sat alone in her office. She poured over her files on Manny, jotting down all the misdeeds she could allege against him, but at best the most she could hope for was her day in court, and that would be a long time in coming, with Manny's team of lawyers using subterfuge and every means in their power to gather what they were entitled to as a defense team and kill off a lot of time. She knew it would be a long and harrowing court case, during which time Manny would behave at his worst. She knew he wouldn't take any attack on him without retribution, and she feared for Arthur's and her father's safety as well as her own. She couldn't rely on her sixth sense to warn her of every impending danger. It didn't always work that way. Sometimes she got insights before the fact, and sometimes after. After wouldn't help if she or Arthur were struck down.

A heaviness settled in her stomach.

Her phone rang. She hesitated until the third ring before picking up.

"Yes."

"Is this Samantha Robbins?"

"Yes." She felt her body unexpectedly tremble.

"I think we should meet in person. I don't do much traveling anymore, so you'd have to come to me."

Samantha turned on the recorder on her desk. "I don't know who I'm talking to. Who are you?"

"I think a person with your abilities does know who you are talking to. Ari said you would."

The name Serino flashed into her mind, but she wanted his name on the recording.

She bluffed. "I have no idea who you are, and will hang up unless you tell me."

She heard her caller snicker. "Two can play the game, Ms. Robbins, but it's really to your advantage to meet with me. Your husband is in danger, and so are you, but I can prevent anything from happening to either of you."

"Then why didn't you protect my secretary? She is in her eighties and no threat to anyone," she said bitterly.

"True. But you're perceived as the real threat to the person we both know. I am not happy with his methods. Simple minds, stupid acts. Bad for business. I can do something about him if you and I can come to terms."

"What terms?"

"Meet with me, and we'll talk.

"Where and when?"

"This Saturday, in New York, over lunch. Get an eleven a.m. flight to La Guardia, look for a driver holding a sign with your name, and he'll transport you, and then he'll bring you back to the airport when we're done. You'll be home by early evening. Will you come?"

"Yes, Mr. Serino, I will come."

She couldn't resist letting Serino know she knew exactly who she was talking to.

THIRTY FIVE

S amantha told Arthur Friday evening that she had to make a day trip
to New York on Saturday to meet a client over a divorce issue, but
would be home in the evening in time to dine out. Arthur didn't like the
sound of it, but he had his own breakfast meeting on tap for ten a.m.
Like most married couples, they told little white lies to each other to
prevent undue concern, but only when each considered it prudent. Their
professions could at times be trying, and they attempted not to cause one
another undue anxiety. This was one of those times.

Arthur was the first to arrive at The New Brothers Deli Saturday
morning. He waved to Ted and Kari, and headed for the same table
he used for his prior meeting. The brothers-in-law were too busy to do
anything but return the wave, as a long line of customers awaited their
turn for service, their trays, with silverware and napkins aboard, sliding
along the counter toward the cash register while the staff behind the
counter worked efficiently and swiftly preparing their orders.

Billie Tsapatsaris and Tony Bottone arrived together, spotted Arthur,
and made their way to the booth. Ken Katte arrived five minutes later,
again wearing his ten gallon hat, stirring up looks and whispers among
the deli patrons, which he apparently enjoyed.

They made their way through the line, ordering all different combi-
nations of eggs and toast, or pancakes, and coffees, with Arthur tagging
the rear, having signaled the cashier by hand to give him the bill for the
four of them.

They again made casual talk until they finished eating. After removal of the dishes and a refill of their coffee cups they were ready to do business.

"How did you get out of the house on a Saturday without Samantha getting suspicious, Arthur? Wasn't she curious about your bugging out?" Billie said.

"She left when I did. She's flying to New York to meet with a client, so I had no problem. What did you tell your wife?"

"I didn't tell her anything," Billie boasted. "I'm the boss. I do what I want when I want."

The comment brought the expected laughs, and the "Oh, sure!" it was meant to.

Arthur got down to business. "Okay, you know the problem. What do you suggest? Who wants to start?"

Tony was the first to answer. "The only way we can prevent anything from happening to Samantha is if we know what might happen and when. We've got to have someone inside to tip us off. But I don't know how to get anyone inside. I don't know those people."

"I do, at least some of them," Billie said, "but you can't get them to spy on Manny. They know Manny would have them killed in a second if he found out, and he would find out. I say bug his home phones, office phones, car phone and cell and we can follow his every move. Can we do that?"

Katte answered. "No. Whether it's legally or illegally done doesn't matter. He has experts from a company he owns sweep his phones, residences, offices and vehicles several times a week. He's always been wary of any type of surveillance, and he's got the best people – tech people – to prevent it. I agree with Tony. We have to have someone inside. He's careful with his people so it won't be easy."

"What about his other lady friends?" Arthur asked. "We can't use the Ashley woman."

"No, he keeps his interest in women separate from his business interests. He doesn't even take any of them to his personal living quarters. He sees them in hotels. It's only this Maria Ashley woman he brings home overnight, but I doubt he confides even in her. He came up the hard way, has a lot to hide. He wouldn't trust his own mother."

"So," Tony said, "We've got a problem."

Arthur agreed. "It looks that way. We've got to do more thinking about this. How do we get somebody inside to talk to us? Anybody have any thoughts?"

Stern faces all had negative headshakes.

"There's no sense kicking a dead horse. Keep thinking," Arthur said. "I'll talk to you all during the week. We'll come up with something. Thanks for coming."

Arthur refilled his coffee cup after they left and hung around a while longer. He sat alone in the booth, worrying that he hadn't really accomplished a lot, and worrying about Samantha. He might have to make a move on his own. An illegal move, but if it would save Samantha…he'd damn well do it.

THIRTY SIX

Samantha was outside the Delta Terminal at La Guardia at twelve fifteen, and spotted a black limo illegally parked directly in front of her. The driver was leaning against the passenger-side door, holding a sign in bold letters with the name ROBBINS. He was talking to a heavy-set monster of a cop who had gladly allowed the driver to wait for his passenger in a no parking zone, and had a new fifty dollar bill tucked deeply in one pant pocket.

Samantha walked over to them.

"Your name please, ma'am," the man holding the sign said.

"Samantha Robbins."

The man smiled. "Welcome to New York, Ms. Robbins." He opened the rear limo door.

Samantha didn't know her way around New York, but knew there must be a main route into the city. She was surprised minutes later when the limo exited the highway, taking a ramp that led into a heavily congested section that was mostly stop and go for the next fifteen minutes.

"There's cold bottled water in the fridge under your seat, ma'am. Please help yourself. We'll be at our destination in another ten minutes or so."

"What's your name?" Samantha said.

"Tony."

"Where are we going, Tony?"

"To a small but excellent Italian restaurant. It's special."

"I'm sure it is. And I assume Mr. Serino owns it."

"Yes, ma'am," came the polite reply.

"Thanks for the offer of water, but I'll wait until we arrive at our destination and have a glass of wine. I'm sure they must have a good Italian wine."

"Only the finest, I promise you," Tony said.

The limo came to a stop minutes later in front of a small, inauspicious store front, sporting the name ROSARIO'S in block letters. "Don't let appearances fool you, ma'am; it really is the best," Tony commented. "It is lunch and dinner by appointment only."

"I'll take your word for it, Tony."

He came around to open the door for her. As she thanked him for the lift, she felt a flash and his mind was open to her, and the answer to herself was "No Way, honey."

He opened the front door to the restaurant. The doorway was apparently equipped with electronic sensors designed to announce any sort of weaponry or metal devices entering the establishment, and she stopped when she heard a buzz.

"Would you step back, hand me your shoulder bag, and enter again please," Tony said. She did and no buzzer sounded. "I'll just store this on the table, Ms. Robbins. You can pick it up on your way out."

She thought perhaps it was her metal compact that had triggered the device. She carried no weapon.

¥

The restaurant was small but lavishly appointed. The front windows were heavily curtained, blocking any outside light from entering – as well as any unwanted eyes from peering in – and the drapes were a multi-layered brocade woolen fabric with raised designs of golden threads. There were recessed lights throughout three separate small dining areas, six tables per room, five of which would accommodate two to four guests, and one round table per room that would easily accommodate a party of eight. All were handsomely table clothed, and preset with fine china, gold silverware and a variety of expensive glassware. Samantha couldn't see how many other rooms were behind several closed doors, but two waiters came out of one of the doors, dressed finely in black tuxedos. They nodded cordially to her. She returned the greeting with a slight nod of her head. She noted there were no other customers in attendance. Apparently Serino wanted this to be a private meeting.

Tony led her to a corner table for four, pulled out an ornately uphol- stered gold fabric club chair and asked her to be seated. "Mr. Serino will be along shortly, Ms. Robbins. May I offer you a beverage in the meantime?"

"No thank you; I'll wait."

Less than five minutes later Mario Serino entered. He was a slim man, with penetrating black eyes, slightly aquiline nose, and perfectly aligned lower and upper front teeth that appeared as he smiled at her. He was of moderately dark complexion, exhibiting his Italian heritage. *Overall a good-looking, grandfatherly type,* Samantha thought. He was expensively dressed, though tieless, and he was accompanied by two young men, also well dressed. The two young men remained just inside the front door, where Tony joined them.

"Ah, Ms. Robbins. How nice to meet you at last. Thank you for coming. I hope your trip was satisfactory." His voice was clear and firm, with no sign of an accent.

"It was, Mr. Serino," she said, accepting his extended hand and shaking it.

"Please call me Mario. May I call you Samantha?"

"Yes," she said simply, as he took a seat beside her.

"May I offer you some wine?"

"That would be fine."

"Do you prefer red or white?" he asked graciously.

"I like them both. Your choice, Mr. ... ah, Mario."

He raised his right hand and immediately a waiter appeared. "Bring a light red and a white, Demetrious. You know what I like. Make sure the white is properly chilled."

Mario turned his attention to the three men in the doorway, made the motion to lock the front door, and a second motion for them to leave the room.

"We have wonderful veal here, Samantha. The best. If I may suggest…"

"Too much for me at lunch time, Mario. I'd prefer a small Caesar salad, perhaps with a small amount of white meat chicken."

"Of course. Whatever you desire." Another hand wave and a second waiter appeared. Mario placed her order, and ordered a Veal Scaloppini for himself.

The first waiter returned with the selected wines, and although she viewed the labels, they meant nothing to her.

"Your choice, Samantha?" Mario gestured.

"I'll start with the white, thank you," and the waiter filled her glass.

"The same," Mario said, seemingly enjoying himself.

With the glasses full and the waiter gone, Mario proposed a toast. "To a good relationship, Samantha."

"To a healthy, meaningful relationship, Mario," she said, seemingly now completely at ease.

He smiled, they touched glasses, and they drank.

¥

The wines and food were excellent, although Samantha didn't come close to finishing her large salad. They made small talk during the meal, with Mario doing most of the talking, telling very little of his wife and children other than the closeness of the family unit. "Family, to an Italian, is the most important thing, as is love and respect, Samantha. Without love and respect life is meaningless."

"True, Mario, but it is important how the two are interpreted. There are people who love and respect, but also harm and murder. I can't liken the two."

He smiled. "There are those that have and those that do not have, the never-bees and the want-to-bees, and that's what makes the world go round. If I didn't do what I did, someone else would. It's as simple as that. But I have cleaned up my act a great deal from the old days, and will do even more. But let's not concern ourselves about that at this time. I asked you to meet with me for a specific reason, and I assume you agreed for a specific reason. Let's get to that now, unless you'd care for dessert and coffee."

"No more food for me, Mario, but coffee would be fine."

He beckoned to Demetrious, and minutes later they sat with freshly brewed coffee in front of them. "Ladies before gentleman, Samantha. What specifically do you have on your mind?"

"In a few words, Manny Antonelli. He's a murderer. He's thoroughly no good, and has, I believe, just abducted and maybe murdered my secretary and very best friend; a harmless, wonderful lady in her eighties that *I* love and respect. I believe he did this simply as a warning to me, and if he decides I need a second warning, he'll go after someone else I care for… perhaps even my husband or my father."

"How do you know that, Samantha?"

She met his eyes. "Knowing things is what I do, Mario. It is who I am. Like you, I won't allow his attack on my family, or my friends, to go unpunished. I won't allow him to hurt anyone else I care for. I'll do whatever I have to to stop him!"

"Ari Alexopoulos talked to me about you, Samantha, and how you saved the life of his wife Kara, and also a fortune of his money. He was very much impressed with you, and I must admit I am as well. I've done some checking on you. You've solved some amazing cases."

"And that doesn't bother you, Mario?"

"No, not at all. I think we could stay out of one-another's hair and co-exist. You're in Boston; I'm in New York."

"Actually you're in Boston and just about everywhere else, Mario."

He smiled. "In a sense, yes. But I could replace Mr. Antonelli with a much more trusted, less…impulsive, individual. A collector and overseer, not a killer. A much better choice for both of us."

"Manny's not just going to walk away…."

"True. But maybe he can be convinced to retire and take a permanent vacation. He could live a long and healthy life in another country. A country far from where he need be a concern for you or your family. That would serve both our purposes."

Samantha said nothing for many moments, then asked, "Do you think that's possible?"

"Oh, very possible. My partners and I are quite convincing when we have to be."

"I'm sure you are," Samantha said. "I would like to see that happen, and have my secretary Pauline returned to me, as quickly as possible."

"I will look into that…"

"Thank you."

"…after Mr. Antonelli is settled in his new villa, learning a new language, far from our shore."

He stood and offered her his hand. "I've enjoyed our talk. Tony will get you back to the airport. It was very nice meeting you. I will have someone get in touch with you in a few days to bring you up to date. Thank you for coming."

THIRTY SEVEN

Samantha arrived in Boston shortly after six p.m. Twenty minutes later she was in her car and on her way home. She called Arthur and arranged to meet him for dinner at Wardhurst.

Arthur was sitting at the bar talking with Bill Brennan, the local historian, when she arrived. She walked over and planted a kiss on Arthur's cheek, offered a smile and warm greeting to Bill, and exchanged a few pleasantries with Jimmy behind the bar. Samantha and Arthur then followed the hostess to a booth in the main dining room, stopping briefly to say hello to several of the long-time waitresses – Anna, Vicky, Donna, Janice – as they made their way to the rear booth that was "their table" whenever it was available. They sat on the same bench, – facing the bar. This allowed them to see the forward sections of the restaurant.

"How was your trip, Samantha?" Arthur said, after they were seated.

"I met with Mario Serino, Arthur. I'm sorry I didn't tell you, but I didn't want you to worry. It was at his request, so I knew there wouldn't be any trouble. The trip was in one word, 'rewarding'. Mr. Serino is quite the elegant gentleman."

"Gentleman?" Arthur said somewhat angrily. "How so? He's a crime boss. He and his partners are all murderers and thieves. I don't think the term 'gentleman' fits."

A waitress stepped up to the table. "Hi, guys. Can I get you a drink?" she asked.

"Hi, Vicky. Another Zinfandel wouldn't hurt," Samantha said.

"And you, Arthur?"

"A Dewars White Label, neat, and if I order another one later, ignore me. I already had one at the bar."

"Gotcha. I'll be right back."

"You must have gotten here early," Samantha said, hoping he would simmer down.

"Forty-five minutes ago," he said after glancing at his watch. "I was anxious to see you."

"That's sweet."

Arthur pressed his lips together, and Samantha knew he wasn't going to be mollified by sweet talk.

"Give me more on this guy Serino," he said.

Samantha leaned toward him and said in almost a whisper, "He's not happy with Manny and intends to replace him."

"You're...you're kidding!" Arthur stammered, looking at her in amazement.

A smile creased Samantha lips.

"No, you're not kidding. Did he tell you why?"

"He and his partners don't like the way Manny is running things. He's too high profile, too 'impulsive'. I gather they don't like the way he generates attention."

"How do they plan to *get rid of* a guy like Manny?"

"Serino said that he would be allowed to retire, in another country. He implied they would more or less look after him, but he would have little choice but to leave."

"And if he doesn't retire willingly, he's dead."

"That's how I see it, Arthur."

"Whoever they replace him with would have to be better for us than Manny, Samantha."

"I would think so. Anyway, Serino said he would be in touch with me shortly, and I kind of rushed out of there. I began feeling uncomfortable, knowing what I then knew."

¥

They dined, had coffees and headed home. They showered together, made love, and fell asleep in each other's arms. A rewarding day for both of them.

THIRTY EIGHT

M anny got a call late that night while watching "Dancing with Wolves" on TV for the third time. He sat in his favorite lounge chair in his downtown Boston apartment. He was in his white terrycloth robe, having showered after a particular strenuous session in bed with Maria. He admired her. She was everything a man could want. Beautiful and hot-blooded. He wondered sometimes where she got the strength. She certainly was a match for him.

Maria was similarly attired, and stretched out on the nearby couch, flipping through her copy of Vogue. She ignored the phone call. She already knew what it was about. Mario had called her earlier and told her of his decision.

"Manny? It's Mario. When can you come into New York? I need to speak with you."

Manny motioned for Maria to leave the room. She gave him a faux hurt look and walked out.

"These phones are secure, Mario. We can speak freely."

"No! I need to see you in person. There are several documents you'll need to read and sign. Congratulations, lad. You're being promoted."

"Promoted? I'm not sure what that means."

"It means that you being admitted into the immediate family, Manny. Are you interested?"

Manny sat up in his recliner. "Yes! I'm interested, but I don't understand...."

"Of course you don't understand, and that's why you need to come to New York. There is a swearing in ritual, in front of me and my partners that you'll have to undergo. We take these things seriously, and so must you, if you want to reach the upper echelon. Frankly, we don't usually accept anyone as young as you are, but the others – and I – believe you deserve it. How about next Saturday?"

"Yes, of course; Saturday. Do I need to come alone or can I bring my main man with me again?"

"You can bring whomever you want, other than a woman. Females are not allowed to view the swearing in. If you want to celebrate afterwards, you can bring a woman, or we'll provide one, but she'll have to go shopping or wait in the hotel until you're free. The whole affair, plus a quick celebratory luncheon, will take three or four hours. Then you're free to stay the weekend as my guest, or do whatever pleases you. That's the way it works."

"I'll bring Giorgio with me. I look forward to getting acquainted with your partners and learn what's expected of me."

"I think that's a good idea, Manny. Come late morning. Tony will pick you up at the airport. Congratulations. Oh! Make sure you tell no one of your promotion. We keep these things to ourselves. The less said the better."

"Of course. Thank you, Mario."

"You are welcome. Good night."

¥

"Who was that calling so late, Manny?" Maria asked when Manny called for her to return. She thought she should at least show a little curiosity.

"No one important. Just a business matter I'll need to attend to in New York over the weekend. I'll be tied up most of the weekend, but if you want to come with me and stay at the hotel I'll catch up with you when I can."

"No, lover. I think not. I have luncheon plans for Saturday and Sunday with some lady friends, and it's really too late for me to call them off."

"Okay. I'll be back Sunday night for dinner. Decide where you want to go."

"Maybe Italian for a change. Spicy Italian," she said and laughed. He laughed as well and pulled her to him.

THIRTY NINE

Manny and Giorgio caught the shuttle to La Guardia Saturday morning. A limo awaited them at the curb. Tony was at the wheel, and a large unsmiling man with a nose that looked like it had been on the receiving end of too many punches sat beside him. Tony introduced him as Angelo. The man said nothing, a dour look on his face. Tony on the other hand greeted them warmly.

"Welcome back to New York, Mr. Antonelli. Hello, Giorgio, nice seeing you again." Addressing Giorgio again, Tony said "Please put the baggage on the rear seat. I'll drop you off at the Waldorf. You'll have the same suite as last time, Giorgio, plus a young lady named Katrina is awaiting your arrival, compliments of Mr. Serino. Mr. Serino said for you to enjoy yourself while your boss is occupied."

Giorgio was all smiles when he took his seat next to Manny.

It took nearly forty five minutes in heavy morning traffic before they reached The Waldorf. Giorgio took his bag and exited the car, still wearing a broad grin with the expectation of having a beautiful woman just minutes away. Manny was smiling too, thinking of the pleasant day ahead of him.

"Enjoy, Giorgio," Manny said. "But don't overdo it. You're not a kid anymore."

"I can handle anything they give me, Manny. When I can't I'll shoot myself in the head."

Both Manny and Tony grinned. Angelo never changed his dour expression.

"Will I have time to wash up before I meet Mr. Serino, Tony? I just need five or ten minutes," Manny said on the way to their destination.

"Of course. You're meeting place has all the facilities. And my congratulations in advance, Mr. Antonelli."

"Thank you, and tell your friend to lighten up. He hasn't spoken a word."

"He'll come out of his shell someday, Mr. Antonelli. In the meantime I prefer him this way," he said.

The remark caused Angelo finally to open his mouth. "Fuck you, Tony," causing both Tony and Manny to laugh.

¥

They arrived at their destination some twenty minutes later, a five story brick building in a section of Brooklyn that was unfamiliar to Manny. The building itself was old, but carefully preserved. The front door was new and stylish. Inside, ferns and floral arrangements decorated the small lobby, and large, gold-framed mirrors and elaborately framed seascape oil paintings lined the walls. Angelo remained in the limo while Tony, carrying Manny's bag, accompanied Manny to a second floor lavatory. The room was ornate. Flowered wallpaper, cloth towels, glass chandelier, four stalls, urinals, and wash basins, and four hand and hair dryers. Bottles of PS Cologne, and combs and hair brushes, properly wrapped, were displayed on a marble shelf above. Each basin had unopened packages of tooth brushes and tooth pastes, disposable Bic Shavers and cans of Barbasol shaving cream. There was a chair in one corner of the room, usually occupied by a male attendant, but he had been excused for this afternoon.

Manny freshened up and rejoined Tony in the hall. They entered one of the two elevators and rode upward to the fourth floor. There were four doorways off the lush-carpeted entryway, and it donned on Manny that these were offices for the four New York bosses.

Tony led him to the second door from the right, knocked gently, and opened it upon hearing "come in."

Mario Serino sat serenely behind a massive desk. Two large well-dressed men Manny had never seen before stood near the paneled wall to his left, their gaze cold upon Manny.

"Welcome back to New York, Manny. Please, come in and sit down." As Manny approached the desk, he was brought a padded bridge chair by the younger of the two men standing nearby. There was no offer of a handshake from Mario, nor an introduction to the two strangers, and Manny sat, beginning to feel uncomfortable.

"There's been a change in our original plans for today, Manny. My partners are unable to join us, but we have discussed you thoroughly and are entirely in agreement. I will speak for us all. And please, no interruptions until I finish. It's been decided that you should retire. We have our reasons for this. I will not discuss them with you. In your retirement, which will be in a place of your choice outside the continental United States, you will receive a – let's call it a – pension for as long as you live in the amount of one million dollars a year, which I'm sure you will admit is quite generous. That is the reason for our meeting today. We hope you find it acceptable."

Manny sat stunned by Mario's speech. For a moment he felt a chill at the two hit men's stares, but then inside he began to boil. He fought successfully not to show it, sitting still fully a minute before he spoke. When he did it was with a calmness he didn't feel. "Am I to be told what I did wrong to deserve this decision?"

"No, Manny. That would not help or change the situation. It's been decided. We know you have plenty of money of your own, but another million a year is nothing to sneeze at. You're young, and have a long life ahead of you if you so choose. We think our offer is quite generous and you should be respectful. The old way would not have granted you this way out."

The threat was there, only mildly disguised. *Get out our way or be eliminated!*

"And I'm not to be told why?" Manny insisted, some of the rage he felt slipping out.

"I've already answered that question. You're walking away rich, young and in good health. You'll be able to live a wonderful life."

Until you decide you no longer want to pay me a million dollars a year and have someone put a bullet in the back of my head. Manny needed time to think and he wasn't going to get it now, or here. He did the smart thing.

"Very well, if that's what you've all decided. How much time do I have to get my things together and make arrangements?"

"One month should be sufficient, Manny. You decide where you want to go and who you want to take with you. We'll help you make the move. You are making a wise decision."

Again Manny noted the veiled threat, and set it aside. "None of my associates will be harmed in any way?"

"That's a promise."

"Is there anything else I should know?"

"No."

"Thank you. May I go now?"

"Yes."

Manny knew he was lucky to get out of there alive. He said little on the drive back to the hotel. And this time Tony was as silent as Angelo.

FORTY

Giorgio said nothing on the drive to the airport after seeing the look on Manny's face and how quiet their driver, Tony, was compared to their drive into the city.

Giorgio had barely finished his first tussle in bed with the beautiful hooker waiting for him in his suite when Manny called and brusquely said they were checking out and to meet him in the hotel lobby in half an hour. Giorgio was disappointed that there would be no time for seconds.

When they reached La Guardia, Manny did not wait for the driver but opened the limo door himself and wordlessly pointed for Giorgio to get their travel bags and follow him. Giorgio did as he was beckoned and followed the fast moving Manny into the terminal as the limo drove off.

Once inside the terminal, Manny stopped, gazed at Giorgio, and said, "We've got some problems. I'll explain on the plane."

Before Giorgio could reply, Manny was on his way again, heading to the ticket counter.

¥

The Delta flight departed for Boston forty minutes later, and once on board, Manny breathed easier. He turned toward Giorgio and spoke barely above a whisper. "They want me to retire, Giorgio. Actually, Serino gave me no choice. I was *told* I was to retire. They want me to leave the country, permanently!"

"Unbelievable," Giorgio said. "Did he give you a reason why?"

"They don't have to give reasons. The nerve of that bastard!"

"What are you going to do, boss?"

"He gave me thirty days to wind up my affairs. I've got some time to think about it."

"Are you going to buck them? We've got plenty of friends who would back you if...."

"Don't talk foolish, Giorgio. There's no way to buck them and live. They have far more resources than I have, and they no doubt have informers – damn spies – working for me who report my every move. At least they didn't put me down while I was in New York, which would have been easy to do. Serino had me alone among several of his henchmen but let me go."

"You're right. That's not the way they did things in the old days. There must be a reason."

"I can't think of one. Giorgio, I've got a question for you. Have Serino or his partners done anything to you or your family to make you turn against me?"

Giorgio looked at him. "There's nothing they could do, or threaten me with, that would make me turn against you, Manny. You're like my own flesh and blood. They would have to kill me to...."

"Okay. I had to ask. I knew they couldn't buy you – you never cared about money, only whores –," he said with a thin-lipped smile, "but everyone has a breaking point. I want to make sure they didn't find yours."

"Never! You and I have been through too much together for anyone to separate us. We're family! I swear to you...."

"I believe you, Giorgio, and I trust you. We'll work this out. Tell no one of this conversation, including your cousin, Leon."

Giorgio caught the inference. "I will tell no one!"

FORTY ONE

Mid-afternoon, back in his private office in the rear of Tully's bar, Manny sat alone, deep in thought. He had called no one upon his return. He hadn't had lunch and was feeling the need for food, but he was too upset to eat. He settled for a cigar from the silver humidor on his desk and a bottle of cold Poland Spring water from the small fridge in the corner. He took frequent turns at each.

His thoughts kept centering on Maria. Beautiful, sensuous Maria. She was too good to be true; undemanding, catering to his every whim. The perfect plant for a man like Serino. He thought back to how they had met on a Saturday evening at a bar in the Liberty Hotel. She had come on to him! Out of nowhere, she was there. A secretary for an insurance firm…owned and operated by two brothers – Italian brothers – who he hadn't bothered to check on to see if they were legit or not. He intended to do that now.

He called Maria on her cell phone an hour later. "Where are you?" he said.

"I'm in the lingerie department at Macy's. Need anything?

"You're very funny."

"What's the matter? You sound upset. Everything go okay in New York? I didn't think you were coming home until tomorrow."

"A change in plans. I'll talk to you about it over dinner tonight."

"Where are we going to dine?"

"At home. You're cooking. Steaks and salad; nothing fancy."

"Damn. I just had my nails done."

"So you'll have them done again. I've got things to discuss with you."

"Okay. I'll be back to the apartment in a couple of hours."

"You didn't have other plans for tonight, did you?"

"No. I had planned to stay in and read."

"I'll see you later then. Bye."

¥

Before Maria could reply, Manny was off the phone. He hadn't sounded right. She thought a call to Uncle Mario was in order.

"Uncle, its Maria."

"I thought you might call, Maria. Is everything all right?"

"You tell me. I didn't expect Manny back until tomorrow. You said...."

"A slight change of plans. I decided it was unnecessary for me to entertain him. I gave him the news of his retirement a day early."

"How did he take it?"

"Rather well. He's smart enough to know he has no choice."

"He called me a few minutes ago, while I was out shopping. He sounded a little strange. He told me we're staying in tonight. He said he wants to talk to me. He *never* wants to stay in on a Saturday night. Is there anything I should know? I don't like surprises."

"Maybe he wants to invite you to go with him wherever he decides to go. You told me he goes for you in a big way."

"I think there's more to it than that. Do you think he knows about our connection?"

"I don't think so. If he does, he wouldn't touch you. He wouldn't dare."

"I'm not so sure."

"You can be sure. If he asks you to go with him wherever he decides to go, would you go with him, Maria?"

She thought a moment. "No. As charming and good looking as he is, I'd be bored within a year. There are too many wealthy, gorgeous men in this world for me to tie myself to just one. Variety is the 'spice of life', isn't it?"

"I wouldn't know, Maria. Your aunt and I have been together a long time."

"Don't tell me she's been the only woman in your life, uncle. I heard stories while I was growing up about you, and…."

"Maria! You mind your manners. Those things are none of your business!"

Maria knew she had gone too far, and changed her tone instantly. "I'm sorry, Uncle Mario. Thinking about my evening tonight alone with Manny has me a little worried, and…."

"There is nothing to worry about! Manny is not stupid. He proved to me how much he values his own skin, but you be careful how you turn him down. Tell him it sounds wonderful, but you'll need time to think. Play him: you're good at that. He's got a month to decide where he's going, and to get there. You're clever enough to keep him at bay and then you opt out. He won't come back for you. He'll settle in with his new life and enjoy it. I'll have people watching him and if he strays I'll know it, and he knows I'll know. You be a good girl and call me tomorrow and let me know how things are going. And don't worry! I have people watching him."

"Do you have people watching me as well?" she said, and then was sorry about it.

Mario took no offense. "Of course I do. You're very special to me, Maria; I'll always watch over you. Goodbye. Remember, call me tomorrow."

FORTY TWO

Maria returned to Manny's apartment before he did. She showered, changed into something seductive, and then set the dining area table for two, using the best table cloth, silverware and china. She placed fresh candles in the ornate silver candle holders, and uncorked a bottle of Robert Mondavi Cabernet Sauvignon and set it on the table. She removed a large sirloin and a small filet mignon from the freezer and set them on the granite kitchen counter to thaw, and readied a package of summer squash – his favorite veggie – and a potato to complete the meal. She still had most of the blueberry pie she had brought home the day before tucked away safely in the refrigerator, and their Keurig coffee maker stood ready. Her menu was set.

She began to think about how the evening would go. *I'll let him carry the entire conversation. I'll agree with everything he says, and see what he reveals. He's upset, and maybe I'll learn all that's on his mind…. I must not anger him!*

¥

Manny arrived home at six fifteen that evening. She could see in his eyes that he had had more than a few drinks, but he wasn't drunk. He never allowed himself to get drunk.

He was quieter than usual, but pleasant. He gave her a tender hug, a lingering kiss on the mouth, excused himself to wash up, and returned to the dining area thirty five minutes later, freshly shaved, showered, and dressed casually in a Patriots tee, designer Levis and leather sandals.

Maria grilled their steaks to the preferred medium-rare, heated the squash, and watched the timer for the baked potato. She smiled at him when he entered the kitchen but said nothing.

"You look beautiful as ever, Maria. Have you had a good day?"

"Yes. Today I was in the mood for shopping, but just for underwear. You should see some of the things they're showing for teenagers. Might just as well wear nothing."

"You could still wear that stuff. You've got the figure for it."

"No thanks. I'm more comfortable in something more substantial. The potato will be done in a few minutes. How about lighting the candles and pouring the wine."

They enjoyed their meal, made small talk, finished the bottle of wine and chose not to open another. They both exhibited a satisfied glow. Manny rose, walked over to kiss her, and said, "Leave the dishes for now. I'll help you with them later. Come into the den; I want to talk to you."

They sat side by side on the couch. She thought he felt the same glow that she did and that they would be making love then and there. It didn't happen; he wanted to talk.

"I've decided to retire, Marie. I've got plenty of money; enough for a lifetime, and my investments will continue to provide more money than I will ever be able to spend. I want to live outside of the United States. I have enemies here that will forget about me if I live abroad, and that's what I have decided to do. I was thinking that once I get settled someplace you would come to live with me; for a while, at least, to see if you liked living abroad. I realize you'd have to give up your job and your local friends but I would provide you with enough funds to equal or better what you're making now, and you could make new friends...."

"Manny, it sounds a little like a marriage proposal."

He hesitated before he answered. "... It isn't a marriage proposal, Maria. I honestly don't know if I could ever marry again, after my horrible marriage with Terri. Love turned to hate, and she tried to kill me. I think I'm forever soured on marriage, and I don't know if I could change. I'm being totally honest with you, Maria."

"Thank you, Manny. Most women wants a successful marriage, but I'm not most women. I don't want kids – I'm selfish and enjoy my freedom too much to want to be tied down. I'm not sure if I'd like living abroad – I enjoy my big city life both in Boston and New York. I'm not sure I could be happy giving it up. I'd – I'd have to think about it for a while. Once you get settled, call me and we'll talk. Maybe I could visit for a few weeks and see. We could try something like that if you want to. I don't know what else to say. This entire business about you leaving comes as a shock. Are you being forced out?"

She regretted the question seconds after she posed it. She wasn't supposed to know much about his businesses and acquaintances, and she was opening up matters she would have been better off staying away from.

Manny didn't seem to notice. "It's by mutual agreement," he said, and with a noticeable grimace added, "My New York associates suggested it and I agreed."

"And you only have a month to – to close up your business ventures here in Boston and move on?"

"You've got the picture, Maria. I have one month."

"Where do you think you'll go?" she said, not knowing how to get away from the subject.

Manny did it for her. "Let's clean up from dinner, watch a little TV and talk about it tomorrow. I've had my fill of it for today."

She had as well. She was happy that she would be able to report to Uncle Mario that Manny was going to do as Mario had ordered.

She was now certain things would work out the way she wanted them to. She would be free to decide how, where, and with whom she wanted to live the next phase of her life.

¥

And Manny now considered that Maria was Mario's spy. She had never mentioned family, other than some friends in New York, and she had too conveniently come upon him at a bar filled with many young, rich, attractive men. Thinking back to their first meeting, she was too attentive, came on too strong and paid no attention to anyone else. In the months after that, she had made many private cell phone calls and, as he thought about it now, never left her cell phone unattended. He had been set up!

FORTY THREE

They made love that night, and again the following morning. It was good, always good; slowly performed, sensual, and highly satisfying. Manny realized it was going to be tough giving Maria up; but wherever he went, he would find someone else who was equally beautiful, equally as good in bed, and hopefully, someone who was trustworthy. He was beginning to think maybe there weren't any women like that, but he knew better. He just hadn't been smart enough to select the right one.

He knew another important thing. Wherever he settled Mario would have someone watching him. Why had Mario let him live? There could only be one reason. Sometime in the future Mario would need him, and remind him that he owed him. There was never something for nothing with these people. They thought ahead, and that was the reason many of them lived to a respectable age. Favors would be called in. He'd been caught off-guard. It wouldn't happen again. The further from New York he went, the less power Mario and his cronies would have over him; and Manny knew about establishing power. If he didn't like the new life Mario had forced on him, he promised himself he would kill Mario and anyone else that got in his way.

FORTY FOUR

⟡

S teve Grant got the call from Weiss on a selected cell phone shortly after eleven a.m. that morning.

"Grant?"

"Yes."

"It's Joe. Can we talk?"

"Yes. I'm alone."

"Good. Our mutual friend wants to meet with you today. Six o'clock this evening, at the bar at The Empire Restaurant. You familiar with the place?"

"Yes. In the Seaport area, near the Convention Center. What's the meeting about?"

"You know better than to ask. Will you be there?"

"Yes. I'll be there."

There wasn't even a "goodbye." Weiss disconnected.

Steve knew he had little choice, and he was curious. Maybe it was about the next installment of money due him and Manny wanted to handle money matters personally. Or maybe ....

Steve changed phones and called Samantha.

"Steve; good morning."

"I hope it is, Samantha. I just got off the line with Weiss. He set up a meeting for me tonight at six p.m. at the bar in The Empire Restaurant in Boston. The main man wants to meet. Do you have any clue as to why?"

"I don't. If you're worried about your safety I don't think it's a problem. As long as you arrive and leave separately he means you no harm. He knows he can get you any time he wants without calling for a meeting."

"Well, that really warms my heart."

She ignored the remark. "I'll want to know about your meeting when it's safe for you to contact me. Maybe we're making headway. Katte called me a half hour ago about a trip Manny took to New York to meet up with Serino. A short meeting, and Manny didn't stay over. I think something of importance is going down."

"What's all of that have to do with me?"

"Probably nothing. Maybe it has to do with me. That's what I hope to find out. Get back to me after your meeting, Steve."

"Yeah. Bye."

Samantha returned the cell phone to the top drawer of her desk. She leaned back in her swivel chair, closed her eyes, and waited. She was disappointed after several minutes when no revelation came. She was in the dark about some phases of the Serino – Antonelli meeting, yet she knew something important had transpired. Sometimes, when she needed it, her sixth sense failed her, but then, when least expected, an epiphany arrived. Hopefully it would do so soon.

Nor did she have the answer about her dear, sweet Pauline. She had had two realistic dreams about Pauline in the past two weeks. *Pauline was calling to her. Was it from another world? No! It was from this world; had to be. She didn't know of other worlds, and yet....*

Samantha took a tissue from the dispenser on her desk. Whenever she thought of Pauline she got teary eyed. *There's more than a possibility she's still alive. But who's keeping her, and why? As a hold over me?* If anyone took Pauline it had to have been on Manny's orders. Yet Manny hadn't contacted her. What was he waiting for?

Too many questions with too few answers. *Please,* she cried out to herself, *please give me the answers!*

¥

The Empire Restaurant was a busy public spot.

At six p.m. it would be crowded with the before dinner crowd and a safe place to meet. The noise would cover any conversation, and they would be able to conduct business without being monitored. Steve considered wearing a wire to record the meeting, but decided it was too risky.

He valet parked his pickup truck in front of the Empire at five fifty p.m. and made his way into the crowded building. He was met immediately by a host. "Can I help you, sir?"

"I'm meeting somebody at the bar. I want to look and see if he's here."

"By all means, sir. If I can be of any assistance let me know."

Steve eyeballed Manny at the far end of the bar, sitting with one of the men who was with him the first time they met in Steve's Salem office. When Steve reached them, and before a word was spoken, the big guy – Giorgio – got up, nodded, and gave his seat to Steve. He walked to the other end of the bar and waited for a bar stool to become vacant. He remained there, observing Manny and Steve, his gaze unwavering.

"Good evening, Steve," Manny said. "I'm glad you could make it. Have trouble getting here?"

"Not really. I left Salem early and beat the traffic."

"Smart." Manny didn't wait for Steve to order a drink. "I'm leaving the country in a few weeks, and I am therefore concluding our business arrangement as of today. You've been helpful, but I no longer have need of your services. You never did find out who wrote those letters, did you?"

"No. I am still working on it."

"If you do I want to hear from you. Otherwise, this ends our business dealings."

"Whatever you say, Mr. Antonelli. Anytime I can help feel free to contact me." Steve was afraid to say more or ask questions, but was surprised at the turn of events.

"I'm going to set up some business ventures overseas, so I may be gone for quite a while. If you come across any information regarding the

Robbins woman that you think would be of interest to me, you contact Weiss and he will contact me. You want a drink?"

"No. I'll have one later. I have a date at eight thirty."

"Good for you. So do I," Manny added without a smile. He reached inside his sport's jacket pocket and withdrew a sealed manila envelope and handed it to Steve. "There's another ten in there, Steve. I think you'll agree that it's not bad for a mere few months' work."

Steve had no intention of quibbling over money. He would have settled for a lot less just to get away from any sort of relationship with Antonelli. He pocketed the envelope. "Thank you, Mr. Antonelli. Is there anything else, or should I go now?"

Manny smiled. He knew the power and fear he wielded, and enjoyed it. "Yes, Steve. You can go. Drive carefully."

Steve headed out of the restaurant, ignored Giorgio when he passed him, and retrieved his vehicle and drove away. He entered the Callahan Tunnel ten minutes later and headed for Route 1A north. When he cleared the tunnel he phoned Samantha. She didn't answer. He left a short message. *Just left our friend. Interesting meeting. Call me. I'll be home after eight.*

FORTY FIVE

Samantha supped alone. Arthur had called to say he was working late. She had two glasses of calming zinfandel, cleaned up after herself and then slipped into her woolen nightgown and terry cloth robe. Stretching out on the couch, she picked up the Boston Globe and began to read but dozed off less than a half hour later. When she awoke, Arthur was in the kitchen grabbing a snack. She checked her array of cell phones for messages and found the one from Steve Grant. She listened to it as she walked into the kitchen to join Arthur.

She smiled and offered a wave with her free hand as she sat down opposite him. He waited until she snapped the phone closed.

"Hi, honey; anything important?"

"As a matter of fact, yes. Steve left me a message that Manny Antonelli gave him his walking papers a few hours ago. Steve is out of a job."

"Wow! Did he say why?"

"That's the interesting part. Manny is leaving the country, supposedly to start up new business ventures elsewhere. But I think that…"

"They are letting him live? Doesn't sound right, Samantha. Something else is going on."

"Exactly! They want Manny out of Boston but don't want him dead. Manny still has value to them. Intriguing!"

"Intriguing? What the hell does that mean?"

"I don't think it has ever happened before. They want Manny out, but not all the way; or maybe just temporarily. Manny must have something on one or more of them for them to come up with that type of an arrangement."

"Maybe it's because of you, Samantha. He must have told them you're holding something over his head, and they want to play it safe. They're getting Manny to go away for a time."

"Hmm. A possibility, Arthur. But I'm not letting him get away."

"Let's think about that for a while, Samantha."

"Think about it all you want. He's not getting off that easy. He's a multiple murderer, rotten in every way, and deserves at the very least life in prison. I intend to see that he gets what he deserves."

"'Heav'n has no rage like love to hatred turn'd, nor hell a fury like a woman scorn'd.'" Arthur said, a smile turning up the corner of his lips.

Samantha raised an eyebrow. "You know Congreve? I'm impressed." She smiled at him in return. "Manny has nothing but contempt for me, so that's scorn. And I feel the same about him. I intend to hound him until he's put away."

"Okay! You know I'll help in any and every way I can."

"I know you will. Did you get a chance to have supper?"

"Yeah. With Tony Bottone. We ate at The Black Lobster. He treated. Said he owed me. I thought he was going to cry when I didn't object."

"You had lobster?"

"No. We had fried clam rolls. I didn't want to take advantage. He sends his regards."

"Thanks. I'm going to call Steve and set up a meeting with him for some time tomorrow. Do you want to be there?"

"Hell, yes. Make it for the evening; some place local."

"I'll try. Mind if I go to bed? I'm bushed."

"NO. Go ahead. Anyone else we should ask?"

"No. I think we should leave Billie and Tony out of this, at least for the time being, until we have more to go on."

"Okay. Goodnight honey. Pleasant dreams."

FORTY SIX

Samantha had anything but pleasant dreams. She was still awake when Arthur slipped into bed more than an hour later, but didn't let him know it. He was snoring ten minutes later. She lay with her eyes open, staring at the ceiling, her mind working overtime to make sense of Manny being removed. She wondered who would replace him, and hoped it was a "new look" business man rather than an old time mobster. She wanted Boston cleaned up, the way the New York guys had cleansed themselves after the passing of Papa Gardello and Lou Adolpho. She did not delude herself with the thought that mob bosses and mobsters would suddenly disappear and crime die out, but if sane business men rather than mindless killers controlled the illicit activities then life would be far more livable.

But it was primarily thoughts of Manny Antonelli that kept her awake. He was a Satan in every manner but appearance. If anyone deserved punishment it was he. *I've got to get him! But how?*

Finally sleep overwhelmed her, and the answer came to her in a dream.

Some dreams are vivid beyond belief. Others are shadowy, ephemeral. Samantha's dream that night was so real that she woke up quivering and in tears. She slipped out of bed without waking Arthur, swiftly made her way to the bathroom, turned on the lights, looked into the mirror, and with a stifled gasp stepped back.

Staring back at her, she saw the face of a woman aged beyond belief – almost unrecognizable. It wasn't her face!

But the image faded, and her real face appeared. She took deep breaths to calm herself. She splashed water on her face and brushed her hair. In a few minutes, she had regained her self-control.

It wasn't a vision. It was just a bad dream. But there's a message there. Manny is going to try to return to the States. When he does I for one am going to hound him and make him the loser he deserves to be!

This last thought made her feel better, and she went back to bed and eventually caught a few hours of sleep.

FORTY SEVEN

Samantha called Ken Katte shortly after ten a.m., reaching him at his office.

"Samantha, how are you? I hope you had a pleasant weekend."

"I wish I could say yes, but I can't. We've had some unexpected developments, Ken, and Arthur and I thought we should meet with you and discuss them. Are you available this evening?"

"I have no special plans. Where and when?"

"I thought we could make the travel easier for you. Do you remember we met last year at the NewBridge Café, on Washington Ave. in Chelsea?"

"Yes. I've been there several times since then. Seven p.m. okay?"

"Perfect. There will just be the three of us."

"See you then. Bye."

¥

Katte beat them to the restaurant. He was sitting at the bar, beer in hand, chatting with two young ladies when they arrived. On sighting Samantha and Arthur, he politely took his leave, and beckoned to the hostess. She led them to a table in a far corner of the room. Addressing Ken, the waitress said "You asked for a quiet table where you could hear yourselves talk and think, but I'm afraid there isn't such a thing at this time in the evening. This table is the best I can do."

"It'll do fine," Ken replied, and slid into one of the sturdy all-wood chairs facing the wall, allowing Samantha and Arthur to take seats facing a ceiling TV.

"Mobbed as usual," Katte said. "She wouldn't give me a table until the whole party showed up. How are you guys?"

"Good," Samantha said, after she and Arthur sat. "There's a lot that's happened over the weekend."

"Uh huh. Some interesting stuff happening on my side too."

Ken stopped talking when the waitress showed up and handed them menus.

He ordered another beer. Arthur ordered the same, but Samantha opted for the restaurant's own brand of diet root beer.

"Let's order first and then we'll talk," Samantha suggested.

"I'm going for the full rack of baby back ribs, and fries," Ken said. "I've been thinking about them all day."

"I'm going for the ribs as well," Arthur said, "but no fries. I'll have a small antipasto salad. A lot less calories that way," he added for Samantha's benefit.

She shook her head. "You both should be ashamed of yourselves for eating all that fat. I'm having the half order of grilled turkey tips with a garden salad. Eat healthy, live healthy, and be healthy. You should both think like that."

Katte glanced at Arthur. "You have to listen to that kind of talk all the time?"

"All the time, Ken."

Samantha rolled her eyes.

The waitress set down a basket of rolls, announcing she'd be right back with their drinks.

Ken had a roll in his hands seconds later. Arthur deferred, not wanting to get that nasty look from Samantha. Samantha, of course, wasn't even tempted.

Their drinks came, and with their meals ordered they were ready for business.

Ken said, "The Ashley woman works for a legitimate business, an insurance company, but the interesting part is the two brothers who run it are cousins to the one and only Mario Serino. The Ashley woman is also related, so we have one big happy family."

"I'm not surprised," Samantha said. "So Mario has been keeping an eye on Manny through Maria Ashley."

"Exactly," Ken said. "Manny was called into New York Saturday to meet with Serino. Our New York people observed Manny and his henchman, Giorgio, being picked up by Serino's people. They dropped Giorgio off at the Waldorf Astoria. Manny stayed in the limo and they took him to a private building in Brooklyn to meet with Serino. We don't know what went on inside, only that they met for barely an hour and then Manny left. They drove back to the Waldorf Astoria and he never got out of the limo. Our people were surprised when his man Giorgio, carrying their two travel bags, got into the limo and they were driven to La Guardia. It appeared they had planned to stay overnight, but their plans for some reason changed."

"The change in plans, Ken, was that Manny was told he was going on a long vacation. He is to get out of the country, and has a month to make his arrangements and do so. Somebody else is going to take over the Boston operations," Samantha explained.

Katte showed his surprise. "How do you know that?"

"Steve Grant was hired by Manny to watch me, to find out what cases I was working on, and to get any information he could pertaining to Manny. Instead Steve teamed up with me and through him I provided Manny with a bunch of no truths and half-truths. Manny met with Steve last night and terminated their arrangement, telling Steve he was leaving the country within the month. Putting two and two together, Serino wants Manny out and someone else to take over in Boston. I'm not sure of the reason or reasons for this, but apparently Manny felt he had no choice and is preparing to leave. My feeling is Manny will be back. He's not the type to be run out of town without a fight."

"I wonder who will be taking over Manny's responsibilities." Katte said.

"I expect we'll soon find out," Arthur said. "Serino will need to send someone within a few days to meet with Manny, and get info on

Manny's people, places and operations. This guy will most likely use Manny's organization until he replaces them or is satisfied their loyalties can be bought. Not an easy thing, but I suppose with the threat of death over their heads the new guy will have a reliable team in a short period of time."

"I agree, Ken," Samantha said. "The Boston team knows they'll be under a magnifying glass for a long time, and won't want to change their lifestyles. Their loyalty to Manny will end as soon as he departs. Anyway, it will be interesting to see who the new Boston Overlord will be. But I'm still concerned about Manny, Ken. Are you going to be able to keep tabs on him once he leaves the country?"

"I honestly don't know. Our agency reach is limited outside the country, and for information abroad we're supposed to team up with the CIA. But the two agencies still don't get along, so how much information I'll be able to get from the few CIA guys I know is questionable. We'll have to see where Manny winds up."

"I was afraid of that," Samantha said.

"He's only one guy, Samantha. And a castaway," Arthur said.

"To me he's not 'only one guy,' Arthur. He's Satan personified!"

FORTY EIGHT

Manny got a call from Serino on a secure line Wednesday evening. "I'm sending my nephew, Tony Cataldo, to Boston tomorrow, Manny. You've met him several times…"

Manny hadn't known Tony's last name, but did now. *The pleasant guy in the limo at the airport!*

"…and he and two others will be staying at the Ritz until they find suitable arrangements for a permanent habitat. If you are interested in selling any of your properties, including your offices, to them – actually, to me – it can be arranged."

"I have several properties I can show him, including my bar. Are you interested in buying that as well? The bar is a profitable business."

"We can work that out. I want as little disruption as possible. One of the people coming with Tony is an accountant. You can work out the sales details with him."

Manny couldn't resist asking. "I assume he's also a relative of yours?"

"Of course. They will make their own arrangements from Logan Airport to the hotel," Mario continued, "and Tony will call you tomorrow evening to make plans to meet you. I will give him your number."

"That's fine."

"Good. I will call to check on your progress. I assume that meets with your satisfaction?"

Manny hid is anger. "Of course, Mr. Serino."

Mario noted the surname usage. Manny was not a happy trooper. "Goodbye, *Mr.* Antonelli."

Manny hung up, got out of his chair and paced the room. He felt helpless, which made him furious. He had successfully called all the shots in Boston for a long time and was now being treated like an unwanted child. He had made millions for these people and they were casting him away like a broken toy. But he was far from broken. He promised himself that he'd regain everything, and more. Heads would have to fall, and the first would be that patronizing dick Mario Serino. And then Ari Alexopoulos, and then Maria Ashley and Samantha Robbins. They had all betrayed him, and he would set things straight.

But their deaths would have to appear to be from natural causes. If they were simply murdered, the repercussions towards him would be endless. He needed allies – people he could trust – and they would be difficult to come by, considering the opposition. But he would find them: it would just take time.

Manny returned to his swivel chair, sat, and for the first time in hours smiled. He, an undereducated kid from a slum in Boston would be taking on highly educated individuals, even one who was purportedly a psychic, and he would ultimately win. These privileged pricks could dish out hurt, but could they take it? He'd taken beatings, been knifed, even shot–but he always came out on top. He would again. The challenge was everything he could ever want. What greater glory could there be?

His twisted mind could think of none!

FORTY NINE

Tony Cataldo and the accountant, Joseph Cusolito, joined Manny in his office Friday morning. The third member of their group, the dour faced Tito, was told by Tony to wait in the restaurant. Tito did as he was told, expressing no feeling for his exclusion from the group.

¥

Giorgio eyed Tito with displeasure when Tito approached him at a corner table where he had been enjoying his third cup of morning coffee and the remnants of a prune Danish.

"Can I join you?" Tito said. "I don't see much sense of my sitting alone and staring at the walls and ceiling."

"Suit yourself," Giorgio answered, displaying a little of the animosity he felt for this jerk. "You want coffee?"

"Yeah. Thanks," Tito said as he dropped into a chair alongside Giorgio.

Giorgio wordlessly signaled Frankie behind the bar for a coffee for Tito and a refill for himself.

They sat without conversation for the few minutes it took Frankie to find a mug for Tito and bring a Silex coffee pot to the table. Frankie said nothing as he filled the mug for the stranger and topped off Giorgio's cup. Tito took two sugars and two creams from the bowl on the table while Giorgio used no additives.

"Are you going with your boss out of the country?" Tito said, trying to get some kind of conversation going.

"I expect so."

"Do you know where you're going?"

"Someplace with good food and plenty of broads."

Tito smile politely. *The guy has a sense of humor.* "Doesn't sound like such a bad deal," Tito said.

"That's right," was the limited response Giorgio gave.

"You want to play some gin rummy while we're waiting? Might help to pass the time."

"How do you know I won't cheat?" Giorgio snapped.

"Okay. So I was out of line. I apologized, didn't I?"

"Yeah, but not willingly."

"So I apologize again; this time willingly. You name the stakes."

"No money. I couldn't stand to see you cry."

"You don't let up, old man, do you? Let's play 100 points for fifty bucks."

"Are you sure?"

"Yeah."

"Frankie," Giorgio bellowed, "throw me a fresh deck of cards."

¥

In Manny's office the three men were all business. Tony sat quietly, listening to Manny and Joe Cusolito discussing properties and prices. Joe had his laptop and sheets of Boston Real Estate properties and prices to refer to and obviously knew his business. He was willing to buy, sight unseen, all of Manny's properties, and was apparently told by Serino to be more than fair with the pricing. Manny expected that. *If you're a billionaire like Serino you don't worry about money.*

¥

Manny had decided to sell everything. Money was not going to be a problem. Keeping alive was. He no more trusted Serino and his partners than they apparently trusted him. But he intended to survive – and have his revenge.

It took two hours to discuss and put a value on each property. Cusolito went through the motion of speaking to Serino before signing off on all the deals although Manny suspected he didn't have to. The prices were fair, and Manny came out with more than forty million dollars, but at this point, only on paper.

¥

Tony cornered Manny alone when Joe excused himself to use the wash room.

"You know, Manny, this was none of my doing. I was happy where I was, but Mario gave me no choice. I imagine that's what he gave you. I hope you don't hold any grudge. I'm just doing as I'm told."

"I know that, Tony, and so am I. Don't worry about it. You heard the money I'll be getting. I'll lead a good life."

"I guess so. Anyway, good luck. I'd like to start on Monday viewing everything and meeting everybody. That suit you?"

"Absolutely. Sorry I can't entertain you over the weekend, but I have a number of things I have to get out of the way. I'll speak to you Sunday evening, and set up a time to meet on Monday, okay?"

"Sounds good."

They joined Tito and Giorgio in the restaurant. Giorgio was smiling, and holding the two hundred dollars he had won from Tito. Tito wasn't smiling, but he wasn't angry as he looked at Manny and said, "I'll remember not to play cards with this guy again."

FIFTY

M anny sat with Giorgio in the bar drinking coffee. Giorgio was pretty much saturated with coffee, but wanted to hear what Manny was willing to tell him about the meeting.

"Everything go okay, boss?"

"Yes, Giorgio. They bought all my properties, and once I spend a week or two with Tony showing him the ropes, we'll be able to take off, and with a ton of money."

"Sounds good. Where are we going?"

"London. I've made inquiries. We'll live separately, but not far apart. That way all the broads you bring home won't disturb me. I think we'll open up a fancy speakeasy or bar room, or whatever they call it over there, while we scout out what opportunities there are for gentlemen of our particular talents. You'll be in charge of hiring all the dancers, so you should have a ball...."

Giorgio smiled.

¥

That evening, Manny took Maria to Abe and Louie's for dinner. They sat at their usual table, ordered their dinners, and Manny ordered a bottle of particularly expensive champagne.

Maria thought Manny had been in an especially good mood when he returned to the apartment earlier that afternoon. She had asked how his meeting went, and he seemed effusive in his joy over the event. "I've got big money coming to me, Maria; really big money. I'm going to settle down in Madrid and see what opportunities are available for a big spender. It should be a blast...."

They ate a lot, drank a lot, talked a lot, and when they got back to the apartment made love–a lot of love.

¥

Manny had told Giorgio London and Maria Madrid. He told Mario nothing. He was hoping Mario would slip up and wish him good luck in Madrid, and not mention London. Then he could be sure of Giorgio. He needed to have at least one person he could trust. His life might depend upon it.

FIFTY ONE

Samantha got the word from Ken Katte, who had been informed by one of the FBI agents in New York. Tony Cataldo was moving to Boston to replace Manny Antonelli.

¥

The New York FBI had almost nothing on Cataldo, other than he was a nephew to Mario Serino. He was in his early thirties, married, with two kids in elementary school. He had no arrest or conviction records. Whether Tony was a temporary replacement or a permanent one for Boston was the question. For some reason, the New York bosses wanted Manny Antonelli out of Boston fast. And Manny was obliging; selling out everything. FBI New York had lots of questions and few answers.

¥

Mario called Tony every evening at six.

"Is he cooperating, Tony?"

"More than I expected, Uncle Mario. He…."

"You can drop the 'uncle' reference, Tony. You're a big man now, and I expect big things from you. Call me as often as you want if you need advice, but I expect you to manage by yourself, and manage wisely for the family. Choose your associates wisely, Tony, and keep tabs on that private investigator from Pemberton. She could be a problem. Leave her alone for now, but keep an eye on her."

"I will, Uncle…I mean Mario. Manny told me he thinks she's a real problem…with all that supposed ESP crap. He believes in it."

"Manny may be blaming his own failures on that bull crap, but don't take her lightly. She's a good detective and perhaps has more than her share of a woman's intuition. It's difficult to know about those things. Like I said, watch her."

"I will, Mario."

"Have you seen Maria?"

"A couple of times. We're still playing the strangers bit."

"Keep it that way. I want Manny in the dark about you two."

"We know."

"Is she going overseas with him?"

"Not at first. He wants a month to get settled, and then she'll decide."

"You tell Manny you want to meet up with Police Captain Weiss, Tony. I want Weiss to be at your beck and call."

"Funny you should bring that up. Weiss is having dinner with us tonight. Manny suggested it."

"Good. When Manny leaves town you meet with this cop personally and make sure he understands Manny is out and you're in, and his only loyalty is to you. I'll talk to you tomorrow. Goodbye."

Tony said goodbye to the dial tone.

¥

Mario thought events were progressing smoothly. He sat in his office and looked out the window…and saw nothing. When he was deep in thought like this, Mario's mind thought of the world as he wished to see it – under his control.

He was still in his office. Darkness had crept in, and he was ready to go home. Well, almost ready. Two of his people waited patiently for him downstairs to drive him, and they never complained. They were afraid to. They had been with him a long time and remembered well some former complainers that suddenly and permanently disappeared. One was even a relative. Mario Serino, the grandfatherly type, the gentlemanly type, the warm, smiling type, could be as deadly as a fanged cobra!

¥

Mario was deep in thought. *Maria says Manny's going to Madrid. But he bought two airline tickets to London. He doesn't trust Maria, but does he know about Maria's connection to me? And Giorgio's traveling with him. He trusts Giorgio. I'll ask Manny where he's going and see what he tells me. I'm getting tired of playing games. But I may need Manny! I'm not sure Tony or anyone else I have in mind can control Boston and the New England area as well as Manny has. And yet, maybe I won't. Maybe I'll just have him buried overseas.*

FIFTY TWO

Antonelli, Cataldo, and Weiss had dinner in Manny's office at Tully's. Weiss and Cataldo arrived separately, and were admitted through the rear entrance by a stern-appearing Giorgio. The menu was simple; baked potato, sirloin steak, peas and carrots, with a side garden salad. Scotch, bourbon and a 2004 Mondavi Merlot wine was served by the two young look-alike waitresses, who captured the attention of Weiss and Cataldo but were ignored by Manny.

Manny made a quick introduction, telling Cataldo that Weiss was invaluable and should be treated with due respect – and money. Joe Weiss was all smiles. Cataldo said to Weiss "I'd welcome your help, and I'll keep you happy."

Weiss did most of the talking that evening, attempting to ingratiate himself with the new Boston mob boss, and Manny allowed him to do so. Weiss was a kiss-ass and would serve anyone who would pay him. Weiss would wind up missing some day, and Manny looked forward to making it happen.

After dessert and coffee, Manny got rid of both of them. He drove to his apartment, gave the questioning Maria Ashley a little nothing about "his important meeting," accepted her love-making to make her think he was still interested, and went to sleep.

The next morning, Manny called Mario Serino.

"Good morning, Mr. Serino. I feel I've given Tony all he needs to know about the Boston operation. He should be ready to get by on his own. We had a private dinner last night with my police contact and they seemed to get along fine. I know Weiss will be of help, and Tony understands the financial arrangements. Tony and your accountant seem to have a complete understanding of my former business arrangements and properties and they both have cell phone numbers which they can use to contact me if they need to. If it's okay with you, I'll leave Boston in the next few days."

"That's fine," Serino said. "I talked to Tony earlier this morning and he seemed pleased with the way things were going. He feels he is ready to be on his own. This cop Weiss; can he be trusted?"

"As long as you pay him, the answer is yes. He carries his own weight with the department, knows everyone, and can get all kinds of information to keep you on tap with what's going on in the city. He also has a few FBI connections in Boston that are hard to come by and will keep abreast of their movements."

"Sounds good," Serino said. "Are you travelling alone?"

"No," Manny said, but didn't say who he was going with.

Serino pressed the issue. "Who's going with you?"

"My longtime associate, Giorgio."

"Anyone else?"

"Possible Giorgio's relative, Leon, if I can convince him to come."

"That's it?"

"Yes."

"Where are you going, Manny?"

There it was, the question that Manny had been waiting for. "I have two first choices, Mr. Serino. One is London, the other I haven't decided. Maybe to Spain. I'll make up my mind in the next couple of days."

"You'll like Madrid, Manny. Enjoy your retirement. Let me know what bank you want your money sent to and I'll send you half of it in two weeks, and the rest of it the following month. Goodbye, Manny."

"Goodbye Mr. Serino."

After hanging up, Manny went to the refrigerator and poured himself a tall glass of low-acid Tropicana orange juice. He returned to his desk, sat, gulped down a generous amount, put the glass on the Red Sox coaster resting on his desk, and smiled. He had told Maria he was going to Madrid and he had told Giorgio London. The only name Serino had used was Madrid, as if it was for sure the given destination. It was Maria who had to have told him that.

Manny walked into the bar area and found Giorgio and Leon in their usual spots, coffee mugs in hand.

"You guys shouldn't drink all that coffee. You'll wind up peeing twelve times a day."

Giorgio snickered. "I do that anyway."

Leon smiled at the comment. "It doesn't bother me, Mr. Antonelli; just keeps me sharp."

"It doesn't bother you because you're still young. A few years down the road you'll find out differently."

"That's what Giorgio told me about sex," Mr. Antonelli," Leon said. "But he can't seem to get enough of it."

"Wise ass," Giorgio responded, his smile as big as the others.

"One question, Leon. Have you decided to join us?"

"Yes. With you and Giorgio gone, they won't give me anything of importance to do. I'd rather stay with you."

"Glad to have you, Leon. You'll be happy you made that decision."

"That's what Giorgio said, Mr. Antonelli."

Manny smiled. *That's if you don't wind up dead!*

FIFTY THREE

Samantha sat in her Pemberton office, her door closed to cut off the sound of the rock music playing on Lucy's – her temp's – radio. Lucy claimed she "couldn't live or work without it," and had forgotten her ear phones. Samantha suggested she not forget her ear phones again.

Samantha was spending more time in her office because she experienced her epiphanies more frequently there. She had had two the prior week. Her first vision had been about Pauline. She was now sure Pauline was still alive, being held but being treated well.

Her second vision was about Manny Antonelli. Manny was at Logan Airport with Giorgio and another much younger man awaiting their flight to somewhere. Katte had filled her in a bit about Manny's replacement, Tony Cataldo, but only to the extent that Tony was a close associate of Serino as well as a nephew, and had no record with the police or FBI. He was therefore classified as an unknown quantity for the time being. There was still some speculation about why Manny was leaving, but the rumor was strong that he had been kicked out. Katte suggested to Samantha that the reason may have been because New York wanted the Boston killings to stop.

With Manny out of the country he would be more difficult to track, and she didn't want to lose sight of him. She would find out where he settled and then find someone who could keep tabs on him for her. He was – and always would be – a threat to her and to anyone who got in his way. She needed Manny in jail. She knew he had enemies, and now apparently a major one in Mario Serino. *Maybe that's why Mario is forcing*

Manny to leave the states. There would be much less fanfare if he were to have an "accident" outside of the country. Manny must know this as well.

Her intercom buzzed. "Steve Grant's on line two," Lucy said. "Do you want to take the call?"

"Yes, I do, Lucy. Thank you."

"Hi, Steve. How are you?"

"Good, Samantha. Thought you might want to know that Manny left the country a half hour ago."

"For where, Steve?"

"London. He left with his man Giorgio and a younger guy."

"Yeah."

"Oh? So you already knew?"

"No. I knew Manny was leaving, but I didn't know with whom or to where. Thanks for the info. By the way, if the new Boston guy, Tony Cataldo, contacts you about anything I'd appreciate you letting me know."

"Of course, but if I can help it I don't want to do business with him."

"Rumor has it he's not a killer. He's more of the managerial type."

"I don't go by rumor. I'm just glad I got out of the relationship with Manny as soon and as easily as I did."

"I'm glad you did too, Steve. Keep in touch."

"I will, Samantha. Bye."

Samantha remained at her desk, contemplating. *Manny pulled up stakes because he had to. He was heading to London but she didn't believe he would stay there. If she knew where Manny was, Serino would surely know, and Manny wouldn't live like that. Manny and his entourage would surely disappear in a few days, for parts unknown. And then Manny would be back – for her and probably Serino. But he would need help, lots of help. But from who?*

FIFTY FOUR

A ri wasn't looking for headaches, but he did not intend to be controlled by a bunch of unsophisticated New York Italians. He had already been approached by Mario Serino and was flatly told by him that any further drug business in the States was to be handled through New York, not through Boston and not through Manny Antonelli. Ari played along, not seeing the immediate need to face off against Serino — until he learned more about what was going on between New York and Boston. He had a degree of affection for the suave, young and handsome Antonelli, and little liking for the New York crew of usurpers. But he respected their power.

Ari was aware that Mario surrounded himself with family members whose loyalty was to family. But he also knew that there were always a few who were jealous or unhappy for whatever reason, and possibly open to becoming informants if the stakes were high enough. He had his people working on it, and so far had one possibility in a nephew of Serino's who was far into debt because of his insatiable appetite for gambling. He studied the name on the paper in front of him – Tito Cusolito – and the man's history: Father, dead in a bar room knife fight in 2004. Mother, died of cancer two years prior to the father's passing. No siblings, few friends, chases after whores – a real loser, making a living by the grace of an uncle who isn't overly fond of him.

Sounds like the perfect man. Definitely a weak link. Worth approaching. If he says no, I'll kill him before he reports back to his uncle!

¥

When Lucy announced a Mr. Ari Alexopoulos was calling, Samantha's heart skipped a beat. She took the call.

"Hello, Ari. It's been a while. How's Kara?"

"My beautiful wife is fine, Ms. Robbins…or rather, Samantha. She's a very active woman, with her card playing, shopping sprees, and love for everything different and expensive. And how about you? I assume all is well with you and your husband?"

"Yes. Why the call, Ari?"

"That's what I always admired about you, Samantha. You don't like to waste time."

"That's right, Ari; I don't."

"I think we should meet. We need to have a discussion about a mutual acquaintance, Manny Antonelli. It would be wise …."

"I really don't want to have anything to do with him or his kind, Ari."

"I'm sure you don't, but I know, and you know, he doesn't feel the same way. And now that he's apparently on the outs with New York, a lot of unpleasantness is in the making. Serino called me to dictate new terms. I'm not a fan of Serino and his group and I'm certain you're not either. You could use a strong ally, and I could use guidance from someone with your…remarkable abilities."

"I'll think about it, Ari."

"Of course. I'll call you back in an hour. Goodbye."

In an hour? He was off the line before she could protest. That was Ari's way.

She knew Arthur wouldn't be happy if she met with Ari, but she decided she would have to. Ari was right. She did need the help of someone who was as ruthless as Serino was, and who could keep tabs on both Manny and Serino.

When he called back, she said, "I'll meet with you."

"Good. Come this Friday to West Palm Beach. Bring your husband if you want. We'll make a pleasant weekend of your visit. I told Kara you'd be coming, and she's absolutely thrilled…."

"My husband won't be coming, Ari."

"Whatever you decide. My plane and crew will be waiting for you at Logan Friday morning at 9:00 a.m. Kara and I will meet you when you arrive in Florida. We'll grab lunch someplace on the way to our home. You'll be quite comfortable with us, I assure you."

"I want to return to Boston by noon on Sunday, Ari."

"Whatever you wish. Oh; Terminal E at Logan, Samantha. You tell the people at any desk and they'll get someone to escort you to my plane. Goodbye."

Samantha cradled her phone and sat back in her chair. *More problems,* she thought. *Arthur won't be happy.*

FIFTY FIVE

S amantha deplaned at the West Palm Beach Airport Friday at 12:47
p.m. She was escorted through the terminal by the copilot and
greeted minutes later by Ari and Kara Alexopoulos. Ari had put on weight
around the middle, and added some wrinkles to his still pleasant face. He
displayed the warm smile she remembered. A smile that he could turn on
and off in a second.

Kara was as beautiful as ever. Nearly six feet tall, one hundred and
thirty or so pounds, with curves that every man enjoyed studying, and
with the beautiful complexion of a teenager who had lucked out. She
looked younger than her late thirties. She hugged Samantha like a long-
lost sister. She was thrilled at having Samantha visit for the weekend.

¥

The sleek Cadillac limo deposited Samantha, Kara, and Ari at the front
entrance to The Breakers Hotel in Palm Beach. Samantha excused herself
from Ari and joined a babbling Kara for a visit to the ladies room, and
then the three of them headed toward what Ari announced would be an
informal luncheon in The Beach Club Restaurant.

The view of the surroundings was agreeable as they headed to
the restaurant. There was an outdoor fountain spewing water, and an
oversized swimming pool surrounded by comfortable lounges that were
already well attended.

It was obvious to Samantha the way Ari was catered to inside the
restaurant he was not a stranger to the staff. It was also obvious to her

discerning eyes that there were at least two of Ari's security people – big, ugly and looking out of place with no food or even water glasses at their table – scanning the room and keeping watch over him.

¥

Once seated, Kara ordered a vodka martini with two olives and Ari a Chivas Regal, neat. Samantha asked for a lemonade. She and Kara went along with Ari's suggestion of the Maine Lobster Club.

There was no talk of business over lunch. The conversation was monopolized by Kara, telling all the things she had been doing since she and Samantha had last met; the revamping of her home, the society functions she had become involved with and her vacations and other ventures the past year and a half.

¥

Ari let them talk, taking in the surroundings, the position of his bodyguards, and thinking about what he wanted of Samantha. Their conversation would come later in the afternoon, once he was in the confines of his walled and gated mansion, and the security it afforded. Samantha needed help – and so did he. He had to take on the New York bosses or be run over by them. *Serino has terms? I do also!*

Serino needed him as an ally, not as a foe, but he didn't know for how long and how much Serino would bend. He'd have to gamble to a degree to find out, especially about Mario's new Boston man, Tony Cataldo. Samantha could help with that, if he could pry her a little bit from her obsession with Manny. Looking at her eyes and the tightness of her face, he was unsure he could.

Yes, Serino was going to be a problem for both of them. He'd need convince her of that.

Ari continued to muse silently during lunch. He had had his people checking for weeks for a weakness in Mario's armor, and they had come up with the surly nephew, Tito Cusolito, and now Ari thought of him again. He was sort of a black sheep, according to the report, who tried to fuck away his frustrations through a successive line of whores. *I'll lock him in,* he thought, and the one who could do that for him was a young, pretty hooker named Joan Liston. He had casually befriended her in the past couple of years when in New York on business. She was mid-twenties, tall, slim, beautiful, and with a good head on her shoulders. Joan Liston was an aspiring actress waiting for a break. He had friends off-Broadway who could provide her one. *She would be the perfect enchantress to lure the unhappy, moody Tito into providing him information. I hate using her that way, but he's not a bad looking guy, and she likes men, especially if she can control them. And she likes money even better.* He excused himself, headed for the men's lavatory, and phoned her.

¥

Samantha and Kara were still deep in conversation when Ari returned to the table ten minutes later. He was smiling. Joan hadn't hesitated when he stated what he needed from her. As the arrangement would come with a hefty ten thousand dollar bonus, she was pleased for the opportunity, and had told Ari so. If the guy turned out to be distasteful, she could always opt out.

¥

After their enjoyable two hour lunch, the group reentered the limo and in less than fifteen minutes passed through the manned gates of a magnificent estate. Samantha said nothing as Kara carried the conversation, but noted what real wealth could provide as they traveled two hundred feet to the front door. The home was a mixture of brick and stone, and three stories high. Kara took pride in showing Samantha the spacious hallway entrance, its paintings and sculptures, and was noticeably upset when Ari halted her tour.

"You can show her around later, Kara," he said sternly. "I need to talk with Samantha privately for a bit. You see to having dinner prepared for seven thirty sharp; just the three of us, and then Samantha's yours for the rest of the evening."

Kara glared unhappily for a moment, but then kissed his cheek and walked away.

Ari led Samantha through an ornate hand-carved, angel-covered oak door and into a large room, thirty by thirty-five or forty feet, with two walls of bookcases and two walls of oil paintings. The books didn't interest her, but the paintings did. Wyeth's, Sargent's and…she stopped looking because he directed her to the chair in front of an out-of-place modern glass-topped desk.

"Would you like coffee or tea?" Ari asked.

"Neither, thank you. I'd prefer to hear what you want of me."

He smiled. "That's what I like about you, Samantha. You think and talk like a business man."

"I don't take that as a compliment. I consider myself an astute business *woman*."

"And well you might. Okay, let's get to it. Mario Serino and his partners *say* they want me as a partner now that they ousted Manny. I'm no longer to provide, um, my goods, to Manny but directly to them, working with them and through them, using their people. Once I've tied in, however, I think it's not unlikely that they would in one way or another try to eliminate me. They're looking to consolidate power, not just for New York and Boston but far beyond." He shrugged. "They've finally caught on that today's business world is global. Even the Big Apple is just a small island, and they don't wish to be trapped on it. For now, because of my fleet of ships, planes, and land transport both here in the States and abroad, they would like me as a partner. I suspect a short-term partner. I don't intend to let that happen, and I think you could keep me apprised of impending moves on their part. In return, I would protect you and your husband from them. We could protect each other."

"You make the situation sound quite sinister, Ari."

"That's because it is. They have informants everywhere, muscle every-where, and will destroy anyone who gets in their way. I believe they see us as falling into that category. That's why it makes sense for us to work together."

Samantha intertwined her fingers upon her lap. "Mario also wants to work with me; or so he said."

"So I've heard. Do you think you can trust him?"

Samantha was silent for several seconds, and then said, "No. But I don't think I can trust anybody."

"An honest answer. I feel the same way. But sometimes you have to take a chance, and I am willing to take a chance on you if – and it's a big IF – you'll do the same with me. Think about it. I have more money than I'll ever need. I have a kooky but beautiful wife who I adore. I have everything I want, and don't need anymore. But I don't intend to give what I've worked a lifetime building to a bunch of mobsters who are little more than street thugs in Armani suits. And now it seems these people know about your…gift and suspicions, and rightly so, that it's a threat to them. I see no easy way out for us other than to beat them at their own game. All I am interested in, Samantha, is coming out of this alive, and keeping what is mine."

Samantha said nothing while she studied him. He still looked strong, with broad shoulders and large hands, their fingernails neatly trimmed, but his fingers roughened and scarred by years of hard labor. There were more wrinkles about his eyes, and his hair had thinned, become wispy white. She met his eyes and he did not turn away. His gaze still held an intensity, but he looked tired. She finally spoke. "I believe you, Ari. Okay! We'll put our heads and resources together and see where it leads us."

Ari's face broke into a wide smile. "Exactly what I hoped you would say. Thank you, Samantha. Once more you've come to the rescue."

"We'll see. Frankly, you're the lesser of two evils. I hope we both survive."

"We will. I feel it in my bones."

"But *I* have yet to *see* it, Ari. That's what I'm hoping for."

"Enough talk for now, Samantha. Kara will show you to your room and you can relax for a couple of hours. If there is anything you want, food or drink or whatever, merely pick up the phone and punch seven. Feel free to wander around the house or the grounds; that is of course if you can manage to slip away from Kara. She's tireless, but don't let her smother you. If you're tired, tell her so, and get some rest. I'll see you for dinner at seven-thirty. Tomorrow we'll discuss strategy. That arrangement sound suitable to you?"

"Sounds fine."

"Good. Come, we'll find Kara."

FIFTY SIX

During dinner Ari allowed Kara to monopolize the conversation, excusing himself several times to receive or place phone calls, and left them at ten p.m. to "catch some needed sleep."

Sunday morning Ari and Samantha met at nine o'clock in Ari's office. The meeting was brief and meant to cement their partnership against Mario Serino and his group, with the details of how they would proceed to battle Serino to be decided over the next week. Samantha had had two epiphanies during the night, which she didn't mention; and Ari withheld his plan for using Joan Liston on Mario's nephew Tito for a future time.

Ari's driver had Samantha at the airport an hour later than she wanted, but she would be back in Boston by mid-afternoon, and Arthur shouldn't be too upset.

She would tell him everything.

¥

Driving home from Logan airport, she pondered her latest two visions. The first was the figure of Manny Antonelli firing many rounds into the body of an already dead Mario Serino. The second vision was more obscure. It was a female figure firing a weapon from behind drapery into the back of a standing, indiscernible male figure. The figure could have been ... well, anyone, but in her mind she guessed Serino or Antonelli, or...?

She didn't know, but she had shuddered at the thought. It also could have been her husband Arthur!

She thought back through the years how her visions had affected her. Wonderment, fear, surprise, and credibility were just a few of the thoughts that flashed through her mind when these epiphanies first occurred, and it had taken a great deal of time for her to believe in herself. She had this ability, and the events she saw would come about – always.

She no longer doubted herself. She was only concerned that she interpret these events correctly, and did the right thing.

¥

I'll never allow anyone to harm Arthur, or anyone I believe in and love. Somehow I've got to put a stop to threats from Serino and Antonelli.

She felt herself sweating, though it was a brisk day. The odds were overwhelming, but her epiphanies had swung the advantage in her favor before, and she had managed to come out on top. She was determined to do so again.

¥

Arthur was watching television when she opened the front door, but he was out of his lounge chair as soon as he heard the door open and close. He gave her a welcome home kiss and hug, hung up her fleece-lined leather coat, and walked behind her as she led the way into the den.

"You want a glass of wine, or a beer?" he asked.

"No, not right now, honey. I just want to come to room temperature. Florida was hot, but Boston is cold."

He smiled at the remark. She usually complained of being cold, even when it was warm. "How was your trip?"

"Worthwhile. Ari wants to team up in what he considers to be a coming battle with the New York mob."

"Oh, Jesus! I was afraid of something like that. That puts us in a no win situation, Samantha. If the FBI can't corral those hoods, how in hell does he expect to?"

"He's no dummy, Arthur. He knows he can't do it alone, but he feels the two of us can hold our own against them."

"Oh sure. He hides out in a hidden fortress somewhere, surrounded by his group of thugs twenty-four-seven, while you're out in the open and vulnerable. He's putting you in the line of fire while offering you nothing in return."

"On the contrary, Arthur. He would be helping me to bring down a murderer like Manny Antonelli, and perhaps diminish the arm of the New Yorkers into Boston vice. And if we can wipe out people like Joe Weiss and replace them with clean cops, we lessen mob influence from outsiders, and…."

"And someone else moves in and takes over. They're like weeds, Samantha. Pull one and another grows in its place."

"I understand that, Arthur. But perhaps the newcomers will be less militant and more business oriented. I'd like to prevent the dozen murders or more per year sanctioned by whoever runs Boston's low life thugs…."

"That's wishful thinking rather than reality. There have always been mobs, and bosses, and killings, and thugs, and they aren't going away."

"I hold out for a better world, Arthur. I agree we can't stop all the world's evil, but we can diminish it."

A warm smile crept on his face. "Sam…Samantha, I love you, and you are one in a million. Just because I don't believe in the impossible doesn't mean I won't back you one hundred percent. But don't try to do everything yourself. You push Ari Alexopoulos, you use Steve Grant, you get advice and help from Billie Tsapatsaris, and you keep Ken Katte very much in the picture. To stand any chance, you need to utilize every asset you've got."

"Including you, Arthur."

"Yes, including me and every cop friend I have."

"Thank you."

"Don't thank me. You promise me that you'll take no undue chances on your own."

"I promise. I really believe we can make a difference."

"Where do we start?"

"Ari is searching out Antonelli and putting a surveillance team on him. We'll know every move he makes, who he contacts, and maybe learn what his plans are. Ari I'm sure will soon have someone reliable inside Serino's group reporting on the mob's moves, and that will be a big plus. I've already had a couple of epiphanies about Serino and Manny."

"What kind of visions, Samantha?"

"Do you mind if we don't discuss them today? I'm still sorting them out. It's been a long day, and I have a slight headache. We'll go into details tomorrow, okay?"

Samantha had had headaches before that followed her visions. They concerned Arthur, but she said she's always had them, and it was the price she had to pay. She still considered her ESP ability as a problem she would rather live without, but she knew she had made positive contributions in halting misdeeds by a number of people. She really didn't want to be special. She wanted to be normal, like everyone else. Have a job, a husband...kids. She was afraid to have kids. Who knows what she might pass on to any future generations.

They spent the rest of the evening quietly, with no discussion of Manny, Serino, or Ari.

PART THREE

FIFTY SEVEN

J oan Liston moved into the Morton Square apartment complex a week after Ari called her. She was located in the NYC West Village area, below Chelsea and above SoHo, on the lower west side of Manhattan. The apartment was procured for Ari by a dummy company beholden to Ari but with no direct ties to him. He was careful to keep Joan's cover from someone as unscrupulous as Mario Serino.

This was a dangerous game he was playing. It really wasn't a question of muscle-power – both Ari and Mario could provide that – but more a matter of brain-power. And determination! And pride! Ari believed he could win. And he believed Samantha Robbins could be his ace-in-the-hole. In the meantime, Joan Liston would be in position to do her part if and when he called her into action.

Fifty Eight

It was Monday morning, a week after Samantha's visit with Ari. It was a brisk and clear day, and Samantha made it to her office shortly after nine a.m., after having experienced a restless, troubled night. When she had much on her mind she tended to get agitated, which more often than not resulted in an enlightening vision. What she had experienced the prior evening was not her usual vision, but a dream, a detailed and explicit dream in which she saw and talked to Pauline.

¥

I'm okay, Samantha. I'm in a farmhouse somewhere, being kept by two women and two men. There are no phones, no newspapers, no deliveries made here. Only books and magazines to while away the time. There are no nearby neighbors to my knowledge. The men bring in the food and necessary supplies, but when they leave I'm shackled and locked in my room. It's never longer than an hour or two. When they come back they release me and otherwise treat me fine. They don't blindfold me anymore, and that's a relief. But there is no way I can escape. I wouldn't know which way to go, and I'm too tired to make the attempt. They keep telling me if I behave they'll let me go, but won't give me a timetable. I'm okay, Samantha, but I'm lonely and tired. I know you'll help me when you can. There's a big old wooden barn near the house, with a huge rooster weathervane on the roof. Please find me....

¥

The thought that Pauline was alive and well brought Samantha relief. But Pauline's location was the problem.

A big old wooden barn with a weathervane. That picture became riveted in her mind, and she felt a moment's despair. *There must be hundreds of those found in New England.* Closing her eyes, Samantha pictured the vane again. This one appeared new, made of untarnished copper with a red painted comb and black tail feathers.

She set Lucy the task of locating all the New England companies that manufactured and sold weathervanes. She planned to have Steve Grant take Lucy's compiled list and make shop visits–find who purchased this particular style weathervane in the last year or two.

Another thought entered Samantha's mind. The people holding Pauline were apparently not covering or disguising their faces. That suggested they did not care if Pauline could recognize them. *Could it mean they expected to kill her?*

¥

"Steve, its Samantha."

"Hi. How are things going?"

"Too slowly. I have a job for you, and it's important. It's about my missing secretary, Pauline…."

She explained she had cause to believe Manny had Pauline kidnapped but not murdered. "She's being held in an out-of-the-way New England style farm house not that far away."

It took Samantha no more than ten minutes to paint the picture for Grant, and describe the new weathervane on the roof of the farmhouse barn.

¥

Steve was anxious and willing to perform the search. "Tell your secretary to call me as soon as she has the list. I'll check out who made purchases and do fly overs by helicopter. I've a friend in Beverly, with a copter for lease."

"Sounds good. Thanks."

FIFTY NINE

S amantha was able to help narrow the search. With a searing
headache that yanked her upright in bed at three a.m., she gleaned
the information within a flash of light that held her spellbound, as a
map of New England appeared in her head, blacking out everything but
New Hampshire. Rooster weather vanes popped on and off in different
sections of the State, but no names and no voices.

Samantha opened her eyes, her skin coated with sweat, her breathing
rushed and heavy. She got up and went to the bathroom to cool herself
down to a normal body temperature and regular heartbeat. Her epiphanies usually were not this strong, and she rested her hands on the edge
of the sink until she stopped shaking. It took fifteen minutes before she
felt calm enough to return to bed. She slipped in quietly to keep from
wakening Arthur. She decided not to tell him what occurred, because
he would again insist she quit the investigative business and the stresses
that made her visions worse. But she would not think about retiring as
long as Pauline was missing, and as long as Manny Antonelli and Mario
Serino were still treating the Boston territory as their own feeding trough
and shooting gallery. She couldn't and wouldn't consider throwing in the
towel until she had put them out of business. It was her fate, her destiny,
her right, to shred the evil that men like them caused.

. ¥

Lucy's computer was humming the next couple of days, coming up with
a number of manufacturers and distributors of weathervanes. Samantha

checked the list and her inner eye kept drifting to the list of names in nearby New Hampshire. That was where she would start.

¥

Steve Grant walked out of Samantha's office at three-thirty p.m. that afternoon with vague instructions. *Get your friend with the helicopter to fly over the countryside of eastern New Hampshire, looking for farms with barns, and see if you find any with a shiny new rooster weathervane. I know you will, but there will be more than one there.*

Steve didn't doubt her, but it sounded like he would be searching for the proverbial needle in a haystack. It took three days to prove he was wrong. On the third day, in Conway, New Hampshire he found a barn so equipped.

They landed in an empty field near the farm house. The noise brought out the owner, his wife, and two pre-teen children, who rode to the copters landing point in a Toyota van.

"You guys okay?" the man uttered, not knowing what else to say.

"Yeah," Steve answered. "Have a little engine trouble, and thought it best to put down and check it out. Sorry to disturb you folk. Dan here, my pilot, will need only an hour or so to find and correct the problem." He held out his hand. "Steve Grant," he said, introducing himself.

The farmer didn't hesitate but shook it. "Stan Greene," he said, "and my wife Elaine." Then he shouted at one of the boys who had sidled closer to the helicopter, "Step away, Michael. Let the man do his work."

"That's okay, Stan," Steve said. "He won't bother us none." To the boy he said, "Hi, kid, ever been this close to a helicopter before?"

Michael nodded no, and was obviously excited.

"When Dan finishes with his repairs, you can sit in the helicopter if you like," Steve added.

"Yes, sir," Michael said, returning Steve's smile. The younger boy was silent but nodded excitedly, his eyes wide and round as hens' eggs.

"Meanwhile," Steve continued, "I wonder if I could beg the favor of a cup of coffee. I was a little nervous when Dan reported a problem. He said it was nothing to worry about, but I'm not a mechanic and pilot like he is."

"Sure. C'mon back to the house and we'll fix you one," Elaine said, "and I just pulled some blueberry scones from the oven, if you like them."

"Sure do."

Steve slipped Dan a quick wink. "I'll bring you a cup back in a bit, Dan. Call me on my cell if you need anything."

Dan nodded his head and lifted the back panel over the engine, feigning interest in the unneeded repairs.

Steve entered the van with Stan, Elaine and the boys and headed to the farm house. When they arrived, he pretended to note the weathervane on the barn for the first time.

"Hey, that's a pretty vane you got up there. Where did you find that?"

"Gift from a cousin of mine," Stan said. "We bought this place eleven years ago. We ain't native, just wanted to get away from the rat-race in Massachusetts. Always wanted to farm. Rebuilt the barn a couple years back and Trevor, that's my cousin, got us that cock on the roof."

The boys snickered.

"Weather vanes fascinate me," Steve said. "Any way I could get a closer look at yours?"

"Sure," Stan said. "In the barn there's a ladder to the loft, and a skylight on the roof near the vane. If you don't mind climbing, you can get a real good view."

"Great," Steve said.

"I'll go in and put the coffee on, honey," Elaine said. "Come into the kitchen when you're done."

The boys, distracted by a cartoon of turtles fighting with nunchucks on the television, elected to stay with their mother, and Stan and Steve made their way into the barn alone.

Minutes later, Steve had his head out the sky light, and voiced his admiration for the vane. "It's a beauty, Stan."

"Yeah, it is. Thank you."

Steve had done much more than admire the vane. He had scanned every portion of the barn and saw no hidden rooms or storage area where Pauline could be held. After sipping coffee and complimenting Elaine on her scones, he'd ask for a tour of the farmhouse, and then looked around outside for any type of shed or hiding place. He had the feeling these people were for real, and not hiding anyone, but he was nothing but thorough.

Steve checked in with Dan, for appearances, every half hour. The third call brought the info of a loose wire being the cause of the problem, and all was shipshape again.

Steve was satisfied with his search. Pauline wasn't there. Stan remarked there were a few rooster weather vanes about in the valleys but didn't remember where. Elaine recalled she saw one on the way up to the Mount Washington Hotel, off Route 302, north, in the Bretton Woods area.

The family drove Steve back to Dan, where he kept his promise and allowed the kids to sit in the copter while he explained the instruments to them. He offered the family a ride in return for their graciousness, but both Stan and Elaine were quick to opt out. There was no way they or the kids would fly in a contraption that had just experienced engine trouble.

Minutes later the copter was in the air, following Route 302 north towards Bretton Woods. They were flying at a low altitude, allowing Steve to note every farm in the area. They found one less than a half hour later, with a barn and with a rooster weather vane – and it was shiny new with a red comb and black painted tail feathers.

SIXTY

D an circled the area twice – wide circles, so as not to arouse any interest below. There were two late-model vehicles – one van and one sedan – bearing Massachusetts license plates that Steve espied through high-powered binoculars and wrote down their numbers. They didn't see anyone working the fields.

The farm was about a quarter mile off the main highway, and was the only homestead on the unpaved road that led to it. There was a narrow stream that cut across the farm, and little else that made the area appealing other than a large number of surrounding birch and pine trees. It certainly didn't appear to be an active farm, but one that had long ago served its purpose and had since settled into obscurity as a simple country residence.

There were no farm animals visible. Several large stacks of chopped firewood bordered the main house, and gray curling smoke rose from the chimney which, along with the parked vehicles, were the only indications that the farm was inhabited.

"Let's go back to North Conway, Dan," Steve said, "or better, to the farm where we landed before. I'm pretty sure Stan will be willing to drive us to a car rental place. I'll make up a story that you've called Boston for a part and someone will drive up and bring it to us in a day or so. We'll check into a hotel and stay a day or two. My boss may want to come and join us, and I think it's important that she does."

"Fine with me," Dan said. "A couple of days' paid vacation, including meals? That'll be lovely." He smiled as he pulled back on the cyclic and the copter rose and arced southeast. "I love the countryside 'bout here. People are laid back, friendly." He turned his head a moment to stare back at the retreating farmhouse. "Mostly friendly."

"Good. Let me do all the talking when we get back to Stan's farm. The less they and everybody else knows the better."

SIXTY ONE

"Samantha? It's Steve. I'm calling from the Comfort Inn & Suites in North Conway. I've got a strong feeling I've found your farmhouse."

He told Samantha about their find and gave her the license plate numbers of the vehicles. "It may be worth your taking a ride up here, Samantha. You could most likely get a read on things better than anyone else."

"I'll get back to you in an hour or two, Steve. I'll run down the license plates first. Thanks."

She called Arthur, gave him the plate numbers and received his promise to quickly check them out. He was back to her fifty minutes later. "The van is registered to a gymnasium company in Cambridge, Samantha; and the company is owned by Antonelli! Now give. What's the story?"

She told him, and Arthur exacted her promise that he would be the one who drove her to North Conway the next day.

It was eight that evening when Samantha reached Steve Grant on his cell phone. "Hold tight until Arthur and I get there, Steve. We'll be there before noon tomorrow. Arthur is coordinating with the New Hampshire state police and the FBI. If Pauline's there, kidnapped and taken across State lines, it'll be an FBI case, and that will be fine with me. We've got friends there. Stay away from the farm house until we show up. And Steve, thanks; you've done a great job."

¥

The team of local and State authorities, with the proper warrants, swarmed the farm the following afternoon. They found Pauline in a locked bedroom whose windows had been heavily boarded from the outside. The two men holding her were armed, but they took the men by surprise while they were playing cards at the kitchen table. One man griped he'd had "Gin" as they cuffed him.

Pauline had lost substantial weight, and her face was drawn and fearful when the authorities broke into the room where she'd been held. At the sight of Samantha and Arthur, she broke into tears and rushed into Samantha's arms. "I knew you'd come for me Samantha. I prayed every day and every night...."

"It's over, Pauline. Did they hurt you?"

"No. Nobody really hurt me. They chained me when they went to get supplies. They never told me why they were holding me. They said if I behaved, no harm would come to me, but I didn't believe them. They kept me here so long I almost gave up hope several times. But I knew you would find me...."

Samantha didn't tell her that at first she'd thought she'd been killed. She figured Pauline had enough on her mind rather than deal with that. She wanted Pauline to believe she would always be safe and under her protection. It was the least she could do for her. Now it was time to get her home and back to her normal life. She hoped the people who kidnapped her would finger Manny, and that information would be enough to put Manny behind bars for a long time.

SIXTY TWO

Manny had remained conspicuously in sight in London. He wished to make it easy for Mario's surveillance team to keep tabs on him. He didn't realize a second team—Ari's—was doing so as well.

¥

Giorgio and Leon accompanied Manny when he looked at several properties for sale, both commercial and residential. Manny wished to give the appearance that he was looking to settle in, but he had no intention of doing so. Surreptitiously, he had made plans for leaving London for Madrid, and made sure he was seen doing so.

At night, Manny sent Giorgio, sometimes alone but more often with Leon as company, to visit different pubs with instructions to drink and talk a lot, while searching for the right person to forge credentials for the three of them. They needed fake documents with new names in order to disappear from London and wind up not in Madrid but in Canada. Once in Canada it would be easy to cross the border into the USA.

Uppermost in Manny's mind was settling matters. The longer he remained idle, the more he steamed inside, his anger building to mountainous proportions toward those who had forced him to leave. Number one on his list was Mario Serino, the gentlemanly, smooth-talking, ungrateful bastard who had thrown him out of what was rightfully his. Number two on his list was Maria Ashley, who in all the time they were together had duped him and betrayed him. And then there was

Samantha Robbins, who held information that could possibly jail him, and that wasn't going to happen.

¥

Manny knew Captain Joe Weiss would play both ends. He wouldn't give up on Manny as Serino had expected because Weiss had always been greedy. He knew Manny would reward him for whatever useful information he could supply, and he reached Manny through one of his connections in MI5, the British secret service agency. They knew of Manny's presence in London—which didn't put Manny especially at ease. But he didn't expect to stay in London long.

He knew Weiss could still be a valuable asset. Through Weiss he had learned the FBI had found Samantha's secretary and were interrogating the kidnappers. Manny regretted he hadn't had Pauline killed, just to emphasize his control over matters and as a warning to Samantha. Other than that, he wasn't concerned. The kidnappers were given a job and paid by an unknown individual who paid up front, and the trail would end there. Samantha would know that he could get to anybody she cared for, including her husband. She'd think twice about confronting him in the future. Weiss could also keep Manny on top of Tony Cataldo's moves in Boston.

Manny decided he'd keep in touch with Weiss, but not let him know he was back in the States when he got there. He smiled at the thought of how surprised Weiss would be. And Maria! And Serino! Although the last two wouldn't know until just before he killed them!

Eventually he would have to confront Serino's partners, and he wasn't sure how they would react. Perhaps he could deal with them through Ari Alexopoulos, whose vast holdings would appeal to them as they did to Serino. Perhaps he could strike a deal whereby he reclaimed his Boston territory.

Realistically he knew that could only happen if Mario were dead.

SIXTY THREE

It took five weeks and thirty thousand dollars to get three high quality fake passports and a viable credit card under the name Joseph Weiss. Manny didn't care about the money, and agreed with Giorgio that the passports would pass muster. They tested one a week later when they watched Leon make his way through Heathrow Airport and board a British Airways flight to Toronto, Canada. They contacted him the following day at a Holiday Inn, where he had booked a moderately priced room for his two week stay.

"Any problem on the trip, Leon?" Manny asked.

"None at all. Everything went smooth in boarding and with customs in Canada. Like you said, look them in the eye, show no signs of nervousness in your speech or mannerisms, and it will be a breeze. And it was."

"How about the hotel? Any problem?"

"No. Credit card went through without question. I took a regular room as you suggested."

"Good. We'll be over in three or four days. Keep yourself inconspicuous. Leave the hotel every morning by nine, carry your briefcase and look the part of a young businessman, and don't return to the hotel before four or five in the afternoon. Watch how much you drink, and don't get involved with any hookers. Keep a low profile, understood?"

"Yes. I understand."

"Okay. Book two more rooms for Saturday under our new names. We'll call from the airport when we get in, cab to the hotel, and have a quiet dinner there. Make an eight p.m. reservation."

"Got it."

"Good. Goodbye."

SIXTY FOUR

Manny and Giorgio encountered no problem at Heathrow upon boarding, or at the airport in Toronto upon arriving.

Leon was waiting for them, as planned. They checked into the Holiday Inn at six thirty-five, had time to refresh themselves, and were ready for a hardy meal.

Manny, Giorgio, and Leon sat at a table in the rear of the hotel restaurant. Manny's beard, and Giorgio's and Leon's hair pieces and mustaches were enough of a disguise in their minds that they wouldn't be recognized.

Being a Saturday evening, the restaurant was well attended, and noisy. Manny ordered scotches, neat, for the three of them.

Giorgio, a half hour and two drinks later, brought up the subject of disguises.

"Do you think, boss, before we return to the States we need better disguises?"

Leon, feeling good after the last drink, said laughingly, "how are you supposed to disguise your ugly face?"

Manny couldn't suppress his smile, especially after Giorgio shot Leon a look that would stop a charging lion in its tracks.

"Don't be a smart ass, Leon," Giorgio said gruffly. "I can still kick the shit out of a punk like you."

"Settle down, both of you," Manny said, his smile gone. "Stop shaving and cutting your hair. We're going to hang around in Canada for at least a month, and you no longer will have to look like your passport pictures. We'll skip into the States illegally. I'll make those arrangements. But we're not going back to Boston right away. I'll need to know what Serino is up to once he loses track of us. You can bet your asses he'll be looking. And then we're going to take him and his bitch of a spy out!"

Manny's tone indicated he didn't want any further questions, and Giorgio and Leon obliged.

"Whatever you say, Manny; we're with you," Giorgio said in barely a whisper.

Leon nodded. He was learning when to keep his mouth shut.

"Good! Then relax and enjoy the rest of the evening. Tomorrow we'll meet here for breakfast and I'll tell you how we'll entertain ourselves while in Toronto. Make no phone calls to anyone, here or State side. Understand?"

Both men nodded they did.

SIXTY FIVE

"What do you mean 'they disappeared'? People just don't disappear," Mario shouted into his phone.

"I checked their rooms thoroughly, Mr. Serino. There's nothing in any of them to suggest where they've gone. They never paid their hotel bill, they never indicated to anyone that they were leaving, and...."

"Enough! You've got one day to find them or someone will be looking for *you!* Call me tomorrow." He slammed the phone down on its receiver.

Mario blamed himself for not covering Manny more thoroughly. *Maria had said Manny planned to go to Madrid. "I'll alert my people in Madrid. Somebody better find him soon."*

His people hired British private investigators and swept London, and Spanish private investigators and swept Madrid, pubs to palaces and all the transportation centers, showing pictures of Manny, Giorgio and Leon to low characters and high-brows but came up with nothing.

Round number one to Manny. That son-of-a-bitch, Mario thought. *If he has the gall to return to the States I'll be waiting for him!*

¥

Manny's escape had been perfect. A week passed and no one in Madrid or London could come up with his location. Mario was not happy. He placed a call to Samantha Robbins, and waited impatiently until she got on the line.

"Hello, Mr. Serino. "What can I...?"

"Stop with the amenities," he barked. "I don't have the time. Where's Manny?"

"The last I heard he was in London. What's the problem?"

"The problem is he's *not* in London; or in Madrid; or anywhere else I know about. So you tell me where he is!"

Samantha paused before answering. "I have no idea where he is. I haven't heard from him. He's not in the habit of keeping me informed of his movements; and the less I have to deal with him the better I like it."

"Bull shit. You have the ability to know where he is, and I want to know right now...."

"Mr. Serino. I don't like your tone of voice. I just told you I haven't heard from him or about him, and I'd prefer to keep it that way."

There was an uncomfortable silence. She could hear him breathing heavily over the phone. But when he spoke again he was under control. "Okay, Samantha. I'll take your word for it. Just keep in mind that he will be after you as well, and you are a lot easier to get to than I am.

"If - No – when you locate him, call me. I can save your life...and your husband's. Goodbye."

When Samantha hung up, she closed her eyes, pushed back in her swivel, and prayed for an answer. When it didn't come in the next ten minutes, she opened her eyes, looked at the ceiling, and muttered a curse word.

She called Arthur, reaching him in his office.

"Hi, honey. What's up?"

"I just got a call from Mario Serino. He and his people have lost sight of Manny in London and he was quite upset. He wanted to know if I knew where he was."

"Do you?"

"No. I have no idea."

"What Serino can't control he worries about. I don't blame him. If Manny disappeared, he may be coming back. I'm not happy about that."

"Neither is Serino. He says he'll protect us if I get him Manny's whereabouts."

"I wouldn't bank on it. I'll call Ken Katte and see what he knows. Maybe his group has kept tabs on Manny. I'll call you later. Bye."

¥

Arthur reached Katte on his cell minutes later. Katte professed he was unaware of Manny Antonelli's flight and would make some inquiries and get back to him. This whole unexpected turn of events troubled Arthur. He hoped Samantha would get some answers soon, or he was going to insist she go into hiding.

The problem was, he knew she wouldn't.

SIXTY SIX

Manny moved the three of them to a three room rental on the outskirts of Toronto and stayed there three weeks. He arranged with a helicopter pilot to go sightseeing, and took three flights during that time, sizing up the pilot. On the third flight, he made the pilot an offer he couldn't refuse. The pilot accepted. A week later they flew low over the dark waters of Lake Ontario at night and landed in a quiet area just outside Wilson, New York, about 25 miles north of Buffalo. He paid the pilot with cash, and with a finger tap to his cap, the pilot flew away.

Manny gave Giorgio the credit card made out in the name of Joseph Weiss, and they checked into a motel on the outskirts of Wilson. The next morning the three of them rented a Chevrolet Impala from Budget rent-a car, using Weiss's credit card again, and with a drop-off agreement for Boston's Logan Airport.

¥

It was a bright, cool Thursday morning when Joe Weiss got the call.

"Good morning, Captain Weiss. I hope you are feeling well."

"I'm feeling fine. Is this who I think it is?"

"It is."

"Where are you?"

"You don't need to know. Can you talk on the phone you're using?"

"That's not a good idea. Can I call you back in fifteen minutes?"

"No. I'll call you back in fifteen minutes. Do you have a clean cell?"

"Yes. It's a new number. Only my wife has it."

"Give it to me."

Weiss did.

"I'll call you within twenty minutes. Be somewhere where you can talk."

"Definitely. Bye."

Weiss was out of his downtown Boston office ten minutes later. He walked rapidly to a nearby Deli. It was too early for lunch, and the Deli was pretty much deserted, except for three tables of senior men and women, regulars who passed their time gabbing on a daily basis. Weiss took a table as far away from them as he could. His call came minutes after he ordered a black coffee and jelly doughnut.

"Hello."

"Are you situated okay?" Manny asked.

"Yeah; fine. I assume you're back?"

"Assume nothing, Joe. Tell me what's going on with Tony Cataldo."

"Not much. He called me over a week ago, telling me they had lost sight of you, and he wanted to know if I'd had heard anything. I told him 'no'."

"Keep telling him 'no'. Can I trust you to do that? You can't play both of us on this, Joe. Whatever money he promised you, I'll pay more."

"I know you will, Manny. I don't know these people, but you and I have history, and I trust you to make good. But I have to be careful. I have to convince them I'm working for them."

"So convince them. I'll call you at this number as long as you tell me it's safe. I'll give you more information as to what I'll need and want the next time I call. Goodbye Joe."

Joe hung up, finished his coffee, and then walked back to his office. He was sweating, and it wasn't from the weather.

SIXTY SEVEN

"Ari, I can't find that son-of-a-bitch Antonelli. Your people have any luck?"

"No, Mario; they are still looking. They are concentrating on every means of transportation leaving London: plane, train, bus, and automobile. If we can't find how they left I'm afraid we're not going to find out where they went."

"I've checked the London bank. He hasn't touched any of the money I deposited for him."

"Probably because he has big money tucked away under an assumed name and can draw from that. He's a smart bastard, Mario. We underestimated him. I don't think he's gone off somewhere to hide. I think he's coming back – to Boston or New York. He's a killer, and a nutcase, afraid of nothing or any one. Personally, I'm leaving for parts unknown this week, taking a couple of months' vacation. You might want to do the same, and let your people chase him down."

"That's not the way I do things," Mario snarled. "I'll find the bastard."

"Good luck, Mario. I'll check in with you in a week or so. Bye."

Ari hung up with a smile on his face. He was going on vacation not to run away from Manny but from Serino. He didn't trust Serino, and if Manny somehow could get to him, all the better. He could deal with Manny. Manny still considered him an ally. With Serino there was no way to make a deal. He wanted it all. So Ari was removing himself from where he thought the area of conflict would be, and rooting for Manny.

As Ari expected, Serino didn't trust him, but was trying to use him. In this business of mob domination, no one trusted anyone. That's how they stayed alive. Presently Mario didn't consider Ari to be his major problem; Manny was.

SIXTY EIGHT

"They'll be looking for three people, Giorgio," Manny said, as Leon drove the Avis rental Ford from Logan Airport into the Ted Williams Tunnel, "so I think it best that we split up. Drop me off at South Station, then you and Leon head out on Route 1 north and stay in a motel where you've never stayed before. Keep a low profile. I'm giving you five grand in cash and the Joe Weiss credit card. Use the card for the motel; most people don't pay with cash in motels, and you don't want to arouse any interest, but pay cash for everything else. That card should be safe for a while. I'll tell Joe to make sure his wife doesn't see the bill and ask any questions. You understand what I'm saying?"

"Okay, Manny. You'll keep in touch with us?"

"Every day, Giorgio. Our cell phones are still safe, but we'll change them soon."

"Where are you going to be, Mr. Antonelli?" Leon said, quickly drawing a look of disgust from Giorgio and Manny. "I mean, when can we hook up and learn what we're supposed to do?"

"Soon, Leon. You just rest up. I'll put things together."

"We're going to need weapons," Leon persisted, "and we're going to...."

"Leon, shut up," Giorgio snapped. "I'm sorry, Manny."

Manny smiled. "It takes time, Giorgio, but work on him. I'll call you tomorrow. Remember, keep a low profile, and don't shave. Phone no one! Keep the same look."

Manny exited at South Station, and after Leon drove off and was out of sight, hailed a cab. He checked in to a Comfort Inn barely a mile away from his sister Angela's home in Cambridge. He would check to see if she was being watched and then decide how best to meet with her - and see his son, Gino.

Manny had taken care of his sister financially for years. Her husband, Jack Gold, earned a good living, but who couldn't use more cash. Angela was raising his kid for him – and she could be trusted.

He called her that night, using a code name they had used for years. "Angela, its cousin Alfie. How are you?"

"Alfie! Good hearing from you. It has been a long time. Are you in town?"

"Just got in. I'll be staying a few days. Will you and Jack and the kids be able to meet me for lunch on Saturday?"

Angela knew exactly what to reply. "Jack is taking the older kids to a birthday party in Boston at noon, Alfie. I've got the younger ones and am free. We'd love to meet you."

"Great. How about the usual place at one p.m.? Then I can buy the kids some toys and T-shirts and keep them happy."

"You spoil them, Alfie."

"I know. It's my pleasure."

"Okay. See you one o'clock Saturday."

The "usual" place was McCormick & Schmicks at Faneuil Hall. That area was usually crowded, and patrolled by the Metropolitan Police. In Manny's mind, it was a safe public place to meet.

¥

Manny watched from a distance as Angela, Gino, and Angela's youngest daughter, Sherri – age five – entered the main door of the restaurant. He waited a full five minutes checking the crowd for possible tails before he entered. He saw none. He freed his right hand from the Glock 17 he had been holding in his trench coat pocket, re-armed the safety, and approached the table for four where the threesome had settled.

Angela looked up as he took the vacant chair, staring momentarily before recognizing her brother. "By God, Manny; I would never have known you."

"That's the idea, Angel," he said softly, using the nickname he called her while growing up. "You look terrific."

"Thank you. I wish I could say the same for you. You've lost weight."

"All part of the disguise. Are the kids old enough to understand what's going on?"

"Yes. I explained it to them. They are both smart enough to understand you're in trouble. Especially Gino. He's so much like you he scares me."

Manny studied the young boy's unsmiling face. "Is that right Gino? Are you as tough a guy as I am?"

The boy never smiled. "I guess I am. Did you kill my mother?"

The surprised looks on the faces of Angela, Manny and Sherri said it all. Manny answered quickly, with the lie he lived. "Of course not. It was the mob that killed your mother. Your mother and I had separated because she fell in love with someone else. It happens all the time, but it was the mob that killed her, and that's why I hate the mob. They are now trying to kill me."

The conversation ended as a waiter came to the table. The kids ordered grilled cheese sandwiches, fries, and cokes, Angela a Cobb Salad and coffee, and Manny a cheeseburger and a Coors. Angela and Manny talked as they ate, catching up, while Sherri people-watched and Gino said nothing, but listened attentively to their conversation.

"So why did you come back, Manny? It's dangerous for you here. Someone could spot you."

"I have no intention of living my life on the run, or in fear, Angela. There is no way they intend to allow me the life of a retiree. Serino wanted me out of the country where, in short order, he could make me disappear with little fanfare. It isn't going to happen. I still have a powerful friend who will back me against Serino, and I intend to use him. I don't think there would be much of a backlash from Serino's partners. I believe they would welcome taking over his share of the organization. If I'm wrong, I think I can still avoid confrontation with them. I have the Greek in my corner, and they all want to partner with him."

"It sounds risky, Manny."

"It is. But I really have no choice, Angel."

"I suppose. Is there anything I can do to help?"

"No. I just wanted to see you all again, just in case anything goes wrong. And I want Gino to understand that if I get through this, I'll spend a lot more time with him – with all of you – and we'll have great times together. How does that sound to you, Gino?"

"Yeah, sounds good," Gino said, but his voice lacked enthusiasm.

"That will be great, Manny," Angela said.

Manny showed no disappointment with Gino's answer. He had never been much of a father. He would have to earn the boy's respect and loyalty. IF he got through this, that would be his first priority.

¥

Leaving the restaurant, Manny whispered in Angela's ear. "If things don't work out, I've left you guys a pile of money, and my lawyer will get in touch with you. Either way, Angel, thanks for everything. I love you."

Her eyes filled with moisture. She kissed him on the cheek, and slipped away.

SIXTY NINE

"Manny's back, Arthur," Samantha said excitedly as she quick stepped from their bedroom into the kitchen. "I was making up my face when I got the vision. He was bearded and his eyes glowed like a…a devil's. He's in the Boston area, and probably making plans to do away with his former girlfriend, Marie Ashley, and Serino, and I guess I'm on his list as well."

"Damn!" Arthur said, rising out of his chair to meet her and take her in his arms. You think in that order?"

"I don't know," she said, hugging him back. "But we've got time to thwart his plans, Arthur. Somehow I know that, so don't you be concerned." She attempted to control the slight shudder she felt run through her body, and hoped he hadn't noticed.

If he did, he didn't say anything. "Where's the Ashley woman now, Samantha?"

"She's still in town, helping her cousin Tony settle in. I think she's staying with him. My guess is Manny will go after Serino first."

"Why?"

"He's the most formidable opponent."

"Perhaps. Perhaps not."

Samantha didn't press the point.

"Does Manny have help?" Arthur asked.

"Yes, his main man, Giorgio, and one other. I saw them in the vision with Manny. They're all in the area."

"How do we find them?"

"I'm working on it. Give me a day or two."

SEVENTY

Manny learned from Joe Weiss that Maria was staying in Manny's former downtown penthouse apartment, now owned by Tony Cataldo. He clenched his teeth. Weiss said she was helping Tony line up all of Manny's old personnel, telling them that Tony was now the boss. Weiss said two of Mario Serino's personal guards – big, mean-looking thugs – lived in an apartment below them and accompanied them everywhere.

¥

At four p.m., Manny donned his trench coat, added a spare magazine for his Glock 17 to his left-side coat pocket, next to the weapon's suppressor, and headed for his old digs.

They had changed the alarm code to the apartment, but had not replaced the alarm system that had been made to his personal specifications. He smiled as he entered an override code.

The apartment was empty. He sat in his old bedroom, out of sight from anyone entering the front door and attached the suppressor to his Glock.

It was a few minutes before six p.m. when he heard the front door open – and the voices of Maria Ashley and Tony Cataldo saying goodnight to the two bodyguards assigned to watch over them, as the guards took the stairs to their apartment below. Manny waited until he heard the door close and the rustling as they hung up their coats in the hall closet, and the tap of their feet upon the polished wood floor as they entered the living room. When he stepped out of the master bedroom, weapon in hand, the two stopped, mouths agape.

"No hard feelings, Tony; just business," Manny said and pulled the trigger twice. Tony dropped to the floor, rolled over, and made a gurgling sound as he died.

Maria struggled for words. "Manny – please – we've got to...to talk. Please don't do this. We can work it out. We can...."

"I must admit I don't want to do this. I trusted you, and you used me. What would people say? Manny's gone soft." He shook his head. "That won't do, Maria. See you in hell, darling." He pulled the trigger twice more. Blood spurted from her chest, soaking her beige cashmere sweater.

She made no sound as she slid to the floor, a few feet away from Tony. Manny went to the table in the hall where she had left her Gucci leather bag, put on a thin pair of Italian-made leather gloves that he pulled from his pocket, and went through her pocket book. Her wallet was amply supplied with cash, credit cards, a driver's license and some notes. In the bottom of the bag rested a lady's-sized revolver with a pearl handle.

Probably a gift from Mario, he mused. He put the weapon in his pocket, thinking it was only right that a bullet from it would end Mario's life, and replaced everything else. Minutes later he let himself out, resetting the alarm. He smiled. Let the cops figure this one out.

SEVENTY ONE

Tito made his first phone call to Tony at nine fifteen that evening and was surprised when neither Tony nor Maria answered. He left a message for Tony to call him. When he hadn't heard from Tony by eleven fifteen, he became suspicious. He had dined at The Capital Grille with them earlier that evening, and Tony had remarked he and Maria were heading back to his apartment. He tried Tony's cell and similarly had no success. After four rings it went to the message machine.

Tito called and alerted Maria's and Tony's guards to a possible problem. Fifteen minutes later, they confirmed Tito's fears.

Tito told them to wait until he got there before calling the police. He didn't have Joe Weiss' phone number, but knew Tony kept it coded in a small notebook. He wanted that notebook before the police arrived, and all Tony's and Maria's cell phones and computers.

Tito arrived twenty minutes later, noted the bodies, found Tony's notebook, pocketed it, located three cell phones and Tony's and Maria's laptops, gave them to one of the bodyguards and told him to stash them in his apartment and throw them in the Charles River in the morning. It wasn't going to be a good rest of the evening. As he left, he told the two stunned guards to call the police and report what they found.

When he was back in his car, he called Mario Serino.

"Why are you calling so late?" Serino said angrily. "What's wrong?"

Tito told him.

"Son of a bitch! Do you know who did this?"

"No, but I can guess."

"I can guess too," Serino muttered and slammed down his phone.

¥

Mario rose shortly after five a.m. after a fretful night, slipped out of bed so as to not disturb his wife, put on his robe and headed for the kitchen. With a tall glass of orange juice in hand, he made his way into his den, and closed the door. He sat at his desk, sipping his drink. Then he placed the glass on his desk blotter and, pressing his lips together, punched a four-letter code on the display of his desk monitor which unlocked the bottom right-hand drawer of his desk. Within were several colored cell phones, two Glock 19 revolvers, several full fifteen round 9 mm magazines, and a few personal files, the thicker one labeled MANNY ANTONELLI. Serino had been in this drawer twice the previous day, and into the lengthy Antonelli file. Now he pulled out the file one more time. Today was the day he would notify all his resources to hunt down and kill Manny Antonelli! He wanted Manny Antonelli to disappear forever!

SEVENTY TWO

The hunter and the hunted.

Samantha didn't know who was who, but she did know things were coming to a head. Three times the past night she had been jarred awake by epiphanies. Three times she had been awakened by visions of flashes of gunfire in darkened rooms, and three times she had heard shouts of anger and moans of suffering.

She didn't know who had died or where it had happened. She didn't see faces, but she knew that a man and woman had been murdered.

Her next epiphany gave her more insight. She saw their faces.

She awakened Arthur. They sat in bed in the early morning darkness, she clinging to him as she revealed what she saw. And she shocked him when she said "More people will die, Arthur, and soon. And either Mario or Manny will be dead as well!"

¥

They got up and bathed and dressed. Arthur, being the quicker, had their breakfast on the table when Samantha joined him. She looked tired and strained.

He frowned. She was getting worse. The stress of knowing Antonelli was back and the multiple visions were taking an ever greater toll on her. She had her normal busy life as well as her abnormal second life to contend with, and when both occurred simultaneously....

He shook his head. Now was not the time to discuss it. She wouldn't listen. But he would – again – when things were back to normal. All he could do now was help her, and he intended to, in every way possible.

They remained wordless during breakfast, but as they cleared the table, he spoke. "What can I do, Samantha? I want to help."

"I don't know yet, Arthur. I'm going to isolate myself in my office this morning and hope I get an answer. I'll call you when I do."

She hadn't said "if I do," she had said "when I do," and from past experience he knew it was only a matter of time.

¥

When he arrived at his office, he went to the bottom drawer of a file cabinet, unlocked it with a key attached to the gold chain around his neck, and readied his service revolver and a second, smaller weapon which he fastened to his right leg-just above his ankle.

He had no idea if he would need either weapon, but he would be prepared.

SEVENTY THREE

Mario and four men he selected left for Boston by limo at ten a.m. the same morning. He had told his people to pack bags for a three day stay. The other thing he had told them was this trip was business, and they had all armed themselves appropriately. Having the boss with them on a hit hadn't occurred in years, and his men were wary but excited.

Five hours later, the group entered a large home in Brookline, MA, opposite a large reservoir. The home was cold and unoccupied, but as the group walked around in their coats, hitting multiple thermostats, the heat quickly spread throughout the two story estate. This was one of several safe houses Mario owned, all maintained by elderly couples who vacuumed, dusted, and took care of what else was needed on a regular basis to keep the homes in decent shape.

Mario assigned his henchmen bedrooms on the second floor, and told them to settle in. He then sent two of them to a nearby sub shop to bring back a dozen sandwiches, assorted soft drinks and plenty of potato chips and napkins. "There will be no booze drinking while we're here. I want you all sharp."

Mario left his men, went into the large room he used as an office, and made a phone call.

"World Wide Insurance," the female voice answered. "How may I help you?"

"Is Carmen in?"

"Yes sir. May I tell him who is calling?"

"Yes. His Uncle Fred."

Rita didn't know her boss had an "Uncle Fred," but she didn't know a lot of things.

"Just one moment please; I'll connect you."

Carmen patched in as soon as he heard the name, waited for Rita to disconnect, and spoke excitedly. "Good morning, Uncle. How nice to hear from you. Is...?"

"You just listen," Mario said sternly. "Maria and Tony are dead. That bastard Antonelli got to them. I want you and your brother to leave the office for the Reservoir house. Don't tell anyone where you're going. Make sure you're not followed, and we'll talk when you get here."

"Yes, Uncle. Right away."

¥

Carmen and Luigi barely talked as they made the half-hour drive to the Brookline estate, but each one was concerned with the news. They had been living quiet, happy lives in Boston, and that was about to end. Mario hadn't traveled to Boston for a pleasant visit. They knew trouble had come, and more was sure to follow.

"I don't like the sound of this," Luigi said, breaking the silence. "Mario here? On a revenge hit? Do you think his partners know? They're not going to be happy. They don't like any sort of publicity...."

"Like it or not, they won't intervene," Carmen said. "It's a family matter. Honor and all that. I bet they know about Maria and Tony. They'll keep their distance from this."

"What about us?" Luigi continued. "I like our life in Boston, and so do my wife and kids. Mario is likely to blow it all away by killing Antonelli, and we'll have to relocate and wind up in a shithole."

"Just keep your mouth shut when we get there, and agree with everything he says," Carmen said. "He's brought muscle with him. We're just logistics and support - bystanders."

"You hope," Luigi said.

They pulled up to the driveway entrance, and Carmen gave his name into the box outside the electronic gate. It slowly swung open. He parked in front of the stately brick home and the brothers were admitted as soon as they reached the door. Neither one knew the two men who let them in, and didn't want to. Both were over six feet tall, two hundred fifty plus pounds, and appeared capable of crushing a man's skull with their bare hands.

They were led into the den where Mario sat behind his desk.

He unsmilingly nodded a greeting, and pointed to two chairs.

"I'm sorry to have learned the bad news about Maria and Tony, Mario," Carmen said after he was seated. "How can we be of service?"

Mario barked his answer. "I want you to use every connection you've got to locate Manny Antonelli for me. I want to know where he sleeps, where he eats, and where he hides out during the day. I want a watch on him, and I am personally going to put a hit on him. I'm going to smash his pretty boy face and watch him die!"

No one in the room spoke a word as Mario paused to pick up a glass and sip some water. The silence continued until he spoke again.

"Are there any questions?"

"How do we contact you?" Carmen said, sucking in air after he spoke to control his nerves.

"I'll give you a number. I want a call every hour on the hour to learn of your progress. Don't fail me. I want to know where he is and where he'll be, starting this evening. I want to conclude this business as quickly as possible. I'm relying on you both."

"We won't fail you, Mario," Luigi said boldly.

"Go," Mario indicated with a flick of his hand. "You've got a lot to do in a short time. Here's the phone number you are to call…every hour. You pull this off and you both will be handsomely rewarded. Don't disappoint me."

The brothers couldn't get out of the house fast enough. As they headed back to their office Carmen said, "We pull this off and we'll be made for life."

"But what if we don't?" Luigi said.

Silence stretched for a few seconds between them.

Luigi sighed. "Where do we begin?"

"With Captain Joe Weiss," Carmen said. "Maria said he and Antonelli were constantly in touch. We'll make a date to talk with him this afternoon or tonight. I'll convince him to come. I'll tell him big money is involved."

SEVENTY FOUR

Less than two hours later Carmen was on the phone with Captain Joe Weiss.

"Yes, Mr. Romano, this is Captain Weiss. You told my sergeant you had information concerning the kidnapping of Samantha Robbins' secretary. Just what is the information?"

"I won't discuss it on the phone," Carmen said. "If you'll meet with me privately this evening at a safe place for both of us, I'll give you the information. I don't want to get involved any more than I have to, but I think there's a lot of money to be made when the case is resolved and I want a piece of it."

Carmen had mentioned the key word casually – *money* – and thought that would entice the notorious police captain. He was correct.

"Okay, Mr. Romano, where do you want to meet, and at what time?"

"Someplace public, and outside of Boston proper. How about The Continental Restaurant on Route One in Saugus at eight p.m.?"

"Okay. I haven't been there in a while, and it's a convenient place. Are you coming alone?"

"Yes. And I want you to come alone. Is that a problem?"

"Not at all. How will I recognize you?"

"I'll wear a fedora. Almost nobody wears one anymore."

"Sounds good. I'll see you at eight o'clock tonight. Goodbye."

Carmen knew the captain was a lone wolf, and would come alone. Crooked cops never trusted anyone and believed the fact they toted a police shield was safer than wearing body armor. But Carmen planned to arrive at the restaurant an hour early, with Luigi, and observe Weiss' arrival. If Weiss entered alone, he would enter alone, leaving Luigi in the car as backup. He would order drinks and an appetizer and get out of there as soon as they concluded their business.

¥

Precisely at seven-fifty-five Carmen and Luigi watched an unmarked Ford vehicle pull off Route One and park illegally in front of the bar entrance of the Continental. A tall muscular man got out, lowered his sun visor, displaying, Carmen thought, some sort of police identification card that would allow him to leave his vehicle anywhere he pleased. The man was alone, and headed for the main restaurant entrance.

"Looks like he's alone, Carmen," Luigi observed.

"I told you he would be. He covers his own ass. You keep watch, and call if anything doesn't look right. I'm going in." Carmen donned a felt fedora. "I'll make it as quick as possible. Enjoy your ham sandwich."

"Screw you too." Luigi would have said more but he was nervous. He didn't like having anything to do with the police captain. Having Weiss on one side and his uncle Mario on the other spelled trouble. And then there was Manny to consider.

Carmen entered the bar, walked past it and out to the front of the restaurant.

Weiss eyed the man with the fedora cautiously as he approached, extending his right hand for a firm but brief handshake. "Do you want to get a table or sit at the bar?" Weiss said.

"I think it will be quieter at a table. We'll order drinks and an appetizer or two and make this meeting as brief as possible."

Minutes later they were seated in an oversized leather-cushioned booth. They ordered drinks and fried calamari and an order of steamed clams as appetizers.

As soon as the waitress left, Weiss leaned over the table. "I'm listening, Mr. Romano. Is that your real name?"

"Yes. I'm here to make you an offer that you should be interested in. You're not wired, are you?"

Weiss laughed. "I was about to ask you the same thing. In fact, I want you to casually unbutton the top four buttons of your shirt, lean my way, and briefly spread your shirt apart."

Carmen hesitated a moment, and did as told. Weiss smiled his satisfaction a moment later, and said, "One can never be too careful, Mr. Romano. You're Mario Serino's cousin, aren't you?"

Carmen showed his surprise. "No, I'm one of his many nephews. I see you've done your homework and checked me out."

"Of course. What does Serino want, Mr. Romano?"

"Call me Carmen. He wants to know where he can find Manny Antonelli. He'll pay well for the information, and you'll gain an important friend."

"I have enough friends, Carmen. But I don't have enough money. What kind of money is Serino willing to part with?"

"One hundred thousand in cash, Weiss, in any denomination you want it in."

"Not nearly enough, Carmen. Manny would pay me five times as much just for giving him the information about this meeting."

"Okay. I won't quibble. One million in cash. He wants Antonelli. Manny murdered his niece and nephew. Maria was his favorite, and Tony wasn't far behind."

Weiss pushed back in his cushioned bench. "I think we can reach an agreement. How do I know I'll get the money once you get the information?"

"Half in advance – as early as tomorrow afternoon – the other half when the matter has been settled. Serino's promise is as good as money in the bank."

"I'm sure it is," Weiss answered, but didn't believe it. "You meet me tomorrow at three p.m. on the bridge in the Public Gardens. We'll walk to a nearby bench where you'll give me the money – in one hundred dollar old bills, nothing larger. I want them in a suitcase with wheels, Mr. Romano. You'll open the bag, show me the money, and I'll set up

Antonelli for you either that evening or the next day. I'll tell him I have to see him and he'll tell me where and when. He may not be alone, but that's your problem. That's the best I can do. Is that agreeable?"

"Where does he usually have you meet him, Weiss? Is there more than one place, or is it always the same?"

Weiss smiled and wagged a finger at Carmen. I'll let you know where when he tells me."

"Then we have a deal, Captain Weiss. I'm sure you know without my mentioning it that if you don't keep your end of the bargain there is no place on earth that you and your family will ever be safe again. I say that because my boss wants you to know the seriousness of this arrangement."

"I wouldn't expect otherwise, Mr. Romano. And I'm sure you realize I have enough friends in all walks of life that would reveal information that would trouble Mr. Serino - and you - if anything unwarranted happened to me or my family members. So I think we both understand each other. Do we proceed?"

"Yes. I'll meet you at three p.m. tomorrow, on the bridge."

Carmen stood. "You can cancel the food order, captain. I'm leaving." He put on his coat, and with fedora in hand departed the way he came in.

Weiss beckoned the waitress and told her to make the food order to go. He left the restaurant ten minutes later carrying a large bag. He was angry he was left to pay the tab.

Seventy Five

"How'd it go?" Luigi said after Carmen climbed into the front seat beside him.

"He agreed, but upped the money to a million dollars."

"Mario isn't going to pay that guy a million. How in hell could you agree to that?"

"Mario will agree to anything to get Antonelli. When Antonelli's dead, he'll straighten out Weiss one way or another. That's not our problem."

"You can't just kill a cop, Carmen; especially a big city police captain."

"Cops have accidents, brother, just like anyone else. It wouldn't be difficult."

"I suppose not. Where are we going now?"

"I'll phone Mario and ask. He's got to come up with half the cash before three tomorrow afternoon. Let's see how he wants to handle it."

¥

"He wants half a million in cash by tomorrow afternoon? And you agreed to it?" Mario said. He didn't sound angry.

"I figured you pay him whatever he wanted and then make other arrangements after he gave up Antonelli. I didn't want to scare him off."

"You did the right thing. I'll have somebody drive in from New York overnight with the money. You be here at the house by one p.m.

tomorrow, and bring the suitcase you need. You'll make the delivery only if I can get at Manny tomorrow night or the day after. You understand?"

"Yes, Mario."

"Get a good night's sleep. You're doing good, Carmen, and will be rewarded."

The only reward Carmen wanted was to be left alone. He couldn't say that.

"Thank you, Mario, I'll be there by one."

SEVENTY SIX

L uigi dropped Carmen off at a Charles Street gate entrance at two forty-five p.m. the following day. Carmen rolled his suitcase through a bus load of tourists entering the gate on a beautiful but cool sunny afternoon. He moved slowly, as he was early, and didn't care to stand awkwardly on the bridge for any length of time. He was armed with a Glock under his jacket to protect the money, at Mario's insistence, but he had no intention of fingering the weapon, especially outdoors in a public venue.

¥

Weiss showed up on the bridge five minutes later. He was in civilian clothes and looking anything but a cop. He had been eying Carmen from a distance and sensed that he was alone.

"Let's go back toward Charles Street and find a bench," Weiss said.

Carmen wasn't about to let Weiss make that decision. "No. We'll go the other way. It's quieter over there – a lot less walking traffic."

Weiss didn't object, and Carmen felt better about it. Apparently Weiss wasn't setting him up.

A few minutes later, they selected a bench in the shade in a relatively quiet section of the park.

"Can I examine the suitcase?" Weiss said.

"Of course," Carmen said, lifting the case onto the bench then taking a Boston Globe newspaper from his coat pocket, opening it, and covering the top of the case to shield what was inside from any passersby. Weiss waited for a break in people traffic and quickly checked, by hand and by eye, the contents of the case. Stacks of used hundreds filled the case.

"How much is in there?" Weiss said.

"The agreed upon amount – five-hundred thousand. The rest you'll get wherever you want it delivered after the agreement has been fulfilled."

Weiss wasn't about to quibble. Five hundred thousand dollars in hand was more money than he could earn in four years of police work, and he felt pretty sure the mob would come up with the rest as promised to keep on good terms with him. He had been weighing in his mind whether to get a counter offer from Manny, but decided it was safer to stay on Serino's side. He was far more powerful than Manny. Manny was one person. Serino had an army.

"So how do we find Manny?" Carmen said, bringing Weiss back from his reverie.

"I will set it up for tonight, or tomorrow. I'll call you with the time and place. Manny is cautious, and when I tell him I've got information regarding a meeting between Mario Serino and Ari Alexopoulos, he'll want to know the details. That means he'll want to meet me personally, especially when I tell him I don't have all the information yet. But, as I said, Manny is a cautious guy. He'll tell me where and when to meet him, and he'll have a couple of his goons nearby as protection. You've got to be prepared for that; and I want to be sure I'm not caught up in any cross fire. You understand? You make sure Serino knows I can be valuable to him in the future. I don't want to be included in his takeout plans."

"Serino is aware of your value, Weiss. You're not on his list of adversaries, I promise you."

"I'm taking that chance, because I know I can be an invaluable ally. But he's got to know that."

"Rest assured, he knows that; but I will relay your concern. I'll suggest he contact you personally."

SEVENTY SEVEN

W eiss made his way out of the Public Gardens through an Arlington Street exit. He crossed the street to his parked vehicle, sitting against the curb, motor running and blue lights flashing. The vehicle drew some attention, but no one touched it. Weiss tossed the suitcase on the back seat, got behind the wheel and roared away from the curb, siren blasting. He waited until he cleared the park area before shutting off his flashers and siren, slowed down and made his way to his home, driving now as any normal citizen. As soon as he was parked in his garage, he was out of the front seat, into the back seat, and fondling the packages of bills. He ruffled many packs through his hands, noting they were all real money, and that he was a rich man. He put the bill packs back in the bag, zippered it closed, got out of the back seat and placed the suitcase on a shelf, covering it with an old blanket. He locked the garage, and with a smile on his face entered his home. After changing into his captain's uniform, he left his house and headed to his downtown office after again locking the garage with the suitcase of cash hidden inside. *It's been a good day's work,* he considered. *Now to find Manny and arrange a meeting.*

¥

It was later than five p.m. when Manny's cell rang. He was in an off-beat safe house in Cambridge that was owned by his brother-in-law, Jack Gold. Giorgio and Leon had joined him and were hiding out there with him.

They only left the premises after dark, in disguise, and only when necessary. Manny knew Serino had eyes everywhere, and he had only

Giorgio and Leon, his sister Angela, and the questionably still in the fold Joe Weiss. He knew money was the only thing that kept Weiss in line, and he had provided plenty of it to Weiss. Weiss could trust him, and that's what Manny was counting on.

"Yes, Weiss. I was hoping you'd call," Manny said.

"I wasn't sure this number was still good, and I have to be careful. Serino's men are all over the place. They want you real bad. Offering me all kinds of money if I find you for them. You better be real careful."

"Of course. What else?" he said suspiciously.

"I learned that Ari Alexopoulos and Mario are meeting in Boston tomorrow. I don't know where but I may be able to find out. That information worth anything to you?"

"If I can get to them it would be. Like maybe a million dollars, Joe. Does that interest you?"

Weiss nearly choked when he heard the amount. He knew Manny meant it. Money was not a problem for Manny; staying alive was. He didn't pause long before answering. "I'll get on it right away. Stay out of sight. I'll get back to you as soon as I can."

"Do that, Joe. I'll be waiting for your call. Goodbye."

Weiss called Mario Serino less than an hour later. "Mr. Serino. I thought I should contact you and let you know I got a call from an FBI friend that Ari Alexopoulos' pilot filed a flight plan for Logan Airport for tomorrow. Ari's had dealings with Antonelli for a long time. There may be something brewing.

I thought you should know about it."

Serino played dumb, deciding there was no need to let Weiss know Alexopoulos was coming to meet with him, not Manny. "That's good information, Weiss. I appreciate your letting me know. Where will Ari be staying?"

"I don't know; but if he's on the plane, I'll have people watching him."

"Good. You keep in touch with me. We both will benefit."

"Yes sir. I'll keep in touch."

Weiss felt good, and he did a little happy dance. He could see the money rolling in from both Serino and Antonelli.

SEVENTY EIGHT

⟡

Ari Alexopoulos' private plane touched down at Logan Airport a few minutes past noon on Saturday. Upon deplaning with three associates, Ari entered Terminal E and was greeted by Arthur Lite and Samantha Robbins. Brief nods, but no introductions and the six people hastened to the parking garage and entered Arthur's van. All this was observed by Captain Joe Weiss, again dressed inconspicuously in civilian clothing, and watching from an upper level.

Weiss followed the van out of the airport to Route 1A north, where it traveled over a mile before making a U-turn to enter the Hampton Inn complex.

¥

"Why did you come to Boston, Ari?" Samantha said, once she, Arthur and Ari settled in Ari's room. Her displeasure dripped with every word. "I strongly urged you not to. There's serious trouble brewing here between Serino and Antonelli, and you've obviously picked sides. You are going to make things a lot more difficult for the authorities."

"We do what we have to do, my dear Samantha. I've come to try and make peace between two business partners. And I thought it might help you, since I know you are involved."

"You and I both know better, Ari. For your beautiful wife Kara's sake, don't mix in. Get out of town before the real trouble starts."

"I'm here to prevent trouble, Samantha, not to cause it."

He stopped talking after seeing the fire in her eyes and disgusted look upon her face. His tone changed, and he said softly, "Everyone has to look after themselves, Samantha. I'm here to do just that."

"And what if I were to tell you the outcome will be far different from what you expect. But no, I won't tell you, and you'll only have yourself to blame."

Her remark caused Ari to pause. "Do you know the outcome?"

"Yes I do. That's all I'm saying, Ari. You've had your warning."

¥

"What was that all about, Samantha?" Arthur said, as they drove away from the motel, made the U-turn, and headed north toward home. "You know some things you haven't told me about?"

"No. It was all a bluff on my part. I was trying to dissuade Ari from mixing in. I think he's trying to play both sides, but will wind up supporting Antonelli. He's afraid of Serino and Serino by far has the stronger position. But before a man like Manny goes down he'll cause a lot of damage. I'm afraid of a bloodbath, Arthur, and I don't know how to prevent it."

"For God's sake, Samantha, it's not your job to prevent it. Get Katte, get the whole damn FBI in on it. Let them stop it."

"Katte and the FBI will be involved, but after the fact, not before it. They don't know, or can't prove who killed Maria and Tony. Ari and his group, Serino and his minions, Antonelli and his supporters – all of them at the moment have done nothing – and that includes Weiss – that will cause the FBI to sweep them up, and by the time they do, I fear there will be multiple dead bodies. I'd like to prevent that, but I don't know how."

"You're asking too much of yourself. Be honest. You can't prevent it! Please, honey, offer advice if – if you can foretell something, but stay in the background."

Samantha sighed. "You are right, honey. I just hope I get some answers soon."

¥

Later that day, Samantha called Steve Grant's office. His secretary, Herb Mellon, took the call, said Steve was on another line, and asked for a phone number so Steve could return the call. Twenty-two minutes later he did.

"Sorry it's taken a bit to get back to you, Samantha, but I was with a client, and she was in a talkative mood."

"Not a problem, Steve. Have you heard anything from or about Manny Antonelli?"

"Nothing from him I'm happy to say. About him, yes. From several sources I hear he's back in the area somewhere."

"Any idea where the 'somewhere' is?"

"None whatsoever. It sounds as if you're expecting trouble."

"Big trouble. If you hear anything, call me. Thanks, Steve."

Manny *had* called Grant's office, but refused to leave a callback number. Steve wondered why he didn't tell Samantha that. He hoped Manny didn't call again. He wanted no involvement.

¥

Samantha sat back and stared at the ceiling. Then she closed her eyes – and waited. And it came – the vision she hoped for.

SEVENTY NINE

Katte had arranged for a fellow FBI agent, Austin Jaffe, to keep tabs on the Romano brothers. The brothers were definitely tied to the New York mob, and he wanted to know where they went and who they visited. He was still waiting for permission to wiretap everything they owned – office, cars, and homes – but hadn't received the okay. FBI budget concerns hampered his moves, and he wasn't happy about it. But he had the tie between the Romano's and Serino, and was one of the first to know Serino and some henchmen were visiting Boston.

Samantha had clued him in on the trouble brewing, and she was forever reliable. Scarily so. So many times in the past few years she had cracked cases before anybody else. Many people didn't accept the words of psychics, but Katte wasn't one of them. He had witnessed what she predicted came true. She was invaluable!

FBI agent Austin Jaffe reported to Katte that the Romano brothers had recently visited an estate on Beacon Street, an estate that previously had been mostly unoccupied, according to neighbors. Agents with cameras and high powered telephoto lenses had been deployed to the area and had captured photos of several men who briefly stepped outside of the home to grab a smoke or some fresh air. One shot clearly depicted Mario Serino. That had raised eyebrows. Katte was elated when he had the information.

¥

He wouldn't have been if he knew of the phone call Austin Jaffe made to a private number later that evening.

"It's AJ, Weiss. I thought you would want to know that Serino and some of his people are in town."

Jaffe gave Weiss Serino's Brookline address. After telling AJ to pick up an envelope at the usual drop-off, which was a thousand dollars well spent by Weiss and appreciated by AJ – Weiss phoned Manny Antonelli.

"Yes. What do you have for me?" Antonelli said.

"Just what you wanted. Serino's whereabouts and how many associates he has with him."

"Good! When this matter has been taken care of, you will get what I promised you. Do you trust me?"

"You've always kept your word. Write this down...."

EIGHTY

Giorgio and Leon met Manny at Punks Corner on Revere Beach. Manny picked the spot because there was a lot of open area, and he would be able to observe from a distance if they had been followed.

Manny was dressed in a Boston College hoodie, dungarees, sneakers, and wearing a Red Sox cap. He was mustached and bearded and looked much older. He used a cane as he exited his Ford and hobbled to meet Giorgio and Leon. They were sitting on a bench facing the surf, looking inconspicuous as they read their newspapers.

"Don't look up, gentlemen," Manny instructed as he lowered himself with feigned effort on the end of their bench. "Ignore me for a few minutes, but look around on occasion to see if any vehicles pull over to park near where we're sitting."

Five minutes passed before he spoke again. "We look okay, Giorgio?"

Giorgio folded his paper, rose from the bench, stretched his frame as he rechecked the street, and without looking at Manny responded. "No new cars parked, and there are only a few old ladies walking in the area. We're good."

"Okay, sit," Manny instructed. "Every few minutes get up, stretch and look around. You alternate turns with him, Leon."

"Okay, boss. If I didn't recognize your voice I wouldn't know it was you."

"We can't make any mistakes, Leon; and don't you forget it. Now listen closely. I know where Serino is holed up. He's got four of his muscle men with him. He's also got two nephews – the Romano brothers – in town, so we can figure there are at least seven of them to consider. We've got to take the five of them out in the house; all seven if the Romano's are there when we hit them – and we'll hit them tonight. Leon, you can handle an Uzi?"

"Yeah, no problem."

"That should even us for fire power, and surprise should favor us," Manny said.

"What about the noise?" Giorgio said. "We'll bring in every cop within five miles."

"We'll have to be out of there quickly. We'll arrive in two cars, and leave in two directions, and travel the speed limit. Worst-case scenario we'll leave together in one car. I want each of you to steal a late-model car this afternoon – nothing fancy – and replace their plates with stolen ones from another vehicle. Try the airport long-term parking garage. Most likely no one will notice the change for a couple of days. That's more time than we'll need. Any questions?"

"Where do we meet up tonight?" Giorgio asked.

"You pick me up on the southwest corner of Beacon and Harvard Streets at nine o'clock. Make sure you check out your weapons this afternoon, and wear dark clothing. I'll bring the Uzi. We're going to party."

Eighty One

S amantha, her eyes closed, rubbed her forehead and grimaced. "It's tonight, Arthur. Manny and his team know where Serino and his thugs are hanging out and will hit them tonight. I didn't see where, but it's tonight."

"Damn. We'd better alert Katte…."

She opened her eyes and, at Arthur's look of concern, gave him a strained smile. "I already have, but I didn't have much to give him. I'm not sure where…."

"Samantha. There's still time. Maybe you'll get more info as the day progresses…" He studied her haggard expression. "…but maybe that is not a good thing. How you feeling?"

"Fine, but frustrated. I couldn't see where Serino's holed up. Everything turns red. Blood red. There's going to be a massacre."

Arthur grunted. "Small loss. In my mind, they're all people who deserve it. Good riddance."

Samantha shook her head. "We can't think like that, Arthur. There could be innocents caught up in the exchange."

"Could be, but I doubt it."

She didn't answer. She didn't have the answer. Yet again, she was frustrated that her visions warned her of horrible things about to happen but failed to give her enough information to prevent them. Her psychic ability once more felt like a curse.

¥

The best lead came from Katte. "I've had a watch on the Romano brothers, Samantha. My New York associates have been doing a lot of research on Serino's bloodline, and picked up the Romano's as relations in Boston supposedly running an insurance business. The Ashley woman worked for them. The company does very little business; it's just a front for Serino in Boston. Both brothers have recently made several trips to an estate on Beacon Hill Avenue that has questionable ownership and is usually vacant. It isn't vacant now. We think Serino's people are hiding out there...."

¥

Samantha felt all kinds of vibes that had her moving restlessly in the passenger seat of their Honda as Arthur drove past the Beacon Street reservoir. The closer they got to the address Katte had given them, the more she twitched.

Arthur noted her unrest but said nothing. When she was in this frame of mind she often had series of short epiphanies, small flashes of insight that set her cringing and jerking as if she were having a small seizure. It scared him sometimes, but they needed all the information she could get. She had promised this visit was only to get close enough to observe, and they would not confront anyone. Arthur was armed, as was she, but against how many? There was no way he would chance an armed conflict against a squad of professional killers.

It was dusk when they did a drive by the estate. They noted lights downstairs behind drawn shades. There were no outside lights to welcome visitors.

"They're in there, Arthur," Samantha said while rubbing her temples.

"Who, Samantha? Who's in there?"

"Mario Serino himself, and a number of his men."

"How many?"

"I...I don't know, but there are now two more at the gate."

Arthur stopped the car, turned around and noted a car at the gate, with the shadows of two people in the front seat. He watched as the gate slowly swung open and the car drove in.

243

"An electronically operated gate, Samantha."

"I noticed."

He was about to turn his Honda around for another drive by the gate when he noted a silver Cadillac Escalade with only its parking lights on moving slowly in their direction. They watched as the Escalade passed the gated entrance and continued down the street. The windows of the Escalade were darkened and its passengers could not be seen, but Samantha knew who was inside.

"The Escalade, Arthur! Three people, including Manny!"

"Damn!" Arthur voiced. "Call Katte now."

She reached for her cell phone. "By the time he gets here it could be too late."

"Then call the local cops, Samantha. Tell them to send everybody they got...."

She was only half listening. She didn't know if the authorities would have time to react in force. She called 9-1-1. "He wants to put me on hold, Arthur! HELP!" she yelled into the phone. "There's a murder...." And she gave the address and hung up.

"Go, Arthur. Now!"

"We're not going in until help arrives, Samantha!" He parked, and drew his weapon. "Just sit where you are."

¥

The Escalade had turned around and stopped near the gate entrance.

A Boston Patrol car came down the street. No siren, but lights flashing. It stopped next to the Escalade.

Samantha couldn't make out the faces of the three men in the Escalade – but she knew who they were. Manny and his two henchmen, Giorgio and his young cousin, and the cousin toted an automatic weapon.

She also recognized the man who got out of the patrol car and talked into the intercom at the gate.

¥

"This is Captain Weiss," Joe said. "I need to talk to Mr. Serino immediately. There's serious trouble brewing, enough to cause me to drive out here in person. Let me in now!"

The gate buzzed and slowly began to swing open, but Joe got back into his patrol car and departed. The Escalade drove in instead.

¥

Serino had monitored Weiss' speech. "Let him in," he ordered. "A couple of you meet him at the front door. Check his car. Make sure he's alone."

The two men Serino sent were dead shortly after they exited the home and approached the Escalade. Giorgio shot both men in the head from the back window of the car using a silenced weapon. In the darkened courtyard, Manny felt no one in the house could have seen or heard anything.

The grin on Manny's face was frozen in place. *Two down, five to go, and he would do Serino himself.*

Giorgio led Leon into the massive foyer, and was followed by Manny. Two more well placed silenced shots from Giorgio downed the Romano brothers before they had a chance to raise their weapons.

¥

A loud boom sounded, and Giorgio dropped to his knees as he caught a slug in his left shoulder that spun him about. Leon fired a staccato burst from his automatic weapon that dropped the shooter and another man. Six down, but no sight of Serino.

Sirens warbled in the distance, again breaking the silence of the night.

"We've got to find Serino!" Manny shouted.

"No time boss," Giorgio shouted and grabbed Manny's arm, pulling him back as the sirens grew louder. "We got to get out of here – NOW!"

The three men raced out the front door, Leon jumping behind the wheel of the Escalade. Giorgio, having dropped his weapon, clutched his shoulder, pressing his handkerchief firmly against the wound while climbing into the passenger seat beside Leon. Manny jumped into the back seat. Leon was out the driveway, through the still-opened front gate and into the street moments later, heading away from the sound of the oncoming sirens.

¥

Three police cars raced through the gate and into the courtyard, screeching to a stop near the front of the home. Armed police officers, noting two bloodied men on the ground, warily made their way through the open front door. Two more dead in the hallway, and two dead in the library had all the officers breathing heavily. A lieutenant called out in a loud voice. "Anybody in the house! Speak up! Make yourself known!"

Only a nervous silence followed. The lieutenant spoke again, this time quietly to his men. "Stay in pairs. Search the house. Be cautious. Move out!"

A thorough search of the house found no one else. More police arrived, as well as two FBI agents, who showed their credentials to the questioning lieutenant. Katte said little, other than the FBI had an interest in the people who owned the house.

Arthur drove into the courtyard, showed his badge to the officer at the front door, and he and Samantha joined Katte in the foyer.

¥

Officers were taping off the crime scene, and bagging fallen weapons. Others chalked the position of the bodies, while awaiting the medical examiner and forensic specialists. Murders were not uncommon in the Boston area, but mass murders in wealthy areas were not the norm and required the utmost care and diligence.

¥

Samantha stood in a corner of the foyer, alone, while Arthur conversed with Katte and the lieutenant.

Her thoughts were on not who was dead but who was missing. There was no Mario Serino, and the house had supposedly been thoroughly searched. She knew he'd been there, so how did he get away, and was he with anyone else?

EIGHTY TWO

Serino exited the library through a rear door seconds after hearing the burst of machine gun fire. He climbed swiftly up a back staircase to the second floor, into his master bedroom, and gathered the Glock 19 from under his pillow. He depressed a small panel on his armoire and swung the cabinet aside to enter a hidden passageway. The passageway led to a small, enclosed area above the four-car garage. The room was furnished with a fully-stocked kitchen; a refrigerator, sink, bed, chemical toilet, a supply of weaponry – and a hidden exit to one of three storage sheds to the rear of the home. The garage housed a Jaguar, BMW, Lincoln Town Car, and a Mustang – all in mint condition, all drivable, and all with ignition keys hidden behind a moveable wallboard.

Serino was furious. Someone had betrayed him. That fucker Weiss! He'd pay. He was sure all his men were dead, but it was the attempt on his own life which irked him most. He took a deep breath and let a cold calm steel him. He was better off alone. He would sit it out until things quieted down and then make his escape.

Then he *would* kill Manny Antonelli and Captain Joe Weiss. Manny had probably paid the little weasel more. Weiss had double crossed him, and was as good as dead.

¥

Weiss was worried. When he reappeared at the scene, he was quick to examine the dead bodies and noted that Serino's wasn't among them. Somehow he had slipped away, and that didn't bode well. Weiss knew he was an open target for Serino and the mob as soon as the word got out. It was time for him to disappear. He'd been preparing for it for a long time. He had false papers and his years of illicitly acquired cash had been secreted away off-shore. He regretted leaving his kids, but he had made provision for them. His nagging wife? No problem leaving her. He would find female company in a new environment and live the life he had planned for and long dreamt about. The thought of it made him stand a little straighter, feel a little lighter. He could feel the chains falling away, and smiled.

¥

"What do you think, Samantha?" Arthur asked. "Serino slip away clean?"

"I don't have the answer. There could be several escape exits on this property and he would know them all. If he has gotten off the property he can't have gotten far. I would like you to arrange for me to get back in this house tomorrow. Maybe I'll come up with something."

"Let's talk to Katte. He should be able to swing it. It is out of my jurisdiction."

"See what you can do to charm the right people, Arthur. I've got to sit down and get my head together. I'm tired and can't think straight, but it's important that I check this place out in the morning."

"Sit, honey. I'll be back shortly. Then we'll get out of here and you can get some sleep."

EIGHTY THREE

Katte agreed to Samantha's request to return to the estate in the morning, but insisted on accompanying her.

¥

Samantha arrived at ten a.m. and parked among a bevy of Boston Police vehicles. Katte met her at the front entrance, and confirmed that the bodies had been removed the prior evening, once the coroner gave his okay, and that they were free to search the grounds and home. There was a police dog and his handler on the way and hopefully the dog would find Serino's scent.

"Let's start with Serino's bedroom, Ken," Samantha suggested. "I'll play the part of the police dog."

He knew what she meant.

As soon as they entered the bedroom Samantha knew it had been Serino's. Everything was neat, the bed having been made, clothing in drawers or hanging in the closet, toilet articles neatly arranged in the medicine cabinet....

Why the armoire? There's a walk-in closet in the bedroom! She walked over to the armoire, opened it, and noticed but one item hanging there – a white terrycloth robe. Then she perceived there was no space between the armoire and the wall. She rapped on the rear inside panel of the armoire and noted a hollow sound. She smiled as she closed the door and searched for a mechanism to move the armoire.

Katte showed surprise when he turned and saw the opening in the wall. "I'll be damned! Don't go in, Samantha. I need to get the lieutenant and some flashlights. I'll be right back."

¥

The lieutenant, last name Navarro, was Cuban born, multi-lingual, short of stature at five-foot six, but fearless, well-intentioned and an aggressive cop. He led the way into the passageway, flash light in his left hand, pistol in his right. He was followed by a police corporal, a big guy named Raul Perez – well over six feet and broad-shouldered – who had to double over to move through the passageway. He also carried a flashlight and drawn weapon. Katte was third in line and Samantha silently brought up the rear.

They cautiously moved forward, stopping to listen every five to ten feet, but they heard and saw nothing. Samantha estimated they had gone ninety feet before they came to a door. Upon opening the door, Navarro's flashlight revealed a small but completely outfitted room. There were three empty water bottles and two empty cans of tuna on the kitchen counter, but no human occupant. They switched on all the lights and found a door and stairway that led down to the four-car garage. The door was concealed from inside the garage by a one inch thick sheet of plywood. The back door was unlocked, and Samantha knew how their bird had flown.

EIGHTY FOUR

S erino had walked nearly three blocks before he found a cab. The cab dropped him off at South Station. Ten minutes' later he was on a bus leaving for the Port Authority Terminal in New York

On route he called his wife.

Sophia answered and nervously asked what was going on.

"I'll tell you all about it later," he promised. "Right now I want you to listen carefully without interrupting me. Send Carlos and some of the boys to pick me up at the 42nd Street Port Authority Bus Terminal. I should arrive there by three-forty-five this afternoon. Have them bring me a coat and a pair of gloves. I've only got a sweater and I'm cold. Tell Carlos to make sure they he's not followed. Do you understand, Sophia? Have them keep their eyes open."

"Mario, for God's sakes, what's going on? You...."

"Not now, Sophia!" he said, in a voice she understood. "Just do as you're told. Goodbye!"

¥

The bus ride was uneventful, and Mario sat next to a school girl who did little else other than text messages, which was fine with him. He had time to think – about the attack upon him, about the men he had lost, and about the people who'd betrayed him. His mind was roiling in anger. He knew his partners would be furious over his involvement, but he didn't care. He would just have to watch his back for any retaliation from them or anyone else.

He had hoped to kill Manny himself, but now thought better of it. He had plenty of men who were better at such things. He would send teams of them after Manny if necessary. And after that, he'd get that dirty cop Weiss. His Beacon Hill estate had been secret, secure. He hadn't seen the attack coming. Who could? His lips twisted into a deeper frown as he thought of that woman private investigator. Samantha Robins had failed him, perhaps betrayed him?

She would need to die as well.

¥

The limo circled the Port Authority Bus terminal until it spotted the un-coated middle-aged man standing next to a doorway. Mario welcomed the coat placed over his shoulders by Carlos as he scampered into the rear seat where a man sat pouring a hot cup of coffee from a thermos. No words were exchanged until Mario broke the silence. "Is Sophia at the downtown apartment?"

"Yes."

"Go directly there," Mario ordered, as he sat back and sipped the life-saving beverage.

¥

Sophia stood as Mario entered the apartment. He tossed off the coat, nodded his greeting, and said "make me some toast and coffee. I haven't eaten."

She did. When he returned from a bathroom visit ten minutes later, she had it on the table, along with grape jelly and a butter spread. For the first time in what felt like a long while, he smiled. "I don't remember the last time you made me breakfast, Sophia."

She smiled in return. "It's not much of a breakfast, but once you warm up I can order in whatever you want."

"This will do fine. Sit down; we'll talk."

While slowly eating, Mario related the events of his trip, although modified a bit. Sophia would not be happy if she knew that he went seeking trouble.

"...and I had to be in Boston personally to finalize the deal – a multi-million dollar deal. But I was attacked by that bastard Antonelli and his men. They tried to – to assassinate me. They killed Maria, they killed Tony! The bastard had all my people killed! I was lucky to slip away and make it safely home...."

Sophia had displayed shock initially, but then her eyes narrowed and her lips pursed in an angry brooding expression. "Do you think your partners had any involvement in this attempt, Mario?" she asked. "Do you thing they're after it all?"

He paused, his eyes widening slightly at the suggestion. "An excellent question, Sophia, but one I do not have the answer to. Not yet, anyway. But it is something I'll have to consider. Antonelli is brash enough to try it on his own, but he isn't stupid. He knows I outmuscle him, present setback aside. I wouldn't be surprised if he received encouragement and clandestine support from Lorenzo and Michael. I don't think Gambino is involved. He's always sided with me. I saved his life once. And I don't trust that Greek Ari Alexopoulos either. He's been dealing with Antonelli for years and can be touchy. I will look into it and act accordingly. Thank you, Sophia."

Sophia got up from her side of the table and went to him. Putting her hands on his shoulders, she leaned over and kissed him. "Thank you, Mario, for confiding in me. You haven't told me so much in years."

"It's only because I don't want you to worry. My business is my business, and my concerns are my concerns. I can and I will handle them." He pushed his chair back from the table. "I'm going in to shower, and then take a nap. I'll take no calls until I'm myself again. Plan an early dinner. You call and have it sent in. My preference is Italian, and the choice of what we eat and from where I leave to you."

EIGHTY FIVE

Samantha, Arthur and Ken Katte sat for a late breakfast in Zaftigs Delicatessen on Harvard Street in Brookline. After placing their orders and a sip or two of coffee, Samantha spoke.

"Serino got out of there by himself. I assume he grabbed a cab and was on his way."

"On his way where?" Katte asked.

"Out of Boston. I don't sense him here, and we'd see his men all over the city if he was still casting nets for Manny after the assault on his compound in Brookline. I think he grabbed a train or a bus from South Station and is back in New York, regrouping. Maybe your New York people can locate him. He's likely home licking his wounds and making plans for another hit on Antonelli. It's real personal now. Manny knocked off at least three of his blood relatives."

"I'll check, Samantha," Katte said. "This whole thing is getting out of hand. I'm not happy with what you implied about Joe Weiss. Are you sure he was the one who got Manny into the estate?"

"We saw him, Ken," Arthur said. "He got the gate open for them and then he was out of there, clearing the way for Manny and his group to drive in."

"I'm going to have Weiss picked up and questioned," Katte said. "I *hate* crooked cops. I'll nail his ass to the wall if I can."

"If you can find him, Ken," Samantha said.

"What do you mean 'if I can find him'?" Ken said. "Where in hell is he going?"

"Far away." She rubbed her eyes. "Serino must know Weiss was the one who let Manny in. I would say Weiss is near the top of the list for Serino to deal with. And Weiss knows this. He isn't going to hang around."

"Where's he going to go? He's got a wife and kids. He can't just disappear on such short notice."

"They can't, but he can. And he will."

Katte pulled out his cell phone and made a call. When he finished, he said glumly, "I hope my people get there in time."

"They won't," Samantha said, shaking her head, and reached for a forkful of her western omelet.

¥.

The Feds did not find Weiss at his office or his home. He was gone. Several hours later, his car was found in a parking lot at Logan Airport. His wife was contacted at work and appeared completely oblivious to what was going on. On the kitchen table at home, they found a brief note that he had left for her. "I'll contact you. It will be a while."

EIGHTY SIX

M anny expected Serino and his people would be back for him, and in force. He knew Serino would peg Weiss, so Weiss was a still-walking dead man. What he didn't know was how he could get to Serino. The man had escaped once, but barely, and would now be more wary than ever and determined to have his revenge. If Manny ran and hid, Serino would eventually find him, and he did not want to live with that threat forever. His only way out was to kill Mario Serino and make peace with Serino's partners!

He made his decision. He would disappear for now, but in the city of New York. Mario wouldn't expect that. He would disguise his appearance and hunt Serino down. He would kill Serino in Serino territory when the opportunity presented itself.

He called Giorgio and left a message on his voice mail. "You and Leon go into hiding. Don't try to contact me. After I kill Serino, I'll contact you with an ad in the Globe, calling for a class reunion of The Wayward Brothers, and leave contact information. If you don't hear from me, then Serino likely got to me, and you'll be on your own."

He added where Giorgio could pick up fifty thousand in cash in one of eight briefcases that his sister Angel was holding for him.

He next called Angel and left a coded message on her answering machine, telling her to give Giorgio his birthday gift when he came by.

Serino's people picked up on the message, and the following day, when the kids were in school and Jack and Angela Gold were at work, their home was fire-bombed, and burned to the ground.

Giorgio shook his head in disbelief when he showed up at Angel's home the following evening. He learned from a local cop that the family had survived – no one was at home when the fire started. They were staying in a nearby motel. He didn't know which one. He didn't care which one. The money Manny had left for him was ash.

Giorgio suspected Serino's people were everywhere – watching for him. He and Leon checked out of their motel late that evening and headed for Logan. They stole a car and several license plates in the long term parking area and headed for New Hampshire to hide out. Leon had little money, but Giorgio had always been thrifty, and had a decent poke saved up, which he now wore in a money belt underneath his shirt.

Giorgio's thoughts were on his friend and mentor, Manny Antonelli.

¥

Leon drove the stolen Chevrolet Malibu with its newly attached Rhode Island plates out of the long-term Logan Airport parking area. They headed north on Route 1A, heading for Route 1 north. It wasn't a long trip mileage wise, but it was a slow trip because of the traffic flow. Leon kept within the speed limit, but Giorgio didn't begin to relax until they were on the Spaulding Turnpike in New Hampshire an hour plus later. Then he dozed off while Leon added another stick of gum into his over-worked mouth. One-and-one-half hours later they checked into the Courtyard Hotel in North Conway. They planned to stay a week before moving on to another New Hampshire small town, keeping their eyes on the TV and newspapers for information about Manny Antonelli and Mario Serino. Most important in their minds was to keep themselves invisible from the mob.

¥

Manny, sporting a shaved head and wearing tortoise-shell, non-prescription glasses, toted a suitcase with wheels onto a late night Greyhound bus traveling to the Port Authority terminal in New York. The bus was full of college-age kids with ear phones, I-Pads and I-Phones seemingly everywhere. They ignored him, and he was pleased about that. He was dressed in dungarees, a wool-plaid shirt, white socks and sneakers. Under his shirt he wore a packed-with-cash money belt. In the bag he checked was a loaded Glock automatic, several full magazine ammo clips, and a knife à la Jim Bowie. With these weapons, he would have to get up close to Serino, and that's exactly what he wanted. How he would do so was still in question, but he would find a way or die in the attempt. Enough was enough, and he had had enough.

¥

Month's before, Ari Alexopoulos had offered Manny refuge in his New York City apartment. Manny had used it once. It was a nice apartment a few blocks away from one of Serino's office headquarters, but Manny feared going there. He didn't fully trust Ari. For now, any secondary hotel would serve his purpose as he staked out Serino. He would take his time and find a way to get Serino.

Getting to Serino proved to be nearly impossible. In the first week of Manny's observations, Serino visited only one restaurant for lunch – his own establishment – and with six henchmen in two limos as protection. All other meals were picked up by his people and brought to him. He stayed five nights in his downtown apartment, always heavily guarded. He spent Saturday and Sunday at his Long Island estate with his wife and with ample security, including three Doberman watchdogs that freely roamed the home, even when it was locked down.

Manny chose to go after Serino at his Long Island estate. He wasn't frightened of dogs. Wide open spaces with scalable walls provided the best opportunity for him to gain entrance. There were probably cameras – maybe even trip wires, but he'd observe for a week or two, or more, and watch how deliveries were made and how the gardeners moved about and took care of the vast grassy areas and gardens. He would get in, strike, and get out. And he would do it alone.

Landscaping crews came once a week, on Thursdays. A group of female maids came twice a week, on Monday's and Friday's. UPS and the postal service left packages and mail at the security booth at the front gate. They weren't allowed in. No guests visited during the weeks Manny watched. Apparently Serino wasn't allowing his wife to have any.

Mario showed up at the estate after eight p.m. on Fridays; also by limo. The first week he had two men with him, the second week three. Manny smiled. *He can't find me, and he's getting worried.*

The guard shack usually was manned by two gatekeepers, each armed and working twelve hour shifts. That then changed to three two-man teams for eight-hour shifts.

It was during the fourth week of observation that Manny elected to make his move.

¥

Friday was a dark and dreary day. Sophia hated it. She wanted out of the estate, bored with her incarcerated living conditions for better than a month, and longing for the chatty gossip of her friends. She had to get out. After first pleading and then shouting, Mario finally relented. He hated when she got angry, and a salon appointment didn't seem to be too much for her to ask for. He acceded, with conditions. She left the house promptly at nine-thirty a.m. for a ten-fifteen beauty salon appointment, accompanied by her chauffeur and two members of Mario's security team. The weather was as foul as her mood had been, but it was brightening. She'd treat him special when she got home.

¥

Manny watched her leave. He was dressed comfortably in jeans, an L.L. Bean dark green wool shirt, black sneakers and socks and was wearing a black stocking hat on his shaved pate. Just before sunrise, his backpack over his shoulders, he made his way over the security wall some two hundred feet away from the front gate by means of a sturdy rope ladder and grappling hooks just before sunrise. He left a dead squirrel atop the wire on top of the wall, intending the animal to be the cause of tripping the alarm. He moved quickly from the area, toting his make-shift ladder with him toward the large twin cabanas by the Olympic-sized swimming pool. He hid his ladder in the hedges and watched with night goggles for ten minutes before two men in a near-silent golf cart came into view. They were armed, and toted a wooden ladder on top of their rig. One man climbed the ladder and searched the top of the wall. Manny could only imagine the conversation from this distance, but saw the man on the wall gingerly pick up and toss an object outside the property. Minutes later the ladder, golf cart and men headed back in the direction of the guard shack.

Manny was free and clear, and heard only the sound of the caged Dobermans fussing in their lockup. They would be released to roam about only after the cleaning people left.

It was Manny's intention to hide out in one of the pool cabanas until nightfall and await Mario's arrival. He unpacked his backpack and its two bottles of Poland Spring water, two ham subs with mustard and in a carefully sealed plastic container, three poisoned steaks he had prepared for the Dobermans. He placed these items in the twelve cubic foot refrigerator in the cabana. He had a newspaper and a book with him to pass the time and began to read. His loaded Glock with silencer was at his waist, and his knife on his belt.

The smile on his face turned malicious as he fingered his weapons.

EIGHTY SEVEN

⟡────⟡

"It's coming, guys; and soon," Samantha said to the group gathered at a round table in the main dining room of the Wardhurst Grille. Arthur, at Samantha's request, had invited Steve Grant, Billie Tsapatsaris, Tony Bottone, and Ken Katte to join them for dinner that Friday night. They ordered beers, and the serious conversation began shortly after Samantha asked for their attention.

"Please let me talk without interruption. Most of you are familiar with where my information comes from, and I can't completely explain it myself, but the fact is what I predict happens. Tonight, in New York, at Mario Serino's estate on Long Island, people are going to die. It may be happening now, it may have happened already, or it will be happening soon. I can't stop it. No one can. I saw this less than twenty minutes ago, and though I expected it was coming I didn't know the timetable. I had called for our dinner meeting this morning, having no idea of what I just told you. Ken, you get on the phone with your people in New York. Have them see what they can find out. I expect by the time we finish dinner there will be news, probably all bad, but we'll have an idea how things stand."

Katte excused himself and left the table. He went outside and called his contact in New York. He returned to the table ten minutes later. "He had a lot of questions I couldn't and didn't answer, but I told him I just got a tip from one of my sources. He told me he'd get back to me. What do we do in the meantime?"

"Eat and drink, but not necessarily be merry," Samantha answered. "Now you have an idea what my everyday life is like. Frustrating. The only thing that keeps me going is that most times I can do some good. This time I can't...."

¥

At that precise moment, on the estate of Mario Serino on Long Island, Manny threw the three steaks over the enclosure confining the Dobermans. He didn't wait around to see them pounce on their last supper. He extracted his Glock from his waistband and headed for the open glass door off the veranda. Sophia was at a desk inside and before she could cry out he pistol-whipped her into unconsciousness. He shot one man standing guard in the foyer, and a second at the top of the stairway. Moments' later he opened the door to the master bedroom and walked in.

¥

Mario was standing in front of a full-length mirror, administering the final flourishes to his Windsor knot, when he saw Manny's reflection in the mirror. He turned slowly, and although his heart raced and his blood pressure rose, he showed no concern. "I think we should talk, Manny," he said in a bland voice.

"Talk?" Manny said. "Talk about what? How you and your partners used me and cheated me out of my lifelong position? How you took away what *I* built up and then discarded me like an unfeeling pet? Talk about how I brought in millions of dollars to your group with never a complaint? Is that what you want to talk about? Well it's too late for that, Mario," Manny said, the smile of victory on his face. "Far too late," he added.

"You were beginning to run wild, Manny. Too many killings, too much bad publicity and notoriety. We sent you away to give you time to cool down and see the whole picture – the picture of business men running businesses properly. We let you live because we intended to bring you back, make you a full partner and run all of New England and the entire east coast operation...."

"Sure you did," Manny said mockingly. "You sent me out of the country so I would wind up dead in some area where I would have an accident that would be little publicized. I'd be a forgotten ex-hood of little consequence. It's not going to be that way, Mario."

"Now you listen to me, Manny," Serino blustered. "We're...."
He never got to finish the sentence. Manny pulled the trigger twice and
watched Serino silently crumble to the floor. Seconds later he was out of
the bedroom, into the hall, and moving rapidly to the stairway leading
downstairs to the foyer. The guard just entering the foyer went for his
gun but was too slow. One more man washing the windshield of one of
the limos next fell with a bullet in his brain, not having heard or seen
Manny's approach.

¥

The guardhouse gate started to swing open as Manny slowly approached
in one of Serino's limos. He suddenly gunned the engine and was through
the gate before either guard could respond and fire a shot at him. He made
his way to the highway and pulled off one exit later, parking the limo in a
supermarket lot. He walked a block until he found a cab and headed into
the city. The cab driver wanted to talk, but Manny didn't, and cut off all
attempts. The driver got the message and used his cell phone to call his
wife. The conversation was in Spanish, and Manny ignored it.

The trip took more than forty minutes, which wasn't bad, considering the traffic. Manny made up for his unfriendliness with a more than
ample tip, watched as the cab drove away, then walked several doorways
down to the entrance to Ari Alexopoulos' apartment building.

He made his way to Ari's penthouse, thinking how well things had
gone, and that he would contact Ari and bring him up to date as to
where he was and what he was planning. He wanted Ari to come to New
York and be his intermediary with the three bosses, Lorenzo, Michael
and Gambino, and form a working relationship in which they would
all prosper....

¥

Manny unlocked the door, walked in and was met with a flood of bullets,
all with his name on them. As he dropped to the floor he saw only the
shoes of the assassin. He died without knowing who got him.

¥

Tito, breathing heavily, looked at the dead body, and smiled. How easy it had been. Ari would make him rich, and he'd be honored by the family for avenging Mario's death.

¥

Ari's people traced every move Manny had made for the past three days. They saw Manny crawl over the wall of Serino's estate and immediately reported it to Ari. Ari guessed right – Manny would kill Mario, and then seek safety in Ari's hideaway.

Tito had waited the entire day for Manny in Ari's apartment, hoping he'd show. And he did, And Manny died there.

Tito would be a hero in both camps; Ari's and Serino's.

Eighty Eight

———

Samantha didn't get word until the following morning. A call from Katte at eight a.m. alerted her to Manny's demise. She listened as Katte related the details of the murder. "…and he apparently tried to hide out in an apartment belonging to Ari Alexopoulos after wreaking havoc at Mario Serino's estate. Mario's wife is one of the few survivors, and she positively identified Manny as the one who entered her home and attacked her. He killed a lot of people, as well as three guard dogs. And apparently all on his own. He was a ruthless bastard, Samantha. My people aren't exactly sure how he got in or out, but he managed against some pretty good security arrangements."

"Apparently they were not so good, Ken. Do your people think there will be any serious repercussions within the New York mob because of this?"

"Funny you should ask, because the same thought occurred to me. My contact wouldn't give me a definitive answer. He just said 'we'll have to wait and see how things play out'."

"That's par for the course. Thanks for the info, Ken. We'll talk again soon. Bye."

¥

"I assume that was Katte you were talking with?" Arthur said.

"Yes. Manny's dead. He was gunned down in an apartment owned by Ari Alexopoulos. Four bullets from up close; two in the heart, and two to the face."

"Apparently someone didn't like his handsome face. Sounds like over-kill."

"Sure does, but by whom?"

¥

Every major paper in the United States carried more or less the same version of a mobster war on the east coast, and showed mug shots of the infamous characters involved.

Giorgio heard reference to it on his radio in the motel, and raced out to find a Boston Globe and the local paper. Returning to his room, he spent considerable time reading about the mass murders, and about Manny being gunned down later by an unknown assailant. He was in tears when he opened the connecting door to Leon's room to fill him in.

Leon was sitting on the bed, facing in the opposite direction, phone to his lips, talking. "...and I expect a good sum of money for having giving you Manny's hideout, Tito. Don't play games with me! Five thousand is peanuts. I want twenty-five thousand, and you send it to...."

He never finished the sentence. Giorgio's powerful right arm was around his throat, crushing his windpipe. Leon struggled violently but was no match for his hate-filled cousin. Leon finally stopped struggling, but Giorgio held on nearly a minute longer, his emotions overpowering him.

At long last, he let the body drop to the floor.

He sat in a chair, looking at the dead man with unmitigated hatred. To think someone of his own blood could be the betrayer of the man he loved like a son. That night, after dark, he placed Leon's body in the trunk of their car, checked out of the motel, and drove to the Walmart in North Conway where he bought a spade. On his drive back to Boston, he pulled off the road and buried Leon where he'd never be found.

¥

Arthur and Samantha shared a Cobb salad and a bottle of Joel Gott Cabernet Sauvignon 2011 that evening for dinner. Samantha had been silent all day, and Arthur feared to disturb her. Her color had gotten better though, so over their wine he tentatively asked, "What now, Samantha?"

She looked at him, seeing the concern on his face, his love for her, and she smiled at him. "Tomorrow we'll start a new day, Arthur. The first thing on my agenda will be to start the hunt for Joe Weiss. His greed was the catalyst for much of this, and it bugs me that a dirty cop has gotten away. We find him and put to rest this sordid mess."

EPILOGUE

Tito made an appointment to meet Mario Serino's partner Lorenzo, the youngest of the four, now three, crime bosses of New York City. Lorenzo, Michael and Gambino all were aware that Mario had surrounded himself with family members who were intensely loyal to him. The partners didn't know much about his nephew Tito, other than Lorenzo had mentioned he wasn't a Mario favorite like Tony had been. But Tito *had* killed Manny Antonelli, who had turned out to be a thorn in their side, and no doubt Tito was looking for recognition – and possibly Manny's job. That's why Lorenzo had made the choice of delaying the meeting three days to glean more information about Tito.

He didn't like what he learned. Tito was a compulsive gambler, always in debt. He was a sullen person and few people spoke well of him. When Lorenzo related this information to Michael and Gambino they agreed they were not about to give him the Boston territory. They knew Tito would be unhappy about their decision, and would have to be dealt with.

¥

It didn't come to that.

As Tito entered his apartment that evening, he turned on the light and went through his ritual of setting three locks on the door. He dropped his imitation leather jacket on a chair, entered the kitchen, switching on the light…and froze. Sitting at his table, weapon in hand, was Giorgio. The Glock, silencer attached, was aimed at his head.

"One stupid move and your dead," Giorgio hissed.

"Manny's dead, Giorgio. You ain't gonna bring him back. If I didn't do it, he would have got it from ten other people. You and I can make a deal. You can be my number one man in Boston…"

"Don't think so, Tito. I'm going to Boston, but you're going to hell."

The three quiet coughs from the Glock produced a delta-like configuration on Tito's heart.

"What's fair is fair," Giorgio muttered. He rose, unlocked the door, and let himself out, a satisfied smile on his face.

(THE END)

CPSIA information can be obtained at www.ICGtesting.com
Printed in the USA
BVOW06s1516090615

403351BV00004BC/6/P

9 781495 805448